A Pinch of Peril
A Magical Papillon Cozy Mystery

Sabine Frisch

Thinking Dog Publishing

Contents

Chapter One

The scent of cinnamon sugar danced on the crisp December air, swirling with the giddy anticipation of a thousand beautifully wrapped presents. Snowflakes, fat and fluffy like miniature marshmallows, clung to the gingerbread trim of the Victorian houses lining the streets of Rosewood Hollow. Inside Thompson Hall, Sarah's cozy haven, Christmas cheer threatened to burst from every corner. Fairy lights twinkled like a fallen Milky Way across the fir tree in the den, casting a warm glow on the flurry of activity.

Fourteen-year-old Emma, a whirlwind of blonde braids and boundless energy, strategized the most effective ornament placement, while Cory, his teenage nonchalance a facade barely containing his own excitement, wrestled with a tangled string of popcorn garland. Sarah, her heart brimming with a joy that rivaled the twinkling lights, belted out carols slightly off-key, her mismatched socks a testament to the delightful chaos that was the Anderson's second Christmas in Rosewood Hollow.

"Mom, you sound totally awful," Cory said, making a face, only to start giggling at Sarah's mock crestfallen expression.

"Wow, that high note almost reached the North Pole," he added in a mock-impressed tone. "Headphones? Anyone? Just kidding."

Sarah playfully cuffed him on the arm.

"You know, your father invited you to spend the holidays in Puerto Vallarta with him and his new lady friend; you can still go if you hurry."

"Right, Mom, get real."

Cory gave her one of his famous eye rolls and held up a little Santa Claus statue made with love and many recycled materials in shop class. "Mind if I put this up?"

"Knock yourself out." Sarah pointed toward the mantle in their den, commonly known as the games room, as an assortment of computer games, board games, and books littered the room every time someone walked in. "As long as Amelia doesn't have an issue with it."

Automatically, Cory's eyes went to the corner where the raw stone fireplace edged up against the wood paneling and the outside wall, where Amelia and Simon, the two mischievous ghosts who haunted this house, were known to appear.

"Haven't seen them in a while, have you?"

The question was asked of the room in general, but really, he meant his sister Emma. She had the closest connection to the ghosts of Thompson Hall. They respected and sometimes feared Sarah, but Emma—Emma was their favorite.

"No," Emma said simply, her shoulders slumping a little. "Maybe it has something to do with Christmas."

"They'll be back," Sarah said, giving her daughter's shoulder a quick squeeze. "They could have crossed over long ago and stayed on the other side for good. For some reason, they like us and keep visiting."

Emma managed a thin smile. "I guess."

"Now, hurry. Matthew has a few things to take care of with the sale of his condo, and then he'll be back for dinner. I want to have this Christmas tree finished by then. Do you think we can do it?"

Cory blew out a breath to let her know what he thought of her doubts and bent over the box with Christmas items again.

Sarah pulled a delicate lace angel from the box. That angel had been crocheted by her own mother so many years ago. It had graced the tree in her first married home with the children's father, Michael. It had moved with her when Michael decided he needed more and moved out, and it had come to Rosewood Hollow and their first Christmas tree with them just over a year ago. That angel, she thought, had seen joy, tears, despair, and their first encounter with the ghosts of Thompson Hall.

"May I?" Emma took the delicate angel from her hands and held it almost reverently. "I think it should be on the tree top."

Sarah let go of the figurine.

"But I made this..." Cory held a golden star he had also made in shop class. It had multiple LED lights that could light up in various sequences and patterns, even synchronizing with the beat of nearby music. Sarah silently decided to talk to the shop teachers next year. Cory looked around and finally grinned.

"This one... this one will go on top of the loudspeakers. Really rock out this Christmas."

Sarah hid a grin and retied her long blonde ponytail. "All right then. Now hurry. Lily is coming over in about half an hour too, and she has news."

Both kids groaned in unison.

"Yes, more news about the guy she's dating now—the one who's basically perfect, good-looking, charming, and also old-fashioned and well-mannered," Cory said with huge exaggerated arm gestures. "The one who is a true gem."

"Hey guys, your Aunt Lily has been alone for a long time," Sarah defended her best friend and owner of the Rosewood Hollow bookstore. The kids had taken to calling her Aunt Lily. "She deserves happiness and a guy who is good to her in her life, don't you think?"

"Yes, but does she have to talk about it 24-7?" Cory asked with another eye roll. "And is he really the guy who helped you figure out the canvas collective mystery?"

"Not really," Sarah answered, thinking back to barely a year ago. "He was in the store, and he picked up on our conversation and pointed us toward the art thefts that had been happening. Other than that, I think he's just new in town and a decent guy. So, give your Aunt Lily a break."

"I've met him in the store a couple of times; he's actually okay," Emma said, hanging an ornament and moving it again with a critical eye. The ornament, Sarah noticed, was a tiny little glass ghost.

Just then, she heard the front door slam and Lily's excited melodious voice.

"Sarah, my friend, I have news, and I have prosecco, and they are both meant for you."

Lily stepped into the room on a cloud of vanilla perfume and a riot of color, with two bottles of prosecco in her hand, her red curls bouncing. Today, Sarah noticed, her flowing boho dress was an abstract symphony of green and red, paired with a snow-white coat of faux fur and oversized red-rimmed sunglasses. Lily had never met a bold color she could resist.

"Wow," Emma said, fingering the red, green, and gold scarf of Thai silk that topped the ensemble. "Is that vintage? I love it."

"Luke found it for me, in a vintage store in Philadelphia," Lily said and spun around once for emphasis. "Chic, is it not?"

"Um," Cory mumbled.

Just then, the front door slammed again.

"My darling family, I am officially homeless now, and I'm hoping someone will take me in."

Dr. Matthew Turner, local town historian, history professor, and advisor to the local museum, walked into the games room, holding two bottles of prosecco aloft. "And to celebrate... Oh, I see we are all set in here."

He looked from Lily to Sarah and back and lowered the bottles in his hands.

"Your brand's better than mine," Lily said quickly, lowering her hands. "You go first. And why pray tell are you homeless all of a sudden?"

"Well..." Matthew popped the cork on his bottle and filled glasses for Lily and Sarah. He even held one out to Cory, who made a face and muttered something about fizzy water.

Matthew raised his own glass and grinned. "As of just about an hour ago, a young accountant from New York City seeking the quiet peaceful life, has countersigned the offer on my condo. After Christmas, I shall officially move in here for good, if that's all right with everybody."

"Yes," Cory pumped his arm. "About time. It's been getting a bit hard to ignore you and Mom always sneaking around."

Sarah startled for a second and finally grinned, touching her glass to Matthew's.

"I see it's not been a secret."

"For a long time," Cory groaned and elbowed Matthew in the side. He'd found the father figure he had always wanted in the town historian, and as a part-time professor, Matthew knew more than just a few things about dealing with teens and young adults.

Sarah squinted over her glass at Cory, almost seventeen now. He wore the baggy jeans and slogan T-shirts favored among his age group. His brown hair was too long and forever fell across his face, and when mad, he withdrew into the depths of some dark-colored hoodie. But he was a good kid—scratch that, a great kid—since meeting Matthew.

"Is Michael going to have an opinion about Matthew moving in," Lily whispered by her side, and Sarah shook her head.

She imagined the kids' dad with his ever-revolving cast of young girlfriends, jet-setting to the most amazing places in the world, and finally grinned.

"Nah. He actually mentioned after their last visit how well-adjusted Cory and Emma were."

"His way of saying what a good job you did with them?"

"Hide your mouth, Lily Morrison. He would never say such a thing, but yes, I have a feeling that is what he meant. Even if he is kind of relieved to spend the holidays in Mexico alone with his latest flame."

"What are you girls whispering," Matthew came around with the bottle of sparkling wine, refilling their glasses. "Making Christmas plans?"

Sarah put her glass on a nearby small table and raised her index fingers the way she had seen him do in front of class quite frequently.

"Let's just all agree here. The only thing that will happen this Christmas at Thompson Hall is a joyous, quiet Christmas, baking, snow, presents, eating way too much, and going for long walks in the snow. Is that agreed?"

Matthew opened his mouth to agree when someone behind them suddenly laughed.

The kids were still discussing ornament placements, and Matthew and Lily stood right by her. Sarah closed her eyes, put her hands together, and turned around slowly.

"Yes?"

A shadow detached itself from the corner of the fireplace, flickered, and became brighter ever so slowly. A gentle chilly breeze stirred the flames in the fireplace, and she knew what was to come. Sarah had purchased the house just over a year ago, and with it came two unexpected residents, Amelia and Simon, a pair of friendly ghosts eternally bound to the year 1901.

When and why they chose to visit the plane of the living always remained a mystery, even though they had a singular talent for stirring up trouble.

A translucent, shimmering figure materialized beside the fireplace. Amelia, a wisp of a woman in a mint-green dress that shimmered like moonlight on water, beamed at Sarah. Her smile, as always, held a hint of mischief and a warmth that defied her spectral state. In her hand, she clutched a small, ornately wrapped package. The fire crackled merrily as if in response.

"Happy almost Christmas, Sarah!" Amelia chirped, her voice a melodic whisper, and the air shimmered slightly as she spoke. Beside Amelia, another figure shimmered into view. Simon, Amelia's spectral companion, materialized in a dark suit and cravat, a hint of a smile playing on his lips. Just then, they looked less like spooky apparitions and more like faded photographs come to life, their clothes slightly out of fashion but their smiles genuine.

"She's outdone herself this year, wouldn't you agree, Simon?" Amelia said, her voice lilting, a fluttering wisp of an arm pointing at the Christmas tree. Simon chuckled, a deep, rich sound that seemed to resonate from the very floorboards. Sarah couldn't help but grin.

"We couldn't help overhear," Amelia said in a soft, rasping voice and glided on a cloud of sparkling white toward Matthew, who, as always, took a careful step back and put his glass down.

"You will be part of our little family here," Simon said, and Sarah could have sworn the ghost winked. "Welcome to Thompson Hall."

"Um…"

As always, Matthew found his words lacking when the ghosts were around.

"Welcome to Thompson Hall," Amelia echoed regally and held out the present to Matthew.

He should have known better, Sarah thought. Of course, he should have known better, but he reached for the ornately wrapped little box. The ghosts couldn't manipulate material objects on their plane very well, and vice versa. His hand went straight through the little gift, eliciting a shower of white and golden sparks.

Matthew pulled his hand back quickly and tried to be circumspect about checking his fingers.

Amelia, however, turned around and unloaded on Simon. As always, when they spoke to one another, Sarah could only perceive a rush of hissing and crackling static that told her the two were communicating in their own way. Perhaps one day, she always thought, when she figured out her own abilities to the fullest, she would be able to listen in the same way the ghosts did.

Amelia pulled back her hand and glowed bright orange for a moment.

"I shall return," she said, same as always, and both of them blinked out of existence in an instant.

Matthew exhaled, took a massive gulp of champagne, and sat on one of the comfortable overstuffed couches in the games room.

"That... always unnerves me."

The doggie door into the yard flapped gently, and Pixie, their tiny white and sable Papillon dog, hopped in and gracefully strode into the den and games room like the little princess she was. She shook out her silky fur and plumed tail and took a spot on a plump cushion, surveying the room.

Nice job on the Christmas tree, Sarah heard in her mind as Pixie sat regally, curling her fluffy white tail around her legs, looking the tree up and down.

And without your help, Sarah automatically answered. Long ago, she had become used to one of her many uncanny abilities, which included communicating with the precious soul she had rescued from the local pound, Pixie.

I was busy with a gang of marauding squirrels, Pixie said, licking a paw.

Then she walked up to the Christmas tree, adjusted a low-hanging ornament with a delicate paw, and turned around again.

"Everything meets with your approval, Pixie," Cory asked, scooping the little dog into his arms.

"Yes," Sarah said automatically, knowing her son couldn't hear Pixie. "Everything is perfect. Just perfect."

She touched her glass to Matthew's and Lily's, and the Christmas tree at Thompson Hall was not the only thing she meant with that statement.

Just at that moment, everything was perfect in her home and her life.

Hold that moment, she thought to herself. *They'll never be fourteen and seventeen; Matthew will never just move in. Hold life right here.*

But, of course, life wouldn't. It never did.

Lily emptied her glass and peered into it as if wondering where it had all gone. Matthew held up the bottle, but for once, Lily shook her head.

"I better not. I'm meeting Luke and letting him into the store so he can work on my furnace. It's kicking up a fuss again. Meanwhile, I want to check on my great aunt Tami, she left me a strange message. She's likely just lonely, but I better check."

"Busy lady," Sarah said and hugged her friend. "Everything okay?"

"Oh, yeah," Lily put down her glass and looked around for her coat again. The face she made belied her words. "You know me." She wouldn't look Sarah in the eyes. "Every time something is going really well, I keep looking for the hair in the soup, keep waiting for something really awful to come to light, and it's irritating me, that's all."

She forced a smile and finally returned the hug.

"Truly, that's all."

"But you said everything is great with Luke."

"It's just me... Matthew, congrats on the sale." She gave him a quick peck on the cheek. "In this market, and just before Christmas... it's a miracle you pulled it off. Have a fantastic evening. Emma, can I count on you to help me at the store tomorrow? Say nine?"

Emma, deeply involved in the intricacies of arranging a group of felt Santa Claus figurines of various sizes, gave a quick thumbs up.

"Sure thing."

"Well," Matthew said, setting down his glass and putting his arms around Sarah. "How about you and I take a little walk? It's just started to snow, and the kids can finish decorating. Besides..."

"Besides?"

"There are a few things I'd rather the ghosts didn't listen in on," he whispered in her ear and winked, and Sarah had to work to hide a huge grin.

Simon and Amelia could be quite selective about what they chose to listen in on, even though they could be entirely invisible if they wished to be so. Naturally, the conversations you wished they didn't hear were the ones that interested them the most.

Sarah shrugged into the coat Matthew held for her. She and Amelia had had their arguments in the past, and they were usually settled with an impressive display of Sarah's powers and acquiescence from the ghosts.

Now, if she could just figure out where these powers came from that suddenly flowed through her hands, she thought, how to use them, and most of all, where the limits were.

❧

The kids didn't even notice them leaving, and they quietly slipped out into the early evening snowfall, holding hands as they strolled down toward the main street of Rosewood Hollow. Sarah snuggled her arm around Matthew's waist, reveling in the way their opposite builds complemented each other: her petite frame tucked perfectly against his tall, lean physique.

"I'm glad Emma is enjoying her work at the bookstore," Matthew said. "At least she gets out and amongst people her own age. "Sometimes I get the feeling she could spend most of her life in a book somewhere instead of getting to know people."

Sarah squeezed his hand and grinned. "She knew her dad could get irritated easily, so she fell in love with the quietest thing on earth, reading."

"I don't think I've ever heard anything more than a polite laugh from Emma."

"Oh, you just wait," Sarah laughed. "Now that she knows you. When we walked into Lily's bookstore our first day in Rosewood Hollow, she stood there and said, Mom, this is the most perfect spot in the world. Lily adores her, and especially at Christmas time, she can use the help in the store."

Sarah suspected Emma would work at the bookstore for free, but most of the money she earned was put into the next book haul anyway.

"You want to buy her Christmas presents, buy books," Sarah chuckled. "I wouldn't be surprised if she asks Lily to work full-time one day. It would be her dream."

Matthew stopped and took her hand.

"Listen," he said softly, and Sarah cocked her head.

From somewhere in the direction of Rosewood Hollow she could hear the sweet sound of a small children's choir performing.

"Carolers," she said and grinned, squeezing Matthew's hand. "How beautiful."

Chapter Two

Sarah woke early the following day.

Last night Lily had told her that, with school out and Christmas sales looming, she could use Emma every day—all day. And a few minutes later, Emma stormed down the wooden stairs, bundled in a scarlet cable-knit sweater and a thick woolen skirt, a picture of winter cheer. Her book bag already swung from her arm and her thick blonde curls were tied in a neat braid.

Last night's snowfall had dusted the world in pristine white, and Sarah, a creature of habit, instinctively reached for the car keys.

"Ready?"

"No need to dig out the car, Mom," Emma said, giving Sarah a bright smile. "It's just a dusting. Fifteen minutes, and I'll be there, warm and toasty with a hot cocoa in hand. Besides, Cory hasn't shoveled the driveway, and Lily wouldn't forgive me for being late on one of the busiest days of the year!"

A smile tugged at Sarah's lips. If she insisted, Emma would likely launch into a lecture about pollution and driving short distances. Besides, Lily could drive her home if the weather became worse. Still, a shiver, unexplainable and out of place in the warm room, crawled down her spine.

"Alright, sweetheart," she conceded, forcing lightness into her voice. "But be careful. The roads might be slick. And call me when you get there."

Emma winked, a little glint in her bright blue eyes.

"Always am," she promised before disappearing into the snow-laden morning, a red blur against the white canvas. Sarah watched her go, touching a finger to her lips. A girl on her way to her happy place, a world of endless stories and imagination. But an unsettling feeling, a cold whisper at the edges of her mind, refused to be quelled. Something about the seemingly ordinary winter morning felt... off.

Something is strange, isn't it?

Sarah looked down and found Pixie right by her foot.

Yes. Everything seems fine, and yet...

Maybe a storm coming in.

Pixie possessed an uncanny knack for sensing the subtle shifts in the air, the undercurrents of emotions, and the vibrations of the world around her. Some might call it intuition, but for Pixie, it was simply part of her essence. If a looming storm was indeed gathering over the quaint town, Pixie would have remained unfazed.

About breakfast?

Little glutton. Sarah grinned her worry forgotten. "With all the treats you've been getting at the Christmas parties, I think it's time for a weigh-in. We should see the vet..."

No need... everything's fine.

Though Pixie was no ordinary Papillon, and an ancient antique store owner had called her a *high spirit* she harbored the same resentments all dogs did: vets, weigh-ins, baths, and nail clipping.

Sarah reached down and scratched the little dog behind the ears just as Matthew entered the kitchen.

"Did we wake you?"

"Not really." Matthew dug through the box of specialty teas he kept on the counter, checked and dismissed a few, and finally selected one.

"I only have a few things to do in the office later, and Cory is at hockey camp all day. I thought perhaps we could drive over to Claremont, see the Christmas market, have a nice lunch there?"

Claremont. A pretty little town not far from Rosewood. The Christmas market was said to be stunning, even if Sarah's memories of the town were not.

"We'll stay away from the courthouse," Matthew said with a little wink.

"I have no intentions of reliving the moment when someone stole Pixie, and we were nearly trampled to death in the plaza."

"Not on my watch." Matthew solemnly raised a hand.

"All right. We can—"

Just then, she heard her cell phone chime in the den, and all at once, that feeling that something was off hit her in the stomach big time again. Matthew cocked his head when he saw Sarah make a fist with her right hand and bring it into her chest with the other.

"Something wrong?"

The phone continued ringing.

"This is not good news. This is not good news." Sarah heard the phrase repeatedly, whispering from all sides like nails scrabbling on wooden boards, and she set her shoulders.

"I'm just irritated today—about what I don't know. Maybe it's the weather," she said louder than she had to and rushed into the den to grab her phone.

"It's just Emma," she called out with a massive exhale. "Letting me know she got to the store. Hi sweetie."

But instead of saying, *Made it, Mom, love you*, Emma blew out a frustrated breath.

"Mom, did Lily say anything about opening late this morning?"

"Not to me, and why would she? It's the middle of the Christmas season. Isn't she there?"

"No. The store is locked up tight, I don't have a key, the back is locked, and Aunt Lily isn't answering the phone."

Even over the phone, Sarah could hear Emma stomping her cold feet to keep warm.

"Hey, I'll come and get you," she said quickly. "Hang tight, two minutes. Meanwhile, Matthew can try to get a hold of Lily again."

Matthew cocked his head when she hung up and grabbed her purse and car keys in one smooth movement.

"I have to get Emma. She's standing out front of Lily's, and the store is closed. Bloody irresponsible. Can you try and get a hold of her, see why she's not opening?"

"Let me come with, we need a few things in town anyway, at least we're not going twice."

Sarah only nodded, in too much of a hurry to get Emma out of the cold. Walking ten minutes was one thing, standing in the icy cold, waiting for Lily...

She drove faster than she usually did, and it was not lost on her that Matthew peered over at the speedometer now and then, holding on to Pixie in his lap.

"You know, she's not going to freeze to death in these five minutes, and I assume she has the sense to go into one of the other stores around. Careful on that turn..."

"I know that. Please don't lecture me. I'm just angry that my child…"

Matthew reached over and put his hand over hers on the steering wheel without another word. Sarah nodded, pressed her lips together hard, and slowed down.

The store in the same building as the Rosewood Hollow Bookstore had once been an art gallery but had sat empty for months. By the time Sarah arrived, Emma had gone across the road into a small travel agency and waited, peering out the window.

"Sorry," she mumbled when Sarah put her arms around her. "I know I worried you and…"

"It's fine. It's not like Lily to be late; come on."

Sarah nodded a thank you to the ladies in the travel agency, and a moment later, they all sat in the station wagon again with the heater up on high.

"Still no answer from Lily?" Sarah asked with a sideways look at Matthew. He only shook his head.

"No," he mouthed quietly. "I'm trying Katelyn just now."

Katelyn, a family friend, was about the only friend Matthew knew he and Lily had in common.

"Maybe she just caught a cold and doesn't want to spread it," Emma said, huddling deeper into her sweater. "I feel awful making a fuss, just because."

"No worries, it's—"

Just then, Sarah's cell phone chimed again with an unknown number. Unknown numbers automatically made her uncomfortable, and together with the nagging unease that had plagued her all morning, her finger hovered just over the reject button.

Don't.

It was Pixie with her paw on Sarah's wrist, and she answered the call.

"Anderson."

"Sarah? It's Tyler, the Rosewood UPS driver."

"Tyler?" Sarah looked at Matthew, her brows knitted. "I'm not expecting a delivery, am I? Unless I missed something?"

"You're not, Sarah, my apologies, but I have a huge shipment of books for Ms. Morrison. I've visited her store three times this morning, but she's always closed. I made all of the other drop-offs in Rosewood, and I don't want to take these books back. Lily paid extra for a delivery today. Do you think you could accept them for her?"

Small-town living. Through her rising panic, Sarah forced a grin. Only in Rosewood would your delivery driver come back three times and then call a neighbor so you wouldn't miss a shipment.

"I'm actually in town right now," she said, looking out toward the village green to see if she could spot his van. "I don't have the keys to Lily's store, but if you're at the end of your shift, leave them on my porch. We'll work it out."

"Thank you, Sarah, I owe you one."

Sarah let the hand with her phone sink into her lap and looked at Pixie.

Something is wrong here, they both thought at the same time.

"Sarah, Lily likely slept in or is ill—"

"No, Matthew." Suddenly, Emma piped up from the back seat. "Now I feel it, too."

"Can you two—" Matthew stopped because Pixie had jumped into his lap again and fixed him with an unwavering stare from dark, chocolate brown eyes.

"I'll go see about that door," he said with a slight nod and opened the car door. Looking left and right, he darted across the road and fiddled with the door to the bookstore for a while. After a few minutes, he returned and blew into his stiff, red hands.

"Not a chance. The door is locked solid, and there is not a soul in sight."

Sarah leaned back and brushed the hair out of her face. "Now what?"

"Now we go back home, take those books Tyler is bringing, and wait for Lily to call you. Eventually, she'll surface again; she has to."

Emma tore a page out of her notebook to paste to the door and not half an hour later, they were all back at Thompson Hall.

Chapter Three

N ot a chance of going for an outing to the Claremont Christmas market now, Sarah thought, pacing the front room to release some of her pent-up nervous energy.

"Everything is probably fine," Matthew attempted for the 100th time. "Lily got carried away, lost track of time, forgot an appointment. Heck, maybe..."

"Not Lily," Sarah argued, turning again to cross the den. Pixie sat on a footstool, looking quite regal, her fluffy white tail draped elegantly over her paws.

You will wear yourself out, pacing like that.

You, too, noticed something was off, remember?

Yes, but you are not solving anything by wearing a track on the rug. All you can do is wait.

"How long before you can report someone as missing?" Sarah suddenly asked, stopping right in front of Matthew.

"I don't think you can report Lily as missing. She is an adult; she only missed one appointment..."

"And I know something is wrong. So? How long?"

Just then, the phone in Sarah's pocket chimed, and she pulled it out, had a look, and answered the call in one fluid motion.

"Lily Morrison, I was worried sick about you; if you were standing in front of me right now, I would—what?"

Sarah listened for a moment, backed up, and sat on the footstool beside Pixie, automatically putting her hand on Pixie's head.

"Okay, we'll be right down," she finally said. "Maybe Matthew can help. Oh, I have a bunch of books for you, too."

Slowly, she slid her phone into the pocket of her jeans again and made a face.

"Looks like I owe you an apology," she said to Matthew. "Emma. Lily's fine."

Emma had heard the phone and came downstairs from where she'd been reading in her room.

"What happened?"

"Lily-style chaos." Sarah dragged her hands over her face and grimaced. "From the thirty-second download I just got, she went to see her great-aunt Tami last night because she was worried about her and ended up locking her phone and her keys into her car. And because Tami lives in the middle of nowhere—"

"She couldn't call, and it took forever for the locksmith service to get there," Matthew finished. "Got it. You see, no disaster."

"Sorry."

"No, you worried about Lily, it's understandable. But why are we supposed to go down there right now? Other than Emma, who likely has to help in the shop."

"That's the thing." Sarah held out a hand so Matthew could pull her up from the footstool. "She's outside her store and says her keys won't fit? Or do they fit, and they are not locking? I don't know either, but there's trouble with the door, and I said you... maybe, could help?"

She looked down at her shoes and scrunched up her face until Matthew squeezed her arm.

"The trouble with having a store in a building as old as Lily's," Matthew sighed. "I already checked earlier, but I will try if it makes you happy. Perhaps keep the number for that locksmith handy, would you."

Sarah only nodded and bundled Pixie into a stylish little wool coat the tiny papillon hated, even though it made her look quite regal.

Only two hours after they had left Rosewood Hollow initially, they were back in front of the charming little bookstore. This time, Lily and Walter Becker from the Rosewood Hardware store fiddled with the door, and a few customers provided a running commentary.

"Sarah," Lily gave her a quick hug. "I'm sorry I worried you… and Emma."

"She was ready to report you missing," Matthew said with the tiniest of eye rolls.

"Yikes. Forgive me, even though I am touched that you would worry."

More customers joined the group outside of the store. It was almost Christmas, and they all had things to do, but something strange was happening here. And anytime something weird happened in Rosewood, it had to be observed, talked about, and documented by all in the vicinity.

Sarah watched with a mix of amusement and apprehension as Matthew and Walter, whom everybody called Grandpa Becker, wrestled with the ornately carved oak door while discussing the merits of various tools.

Nestled amidst the quaint brick buildings of Rosewood Hollow, the bookstore exuded a timeless charm. Its weathered sign, boasting Rosewood Hollow Books in faded gold lettering, promised an adventure within.

But the adventure seemed to have begun right at the entrance. The brass doorknob, tarnished with age, refused to budge under their combined efforts. In her striking coat, Pixie garnered just as much attention as the two men and their tools, and she clearly loved it.

"Guys, I don't know," Sarah said, hanging onto Pixie so she wouldn't get too many treats. "That's an ancient door. You think maybe I should call that locksmith?"

Matthew grunted, his brow furrowed in concentration, while Walter, the owner of a perpetually mischievous grin, muttered under his breath, fiddling with a rusty keyhole cover. A collective grunt escaped them as they heaved against the door. Suddenly, with a gut-wrenching groan, the entire mechanism gave way.

Sarah flinched, bracing for the worst. Instead, with the harsh crack of an old mechanism finally breaking, the door creaked open, and the little bell over the frame chimed, inviting them inside.

A hush fell over the trio, surprise etched on their faces. Even the mischievous glint in Walter's eyes seemed momentarily extinguished, replaced by a sense of confusion.

"I'll be. Will you look at that, Lily? I think that door was locked from the inside. No wonder it wouldn't open." He stared at the remnants of the locking mechanism in his hands and shook his head. "You really ought to remember."

Then, it hit them all at the same time. Who had locked the door if Lily was standing outside on the sidewalk with them?

Lily, more confused than anyone, hurried inside and turned on all the old-fashioned light fixtures.

"Weird, but we'll figure it out. Come on in," she said, a little flustered. Listening for the deep rumble of her oil furnace, she grinned. "Sounds like Luke managed to fix it. He did say he'd just fixed that very same model at a restaurant somewhere in town. Tricky bugger, he called it. Come on, everybody, I'll make cappuccino for you all to make up for the floor show on the sidewalk."

With Lily's chatter and the hiss of her espresso machine, the confusion at the door to her store had faded into laughter and animated conversations. Enchanted customers, a mix of locals and tourists, browsed the labyrinthine shelves, fingertips trailing along worn spines.

Lily had not even bothered to remove her coat; it hung draped over one of the nearby chairs, and Pixie had made a little nest in the crimson woolen folds.

Sarah watched with a contented smile as Matthew, his earlier frustration forgotten, accepted a mug of tea from Lily. A woman with a mane of red hair and dozens of gold bangles that chimed every time she moved, Lily exuded a warmth that instantly drew people in. Already balanced precariously on a stepladder, Emma retrieved a hefty tome for a bespectacled gentleman. The air itself hummed with a comforting serenity, punctuated only by the soft rustle of turning pages and hushed whispers of literary discovery.

The bell above the bookstore door chimed merrily as new customers entered, joining in the impromptu gathering. But Pixie, content in the nest of Lily's coat, suddenly stiffened. Her head rose, her nose tested the air, and the tip of her tail began glowing with a faint golden shimmer. Visible shivers ran down her tiny spine, and the fur on her neck bristled.

Watch out, watch out there is a...

Sarah scratched her behind the ear and accepted a cup of coffee.

Pixie darted in and out between Sarah's legs, whining and pawing at her knee. Sarah inhaled the steam from her cup, passed the cookie plate to another customer, and barely registered the frantic nips.

"Shh, Pixie," she murmured. "It's okay, everything turned out to be alright."

Undeterred, Pixie pivoted and raced towards Lily and Emma, yapping in a frenzy. Her normally bright eyes held a panicked glint, her tail tucked low between her legs. But for once, the little papillon's antics were lost to hushed conversations and Lily's joking announcement that she needed a new door now.

Suddenly, Matthew snapped his fingers.

"Oh, I almost forgot," he said to Lily, "I still have that book delivery out in the car for you." He flashed Sarah a quick, reassuring smile before exiting.

"Oh, thanks, guys, that's my Christmas order," Lily called after him. "Just leave the books right out here and pop the invoice in my office, would you? Pixie is pawing at it already."

Sarah couldn't resist the beautiful cards and shiny coffee table books that spilled from the box. Pixie now sat strangely silent and tried to get her attention while Sarah was busy showing Emma the cookbook she had discovered.

"Look, why go to Claremont? We have just as many beautiful stores right here."

Moments later, Matthew reappeared, his face suddenly a mask of stark horror, both hands raised. The playful atmosphere shattered like a dropped teacup. Silence descended, thick and heavy—his voice cut through the stillness, devoid of its usual warmth.

"Everyone," he began, his voice barely above a whisper. I need you all to leave... now." Customers looked up and saw the terror in his eyes, and Sarah's heart hammered hard against her ribs.

"There's... there's been an incident. In the office." His eyes darted back towards the office; an area usually closed up, Lily's private domain. Panic, cold and sharp, clawed at Sarah's throat. Accident? What accident? Her eyes darted around, but Emma, Lily, and Matthew, the people who mattered most to her, were right here in the room.

Silence, thicker than molasses, choked the room. Every creak of the floorboards, every whisper of fabric, sent Sarah's mind into overdrive, conjuring a parade of horrors. Matthew's strained voice, a distant echo, offered no comfort.

"Could you...?" His voice failed in the face of the raw terror etched on his face. "Call the police. Please."

He shook his head and put out his arm to bar Lily from entering the office when she wanted to check.

"Don't. Lily, please don't. You don't want to..."

A frantic flurry of activity shattered the peaceful quiet of the bookstore at the word police. Customers either rushed out or thronged to Lily and the cash register to get their purchases in a hurry. Lily's fingers flew over the register keys in a frantic blur.

⌘

Officer Penny Harding appeared not ten minutes later. A woman with a no-nonsense demeanor and a shock of gray hair bustled in, her uniform a stark contrast to the bookstore's warm ambiance.

The last of the customers clutched their book bags and shuffled out under the officer's firm but gentle direction. Sarah watched them go, a part of her desperately longing to join the exodus.

Lily, her earlier vibrancy extinguished, clung to Emma's arm. Her eyes were clouded with worry, and she was torn between running back to the office and knowing she shouldn't. Matthew hovered near Officer Harding, his face a canvas of conflicting emotions. Sarah felt a surge of protectiveness towards him, the playful banter of moments ago replaced by a chilling fear.

Finally, Officer Harding pushed past the plain panel door that separated the customer area from the office. Silence stretched, punctuated only by the officer's muffled movements. Sarah strained to hear; her breath caught in her throat. Then, a gasp, sharp and sudden, sliced through the stillness. A string of muttered curses followed it. Officer Harding's voice tinged with a tremor of shock.

A cold dread seeped into Sarah's bones. No, this was not a simple accident. The idyllic bookstore, once a haven of comforting familiarity, now was anything but. The playful scent of old paper had been replaced by a metallic tang that made her stomach churn. How had she missed this before? Images, unwelcome and vivid, flooded her mind. Lily's office, usually a sanctuary of books and teacups, transformed into a scene of violence.

Then, Officer Harding emerged again, her face pale and drawn. A beat of stunned silence followed, broken only by the officer's ragged breaths. Lily, her relief morphing into a dawning dread, took a tentative step forward.

"Penny? What is it?"

The officer's voice, when she finally spoke, was barely a whisper.

"Lily... you need to see this." With a trembling hand, she motioned to Lily.

Lily's scream shattered the tense silence. It was a primal shriek of pure terror and grief.

Chapter Four

Sarah whirled around, heart hammering against her ribs. In the harsh glare of the overhead light, she saw him: Luke—Lily's boyfriend—sprawled on the plush rug, his short buzz cut stark against the crimson stain blossoming on his fatigues. His eyes, forever vacant, staring sightlessly at the ceiling. Sarah felt her blood turn to ice. She'd only ever seen a dead body at the movies or on TV, safe in the knowledge it was fake. And the discovery, shrouded in mystery and confusion, hinted at a darkness deeper and more terrifying than anything she'd ever encountered.

"Matthew, you'd better take Sarah and Emma home. I'll want to talk to them later." Penny Harding's arms were spread just enough to prevent anyone else from entering

"Lily?" Sarah asked.

"I'll need to talk to her first." Penny shook her head. "Go home, make some tea. When I'm done with Lily, you'll need to be there for her. Can you do that?"

Sarah nodded, and Matthew answered for her. He found their coats and Pixie's carrier and gently guided them outside.

As they stepped out of the bookstore, the local fire department and ambulance had joined the police cruiser by the curb.

I tried to tell you.

Sarah only patted Pixie's head over and over, unable to answer.

◦~◦

At home, Matthew settled Sarah in the den with a plush blanket and Pixie by her side while he went to make tea. Sarah stared at the Christmas tree, its cheerful decorations now garish and seeming completely out of place.

I told you something was wrong, Pixie said again. *I could smell it. With dead bodies go—*

Please don't tell me you have experience with dead bodies.

Pixie climbed up into her lap, and from there into the crook of her elbow, sharing the warmth of her body with Sarah, who still trembled.

I was there when my original Mom passed away, Pixie said, pushing the blanket up a bit with an impatient jerk of her little mouth. *Other than that, no.*

Serena, Pixie's original owner.

For a moment, Sarah hugged the little dog a bit tighter.

What killed him? she finally asked.

You mean who killed him. Luke was stabbed. Pixie stretched and leaned into the embrace.

And you know this how?

Sarah accepted a mug of tea from Matthew and took a generous sip, scalding her tongue on the hot tea, needing the warmth anyway. Pixie pawed at her to have her little white tummy rubbed and turned the large, fringed ears papillon dogs were so famous for, this way and that.

You forget these? I heard Penny say stabbed, although I'm pretty sure she didn't mean for any of you to hear it. That and the look of the crime scene—it was pretty obvious.

Sarah shivered, pulled up her shoulders and blew on her tea.

"Where is Emma?" she asked out loud." I don't think she should be alone in her room after all of this."

"I told her as much," Matthew answered and settled on the couch beside her. "She's gone upstairs to change and grab an extra blanket. How about you? How are you feeling?"

"I..." Blank. Nothing. She couldn't put into words what was going on inside of her and threaded her fingers through Pixie's coat again. With a calmness that seemed to emanate from her very being, the little papillon offered a sense of peace, understanding, and comfort. When Emma came downstairs and snuggled beside her mother, Matthew stood and straightened ornaments on the tree that didn't need straightening.

"We have to tell Cory," Emma said and Sarah put an arm around her daughter.

"Leave it be for now. Let him enjoy his hockey camp, at least for a bit."

All too soon the innocence of a boisterous game on skates would be shattered.

They sat in silence, staring into the dancing flames of a fire Matthew had finally lit for another hour until the slamming of the front door heralded the arrival of Lily. Pixie ran to greet her friend.

Lily's hair looked orange suddenly, against the stark white of her face, Sarah thought, and she had tied and retied her braid a dozen times until it stood out from her head like a fuzzy reed. She undid it again now, shook out her hair, and ran her fingers through it.

"Luke," she said. "Luke. He never... He was new in town for crying out loud."

Matthew brought more tea and another blanket, and they managed to squeeze onto the big couch.

Sarah watched Lily clench her fists, the silver ring on her right hand catching the flickering firelight. Luke, new in town and recent boyfriend of Lily, found dead in her own store, a locked room mystery with Lily possibly the prime suspect? It felt absurd. True, Lily had known Luke better than anyone else in Rosewood Hollow. Lily, ever welcoming, had befriended him easily. But Sarah knew Lily. She wasn't capable of violence.

"Did Penny have any insights?" Sarah asked, at the same time both wanting and dreading the answer.

"Not much," Lily shook her head. "Although she must have asked me five times if I had any reason to be... upset with Luke."

"You? Why you of all people? You didn't."

"Of course, I didn't." Lily jumped up, tossed the blanket aside, and began pacing the den from one end to the other. "It's absurd. But Luke was found dead in my store, and the door was locked, at least until Matthew and Grandpa Becker messed with it, according to her." Lily wiped her hands over her face for a moment and pulled in her shoulders.

"Penny said nobody in town had any reason to resent Luke. I was the only one who knew him at least a little."

"Well, duh. But that's no reason. In your own place." Sarah came out of her blanket now too and blocked Lily's path so she couldn't turn and pace the room again.

"This is silly, we all know you didn't."

"Thanks."

"Besides, you were at your Aunt Tami's."

"Great aunt."

"Whatever." Sarah threw up her arms. "What is wrong with Penny Harding? Why suspect you? She's wrong, dead wrong." Sarah bit her lip for a moment. "Maybe it's just something they have to do."

"According to her, there is a possibility I could have gone to Tami's, rushed back down here to stab Luke real quick and then driven back up to Tami's," Lily sighed. "It makes no sense but there you have it."

Matthew scrolled through something on his tablet, a frown creasing his forehead.

"The news is already buzzing," he finally said. "I wish I hadn't messed with that door."

Sarah could practically hear the town gossip swirling around them like a dust storm. Pitying glances and accusatory whispers were inevitable. She shot a sympathetic look at Lily, who was staring intently at the fire, her face a mask of worry.

"This isn't your fault." Lily put a hand on Matthew's shoulder. "I asked you to open it. And it would have made no difference. They showed me the locking mechanism after it had broken out of the door. There wasn't much left of it, no way to tell. That building is older than this place. And I know, from locking myself out, if the key doesn't work in the lock, that means it's locked from the inside."

"Our own front door can get tricky like that sometimes," Sarah said and sat hard on a footstool as the reality of the situation hit her. "Old mechanisms... But how would you even have gotten out of the room if you were the one that did it. That makes zero sense."

"You got it." Lily nodded. "I guess that there is exactly why Penny Harding thinks the whole locked from the inside bit is nonsense and why I probably did it and waltzed right out the front door. You watch if she doesn't come around asking you if you think I was acting."

"Don't panic right now." Sarah reached for her friend's hand and gave it a quick squeeze. "All Penny has right now is a lot of assumptions and theories. There's no proof and no motive. Why would you?"

A cold breeze swept through the room, and a white, cloudy figure appeared at the corner of the fireplace, slowly forming into the shape of Amelia.

"And that, my dear Sarah, is why Lily is still a free woman at this moment," Amelia said, hovering before Lily. The two coal-dark orbs that used to be her eyes stayed focused on Lily's for a very long time until Amelia slowly glided back.

"You did not commit this terrible thing," she said with the conviction only an immaterial could manage.

"Great. Would you mind testifying in court on my behalf?"

Amelia swept into the corner of the room, gave the Christmas tree a half-hearted glance, and finally came back.

"Do not joke about such things, Lily Morrison," Amelia said in a voice that had a dangerously low rasp. "If you must know, I paid a little visit to the police station of this town. A dreadful little building. But I am privy to the knowledge that Penny Harding presently deems you her prime suspect."

She attempted to fold her ghostly arms in front of her chest, failed, and glided off toward the tree in a huff again.

"But can you not help us, Amelia?"

Emma. Her daughter treated Amelia like one of her friends, Sarah thought. Emma reached out her hands toward the ghost, and Sarah balled hers into tight fists, half raised in case there was the slightest sign of hostility from Amelia. The ghost knew well enough that showing any kind of aggression toward her family brought out powers in Sarah that were no small thing to mess with.

With a sideways glance at Sarah, she closed the distance to Emma and placed her shimmering ghost hands over Emma's, eliciting a small shower of pretty purple sparks.

"Simon and I shall do our utmost," she said with a smile, disappearing like a light when the power was turned off.

Sarah let out a hard breath.

"I wish she wouldn't do that," she complained, folding her arms. "But she's right, Lily. If Penny feels you're her best suspect, you're on thin ice. You need a good lawyer."

"I did leave a panicked message for my lawyer," Lily said, staring at the spot where Amelia had disappeared.

"Is your lawyer a local?"

"What do you think?" Lily rolled her eyes.

"Then he's probably well-versed in wills, real estate law, and town bylaws. I'd prefer you'd get one of those... dream team sharks, you know."

"I might." Lily brought a hand to her mouth and stared at Sarah with lowered eyes. "I just never... thought... This is my home. These are my neighbors. Suddenly, I'm a suspect? This can't be real."

"It is. And Luke is dead." Sarah dropped the sentence like a heavy burden. "If only a few of them are convinced you're guilty..." She didn't need to finish the sentence.

Lily's shoulders sagged even more profoundly, and she sat hard on the footstool Sarah had just vacated.

"First of all, don't give up," Sarah said. "We'll figure out how to help you out of this mess."

"If there even is a way…" Lily's sentence trailed off, and she dragged her fingers down her cheeks again.

Sarah stopped in front of her friend and put her hands on Lily's shoulders. "Look at me, Lily. Yes, there is a way, and we will find it."

"But…"

"But… You have two capable adults, two ghosts, two spunky kids, and a papillon dog with a few tricks up her sleeve on your side. That's more than most accused have. We'll work it out, okay?"

Lily finally managed a weak smile. Sarah noticed that she had lost one of her silver and pearl earrings, and her hand kept going toward her right ear.

"And you, my friend, also have a few tricks up your sleeve."

"I'm here for you."

"We all are," Matthew came to stand with Sarah. "Don't think I've forgotten how much you helped get the sapphire back to the museum when my feet were in hot water."

"Thanks, guys," Lily turned her head and wiped the side of her eyes. "There's just… one more thing."

Sarah waited until Lily started again, her voice all tiny and scared all of a sudden.

"Penny thought it would be better—for the general public perception—if I didn't personally run the store until we've sorted all of this out. Wouldn't want one of the town merchants being a suspected felon now, would we?"

"Keep you from your own store? That's just dumb." Sarah straightened her back and rolled her shoulders, making a snap decision at that very moment.

"Because people will gossip? Let them, for God's sake. It's your store, your dream. I will not let you lose it." She stopped hard and looked around her cozy den, but Lily only shook her head and stared off into things that existed only in her mind.

"OK then," Sarah snapped. "I will do it if they don't want you to run the store. The moment they've cleared the scene, Emma and I will open that store for Christmas business. It will be my message to everybody: go and..."

Matthew's head snapped up, but Sarah let the end of the sentence trail off.

"Thanks, guys. I couldn't do any of this without you."

The three came in for a hug, and Matthew discreetly went to the kitchen for more tea, some type of pastries, and maybe a glass of wine for Lily. Sure, it was early, but being under suspicion for murder makes everything change in a hurry.

Chapter Five

Pixie sat on the back of the couch, her fluffy white tail draped around her paws, as always. Sarah tapped the little nose with a forefinger, but this time, Pixie didn't look up or bat at her with a paw or turn on her back for a tummy rub. She stared at something close to the Christmas tree, seeing without seeing.

What's the matter, Pixie? If you were a person, I'd say you look troubled.

Pixie looked at her briefly, and the tail twitched a little.

I smelled something, she said softly.

I know. The dead body, and I am sorry for not paying attention when you warned me. Everything was in chaos, and then the door finally opened, and I... I didn't see how important it was.

That's not it. Pixie sank down and rested her chin on her front paws. *On Luke. I detected a scent I have never smelled before. And it was fresh.*

A cologne, a person, a food, some drugs? What?

Pixie's eyes closed, and she groaned when Sarah rubbed the little spot between her shoulder blades.

Relax, it will come to you.

Matthew stepped into her field of vision and handed her another cup of tea.

"Thanks. Any more and I'll float away." Still, she accepted the tea carefully and continued rubbing Pixie's shoulder.

It could have been anything, even the polish he used on his shoes yesterday.

Pixie made a little groaning sound and turned over on her back, exposing her little white tummy, and Sarah happily obliged.

∾

Ultimately, Sarah decided Lily should stay with them for a few days. The thought of her friend alone in her apartment, rolling around memories, fears, and worries in her mind, was too much for her.

"The benefit of this huge old house," she said to Lily, "Is that there's always a room for a friend. Up the stairs, drop your stuff in the room beside Cory's. Then we'll go for a walk."

"But I don't want to impose. And Matthew just moved in, and you have your hands full and..."

"And you are a friend who just lost somebody very special to you. Don't you try to hide it. Whenever you talked about Luke, I could see it in your eyes. You were thinking about... more."

Lily lowered her head. "Yes, I could see him in my life... for a long time," she said, turning away too late.

Sarah had seen the glittering tear in the corner of her eye. "And to be accused of his murder, of running a knife into his heart—that's just..."

"It's preposterous."

Sarah and Lily automatically wheeled around. Simon, Amelia's fiancé, had materialized in the corner by the fireplace without the usual cold draft Amelia liked to generate.

"I know. I had to live a lifetime without my beloved. And if it were not for you and the young ones, we would still be separated."

"Thanks, Simon... I think."

Lily pulled her arms closer to her body. Of course, she'd seen the ghosts before, and she knew what they could do. She had spoken to and listened to them, but she still became tight and rigid every time one appeared, and she needed to convince herself they were indeed there.

"The perpetrator was not you. It was a man."

Simon said those words with a finality that made Sarah's mouth go dry. Having said his piece, Simon folded his arms and merely stared. The rumpled brown suit he wore looked decades out of place and hung on his lean, tall frame. A worn leather satchel hung from his shoulder, and a beret perched at a jaunty angle on his head. He stared out the window, his face etched with a kind of wonder Sarah couldn't decipher. The air, usually fresh with the pine cleaner she used, suddenly smelled faintly of pipe tobacco and something... else. Something old and forgotten. *A man...* Sarah's heart hammered against her ribs.

"How do you know," she asked. "You didn't; you weren't there, were you? Did you perhaps see Luke's murder?"

She dared to hope for a moment, but Simon shook his head, a gesture that made him become unfocused for a moment before he leveled a clear look at Lily again.

"Amelia sensed Sarah's distress at the store upon discovering... your fellow, Lily. She sent me to investigate."

Sarah hid a smirk with her hand for a moment. She could just imagine how that conversation had gone. If ghosts indeed had conversations in the afterlife.

"And that told you... what?" she asked, wrinkling her brow. The thought that she shared this connection with Amelia should perhaps have worried her, but she had more important things to think about just then.

"Energy lingers," Simon said, throwing up his hands as if tired of explaining the obvious to an imbecile. "Especially intense emotions like love or hate or…"

"Murder," Lily finished. "And you could… feel it? Who did it? Quick, tell me so I can point Penny Harding in the right direction."

"Alas, it is not that exact, dear Lily. We ghosts can sense the impression a strong emotional event leaves behind. The energy imprint in your store was powerful, violent, and distinctly male. I have an impression of a dark figure rushing off, but I cannot see a picture of the kind you call… movies?"

Lily's shoulders slumped. "So, we still have nothing," she said with a sigh. "Thanks for trying, Simon, and for the vote of confidence, but the impressions of a ghost are, ah… inadmissible in court, I think."

Emma, who'd stared at Simon as if enchanted, now came and took Lily's hand. "But we do have something, Aunt Lily. We have a place to start."

She turned around again and raised a hand toward Simon. Sarah gasped when Emma's hand lit up briefly and passed right through the ghost in a brilliant flash.

"Yes," Emma said softly. "Amelia and Simon will do everything they can to make sure the man who did this to Luke will be found."

Simon glowered for a moment. He quite obviously didn't feel the same connection to the family as Amelia did, but from the looks of it, she called the shots, even in the ghostly realm. Silently as he had come, Simon disappeared, and Lily held her head as if she thought it would explode at any moment.

"Didn't think I'd see the day when I'd be glad to have ghosts on my side."

With a resounding bang, the front door slammed just then, and Cory stormed in without so much as a hello.

"Mom, Lily, is it true? Somebody killed Luke?"

He stood in the den, staring from one to the other.

"Yes," Sarah tried to give him a hug, a move he quickly evaded and stood square in front of Lily. "Why, how, where?"

"In my store, probably last night, and as of right now, the police think I did it."

"That's bull— BS," Cory said, flinging his jacket onto the sofa. "And why didn't anybody tell me? I heard one of the coaches talk about it."

"I wanted you to have fun at hockey without dealing with... this."

"Well, you should have called me. This is Aunt Lily we are talking about." He turned to Lily and raised his arms, a teenage boy, awkward with a hug, frustrated and fumbling for words.

"Not you. Not this guy who..."

"It's okay, bud, thanks. It all just happened," Lily said and squeezed Cory's shoulder. "I'm sure it will all work itself out, and they will find who did it."

"Oh yeah? Remember Katelyn's case," Cory asked, his voice dripping with more sarcasm than a seventeen-year-old should have. "It will all work out, oh yeah. I can see that. Don't trust the police, Lily, please."

"Simon thinks it was a man doing the stabbing," Emma piped up from where she'd been playing with Pixie on the end of the couch.

"Simon? The ghost? He was there," Cory's arms dropped, and he turned to Emma almost in slow motion. "He was there?"

"Not really there-there. It's kind of complicated. I think he can sense what happened."

"Shoot, I missed everything... again," Cory muttered, dropped onto the couch, and began ruffling Pixie's long ear fringe. "And what about you, little devil? You got a suspect in mind?"

Pixie shook her ears free, jumped to put her paws on his chest, and licked his face until Cory giggled.

"Now what," he finally asked, holding Pixie and her busy tongue away from his face for a moment. "What do we do now?"

"For now," Sarah pointed at the jacket, carelessly dangling from the edge of the sofa, and nodded toward the entry hall. "Lily will stay with us for a few days, just so she is with friends at Christmastime and not grieving alone."

"Right, okay," Cory nodded and tickled Pixie under the chin. "Then she'll also be right here while we figure out what happened. I'm not going to let them pin this on you, Lily. First thing I'm going to want to look up..."

"It's Christmas," Sarah sighed and nodded again at the untidy jacket. "I was actually hoping this could be the first holiday where we did not get involved in any kind of crime, and have a peaceful family celebration. That will not happen, but can we at least let the police handle this for now and just... have a nice Christmas?"

Cory finally got the hint, rose with lazy slowness, and took his jacket to hang it up in the hall.

"But Mom..."

"I know it is important, and Lily is my best friend, but Penny Harding is a detective. If there is any way to help, we will help, of course. Did you not promise to volunteer at the Rosewood Hollow Christmas market?"

"Kind of..."

"And you have the youth group at the YMCA for basketball?"

"Yes, but..."

"Let's just have Christmas."

Cory walked away without arguing, clearly not interested in Christmas, volunteering, or family time, but he knew his mother.

Sarah saw Lily standing by the window, staring outside into the snowy yard with slumped shoulders. Her hands were hugged close to her body, and her lips were tight. Sarah leaned her head against the other woman's.

"Don't think about the worst. It won't happen, and you'll make yourself crazy. We'll figure it out." she said softly. "Promise. I know it doesn't feel like it right now, and the last thing on your mind is Christmas, but nobody who really knows you believes you would stab Luke."

Lily only shrugged, and Sarah turned her around gently.

"Nobody, understand? We know you didn't do this."

"You... maybe. But we live in a small town. I grew up here. I know people talk, and they love to gossip and spin crazy theories. It's their favorite thing. And my store, what's going to happen to my business when nobody comes in to shop for a few months because of those rumors."

"Lily, what did I just say about thinking the worst a minute ago? We will figure this out."

A deep gong rang through the house with a deep five-bell sequence, and Lily managed a thin smile.

"Did Matthew finally install that old doorbell I found in Claremont?"

"He did." Sarah grinned. "Neat, isn't it? Suits the house, I think. Emma, can you get the door? Unless it is some nosy neighbor who wants to know about Luke."

It's not a nosy neighbor, Pixie told her, and suddenly, the little papillon sat up straight, shook her ears, and ruffled her fur to make herself look twice as big as her actual five pounds. Her finely tuned senses picked up something at the door—something threatening the house's fragile peace.

"Pixie? Who's at...?"

Through the heavy oak double front doors came Penny Harding, her uniform now more threatening than charming, the cruiser at the curb a physical manifestation of an accusation. Sarah shuddered and forced herself to smile.

"Penny, welcome. What brings you here? Good news, I hope. Did you find something at the store?"

Her words trailed off at Penny's slight headshake. The officer barely looked at Sarah and Emma and focused on Lily.

"Lily? You want to speak in private for a minute?"

Lily shook her head. "This is not good, is it? I do want Sarah to be here."

Sarah clenched her fist. "No problem. Emma, do me a favor and go to your room for a minute while we sort this out."

Emma quietly slipped out of the room with a slight breeze. Was that one of the ghosts, or were Sarah's nerves and worries making her shiver?

"Do you want some water?" she heard herself ask, and Penny shook her head again.

"I would have preferred to find out about Luke's past from you, Lily, not from our police databank. Did you think I would miss it? This is not a good look."

Lily's head snapped up, and she wrinkled her brow.

"What are you talking about? Luke's past? He's new in town, yes, but he's a talented mechanic. And always sincere, polite, and helpful; what else is there to know?"

"Really?" Penny's hand slid down the side of her uniform pants along the seam. Too close, Sarah thought, far too close to the holstered weapon, the stunner, and the emergency radio. "That's all you know?"

"I told you," Lily's voice had an edge suddenly. "He was a mechanic at Dalton's. In his spare time, he helped out at the handyman store. I don't know. He probably got paid in cash a time or two. Is that what this is all about?"

Officer Harding shifted uncomfortably for a moment and looked sideways at Sarah.

"Never mind, Sarah knows everything about me. Penny, what is it you're saying?" Lily's voice breaking now with panic.

Part of Sarah wanted to leave to give them privacy, and another part knew she needed to stay for Lily. Pixie jumped up and stood beside Lily, pushing her little body in close, putting a paw on Lily's foot.

"Luke's... criminal past," Penny finally said, not taking her eyes off Lily's face for a moment. "I am sure you were aware of that, right?"

Sarah tensed, a knot forming in her stomach. From the grim set of Penny's jaw, this didn't sound good.

"Luke Devin didn't have a criminal past," Lily scoffed. "No more than Sarah or I do. That's preposterous."

"Are you sure you want to let that statement stand? Because according to the records down at the station, Luke Devin was released from prison on parole in January of this year, after serving half of his sentence... for manslaughter."

Lily's breath hitched. "Manslaughter? That's impossible! Luke wouldn't hurt a fly!"

The weight of Penny's words hung heavy in the air. Sarah's hands automatically flew to her face. Lily's world had just been turned upside down, and they were caught right in the middle of the mystery.

Sarah! Even without Pixie's warning thoughts, Sarah saw it: Lily, standing straight and defiant, then suddenly crumbling and holding onto the back of a deep reading chair. Sarah jumped to her side, supporting her shoulders and guiding her into the chair. The ticking of the grandfather clock out in the entry hall had become oppressively loud somehow, and with a mechanical whir, it struck five times.

"No, no," Lily whispered. "You must be mistaken. That's not right. You've got the wrong guy. Not Luke."

Pixie jumped into Lily's lap just as her grasping hands needed something to hang onto, and she squeezed the little papillon tight. "The wrong guy," she repeated.

Sarah raised her eyes and looked into the face of Officer Harding—a steady, unflinching gaze. There was no doubt. They did not have the wrong guy: Lily's new love had been an ex-convict.

Chapter Six

Matthew returned from some errands a little while later and found Lily sitting in the den, staring unseeing into the fireplace and the dancing flames, with Pixie on her lap. Her fingers threaded through Pixie's fur, ruffling it in a way that normally irritated the little dog.

Her eyes were empty and red-rimmed, and a pile of mangled tissues sat on the table beside her.

She hadn't spoken since Officer Harding left, no matter what Sarah and the kids had tried. Sarah had heard the car in the driveway and stopped him in the hall with a finger over her lips, leading him into the kitchen. Quietly, she caught him up on the events of the last few hours, and Matthew sat hard on the kitchen chair, a bag of produce and a fresh loaf of bread forgotten on the floor beside him.

"Manslaughter, Sarah?" Matthew asked, glancing upstairs. "For god's sake…"

"Lily swears she didn't know," Sarah hissed, then added, "Lower your voice, please."

"An ex-convict? My god, Luke's been in this house, with your kid s…." Matthew trailed off, running a hand through his hair. "They are not my children, but I still think this is something we should have been told about."

"I know, and thank you," Sarah said, putting her arms around him. "Cory and Emma are like your kids now, too."

Matthew pushed his fingers into his temple and then looked serious. "If this has something to do with Luke's time in jail, who knows, perhaps it's about revenge, and this could get dangerous for us in ways we don't even want to think about."

"I haven't had time to process it," Sarah admitted softly.

"On the other hand, if we are talking revenge," Matthew continued, "then maybe this will finally take the scrutiny off Lily."

"I wish," Sarah sighed. "Penny Harding thinks Lily might have found out about Luke's past and had a motive: revenge, anger, betrayal..."

"I swear to you, Matthew, I didn't know anything about it."

Sarah looked up, and Lily stood in the doorway, cradling Pixie in her arms. She had a blanket slung around her shoulders and looked like she wanted to just drop at any moment.

"Nobody is suggesting that," Sarah said, taking Pixie from her friend and gently steering her toward one of the kitchen chairs.

"I don't know where to go from here," Lily rested her head in her hand and stared unseeing at the tabletop in front of her. "I am just... empty inside. I was so sure I was a good judge of character, of people. I deal with people at my store all day long." She got back to her feet and looked around for her coat. "And then Luke. And this... I-I have to..."

"You have to nothing." Sarah pushed her back down and nodded at Matthew. "It's Christmas. Matthew and I are going to make us something to eat. Then you'll go to sleep upstairs. Tomorrow, everything is going to look different. Emma and I will open your store, and we will figure out a way to get Simon's hint to Officer Harding, okay?"

Lily only nodded, still staring unseen.

Keep an eye on her, Pixie said in Sarah's head. *She's really close to having a complete breakdown.*

Thanks, Pixie. Can you...?

But Pixie had already jumped into Lily's lap and pushed her hand with her little snout to get more tummy rubs.

An hour later, Lily was huddled deep into the worn armchair in the den, her face pale in the flickering firelight. The shockwaves of that day hung heavy in the air, dampening the pre-Christmas cheer that usually filled the house.

Sarah stared uncomprehendingly at the strings of popcorn and cranberries around the mantel, casting a warm, ruby glow on the room and the twinkling lights on the Christmas tree in the corner. Had they only decorated two days ago? Everything seemed strained, the promising sparkle subdued.

Dinner had been a quiet affair. Matthew had whipped up a feast, a hearty vegetarian stew with potatoes and vegetables. Yet, the plates remained mostly untouched. Both kids, usually a bottomless pit for Matthew's cooking, poked listlessly at their food, their eyes filled with a concern that mirrored Lily's own. Even Matthew, his usual easy smile absent, focused on ladling stew with a meticulousness that betrayed his worries.

The only bright spot amidst the gloom was Pixie, a ball of white fur with a perpetually wagging tail. She had curled up on Lily's lap, refusing to leave even through dinner.

We'll get through this, Sarah heard her say. *Like we always do—together.*

Sarah offered Lily a weak smile. "You know, Pixie swears these gingerbread cookies are magical," she said, pushing the plate towards her friend.

Lily forced a small laugh, her voice thick with emotion. "Magical gingerbread cookies, huh?" she croaked, picking up a cookie with a trembling hand. "I think I might need a miracle, not a cookie."

A flicker of defiance sparked in her eyes as she took a bite. It was faint, but it was there. Perhaps it was the cinnamon and ginger, or maybe the unspoken support from Sarah and her family, but a tiny ember of hope rekindled within her.

"I don't know, Sarah," she said, her voice gaining tiny bit of strength. "I still feel lost."

"We'll find the truth, Lily," Sarah promised, her hand resting comfortingly on Lily's shoulder. "And whoever did this to Luke... they'll pay."

Lily put the remainder of the cookie back down and closed her eyes for a long moment.

"I hope so, but I do know one thing," she continued. "Without all of you, I'd be going stark raving mad in my empty apartment. So perhaps your cookies are magical after all."

Chapter Seven

The aroma of freshly brewed coffee did little to dispel the leaden weight in Sarah's stomach. Dawn's vibrant hues of orange and pink mocked the gloom clinging stubbornly to the corners of Rosewood Hollow Bookstore. Unpacking the last of the delivery Tyler had left felt like shoveling sand against the rising tide of dread. Lily, usually an early riser, was conspicuously absent. No surprise there. The revelation about Luke had shattered the comforting routine of her comfortable mornings at the store, leaving a gaping hole filled with swirling questions and a cold, metallic taste of betrayal.

A soft click of tiny claws against wooden floors startled Sarah. Pixie, a normally effervescent ball of white fur, emerged from her carrier, a stark contrast to her usual boundless energy. Today, her bright eyes held a dull reflection of Lily's sleepless night. A low whine escaped the tiny dog, and she nudged Sarah's leg with a wet nose and a tentative paw. Sarah sank to the floor, burying her face in Pixie's soft fur, seeking solace in the familiar warmth.

"I know, girl," she murmured, her voice thick with worry. "I heard you kept Lily company."

Pixie's tail thumped a listless rhythm against the floor. Sarah could almost feel the echoes of Lily's restless tossing and turning through their unspoken bond.

Emma, her cheeks flushed from the harsh wind outside, materialized beside them with a steaming mug of coffee, her usually vibrant eyes mirroring the gloom.

"Strong one, please," she rasped, her voice devoid of its usual cheer and sounding so very grown up. "Did you hear Lily pacing last night?"

Sarah nodded, her eyes closed and her lips a tight line. "Yup. I think she needs some space. I hope she is resting now."

Silence, heavy and oppressive, descended upon them, broken only by the furious hiss of the espresso machine and the mournful howl of the wind outside. The routine tasks of the morning seemed to mock their churning anxieties. The rhythmic tap-tap-tap of police boots echoed through the building from the back room, a constant reminder of the tragedy that had unfolded in the rooms beyond the cozy store. Sarah and Emma exchanged worried glances, the unspoken question hanging heavy in the air: what exactly had happened in this beautiful place?

Finally, the connecting door creaked open, revealing Officer Harding. Her face, etched with fatigue that ran deeper than exhaustion, mirrored the shattered sense of peace within the bookstore.

"Alright, Ms. Anderson," she said, her voice gruff. "You can remove the tape and open for business, if you truly wish to. But remember, the back rooms are still a crime scene. We'll need your full cooperation, understand?"

Sarah nodded, a hollow feeling settling in her stomach. Relief at opening the store was overshadowed by Officer Harding's words, a constant reminder of the darkness lurking just beyond the yellow tape.

The first customer pushed open the door, then another, drawn by a morbid curiosity that hung heavy in the air.

Whispers snaked through the aisles: "Murder... right here..."

Sarah forced a smile, her heart a lead weight in her chest. This haven, once a cozy, charming refuge from the city's chaos, now felt tainted.

But as she met Emma's resolute gaze, a spark of defiance flickered within her. They wouldn't let the rumors win.

∽

Hours stretched before her, punctuated by the occasional sideways glance and hushed conversations that dipped to whispers at her approach. Each one was a prickle against her skin.

The Christmas playlist on Lily's sound system, usually a source of comfort, now felt jarring against the grim reality. The cheery sign on the counter, 'Discount on coffee and cookies today!' seemed like a desperate attempt at normalcy.

As the day went on, her fingers danced across the worn keys of the cash register, a comforting rhythm echoing the steady tick-tock of the old round clock on the wall. Despite the forced cheer, the day stretched on, and Sarah thought she could feel eyes boring into her every time her back was turned.

∽

The afternoon sun cast long shadows through the store windows as the bell over the door suddenly clanged wildly. Cory burst in, a flurry of red cheeks and frantic energy, his breath ragged.

"Mom, gotta show you something—right now!" he blurted, ignoring Sarah's sputtering questions about his sudden arrival and reckless mode of travel on a cold winter's day.

He ripped off his bike helmet, ice crystals clinging to the visor, revealing a manic glint in his eyes.

"No time... gotta see this in private."

Customers craned their necks, their whispers adding to the rising tension. Sarah hustled him away into a quiet corner, the festive displays in the geography and travel section a stark contrast to the urgency etched on her son's face.

"Quiet place? What's going on? The office is still off-limits," she hissed, her gaze darting nervously at the curious onlookers. "Couldn't you have texted me if you needed something? Everyone's already on edge."

Cory barely glanced at the customers, his voice tight with suppressed excitement.

"Whatever. Look!" He thrust his tablet at her, the screen displaying a website with a name that sent a jolt through Sarah—Luke Devin.

"He... he went to some beer festival with his brother-in-law a few years back," Cory sputtered, scrolling down the page with trembling fingers. "Apparently, things got out of hand. Luke caught him... harassing someone."

Sarah's stomach clenched. "Harassing?"

"Yeah, like, hitting on other women right in front of his wife! Luke confronted him and told him to quit being a jerk, but the guy wouldn't back down. Suddenly, this thing turned into a big brawl."

"This is... this is private information, Cory. It's none of our business."

"But Mom, he was defending his sister! And now..." Cory's voice cracked, his eyes mirroring the turmoil within. "It was just an unlucky punch. The guy survived for a bit and... passed away at the hospital. Luke felt horrible about the whole thing. Said he was just drunk, never meant to hurt the guy, just wanted him to stop being a jerk."

"Violence is never the answer. I keep telling you that. Where are you getting all of this information anyway?"

She reached out a hand for the tablet, and Cory swiped it back just as quickly.

"Murderpedia."

"Murder... Cory!" Sarah lowered her head again; the word murder was not one to be used lightly in this store just then.

"Cory," she hissed again. "Do I have to start checking your internet use now?"

"Relax, Mom, it's just a true crime info site. Everybody uses it. And I only went there to look up Luke to help out Aunt Lily." Cory pressed his lips together hard. "She's... a wreck. Just like Katelyn. It's like somebody... let's just say she's not taking it well."

"She adored Luke," Sarah sighed, her voice barely a whisper. When she caught a customer's eye, she pulled Cory a little further into the corner, where the Christmas music from the loudspeaker would mask their conversation.

"I appreciate you trying to help, but the police are investigating. Lily's innocent, and eventually—"

"Innocent, huh? Just like Katelyn was supposed to be?" Cory's voice held a chilling edge.

Sarah threw her hands up, frustration warring with a rising tide of fear. "Didn't we agree on a peaceful holiday?"

"Isn't Aunt Lily your best friend?"

Sarah forced a cheerful smile as a customer approached, a stack of books cradled in her arms.

"Unless you can lend a hand here," she continued hurriedly, "head back home. Keep Lily company. Maybe take her along when you go to hockey practice. We'll talk later, alright?"

❦

The customer smiled, oblivious to the undercurrent of tension. "Afternoon, Mrs. Anderson. Merry Christmas! These are for my niece."

Cory shoved the tablet back into his backpack, his eyes gleaming with a spark of defiance.

"Fine. But remember this, Mom. That wasn't murder. It was an accident. Meaning someone had a different motive for silencing Luke."

Sarah plastered on a smile for the customer. "Mrs. Brightwell! Are you out Christmas shopping today? Let me wrap those for you. Speaking of gifts, we just received a new baking book with recipes to die for!"

The joke hung heavy in the air, a stark contrast to the growing unease in Sarah's gut. Lily had poured her heart and soul into this bookstore. It was her haven, and Sarah wouldn't let anyone take it away.

Throughout the day, Sarah couldn't shake off a chilling sensation, a phantom draft that tugged at her skin now and then. Each time, she'd scan the aisles, searching for Amelia or Simon, but they remained eerily absent. Perhaps it was just the old building creaking its bones, she thought, deciding to keep it from Emma.

However, a new detail gnawed at her. Lily's usually upbeat Christmas playlist had morphed into a somber collection of traditional carols. A shiver ran down her spine. Odd indeed.

❦

And what is it you are doing?

Pixie, usually a champion napper in the bookstore's plush armchairs, had abandoned her usual routine. Today, she was a furry detective, her nose pressed to every shelf, sniffing every corner with a fervor that sent shivers down Sarah's spine.

I told you I smelled something powerful and very strange on Luke when they took him away.

Pixie looked up and let a customer scratch her ears.

Mmmm. I thought I would check if it was something in the store.

And?

Nothing, which is very frustrating.

"She's just the perfect shop dog, isn't she?" a customer behind her chimed in, breaking the silence. Sarah whirled around, her cheeks burning with the sudden realization she'd been caught staring at Pixie.

"Yes, that she is," she stammered, forcing a smile. "Can I help you find something?"

Chapter Eight

S arah pushed open her massive front door, the weight of the day clinging to her shoulders. In the den, Lily and Cory were locked in a lackadaisical game of checkers, while Matthew hunched over his tablet, a forgotten mug of tea sitting beside him.

"About you waltzing into the store with a murder website..." Sarah began, her voice trailing off at the sight of their united front.

"My fault," Lily said without looking up, her pale skin glowing in the dim light of the fireplace. "I asked Cory to use his mad research skills to find out what really happened to Luke."

Sarah pinched the bridge of her nose, frustration warring with a surprising warmth.

"Cory isn't entirely wrong," Matthew chimed in, finally glancing up. "Luke didn't get a fair shake. A good lawyer could have—"

"Guys," Sarah interrupted, desperation creeping into her voice. "Christmas."

Heads snapped up, a flicker of understanding crossing their faces.

"How was the store today?" Lily asked when no one had jumped into the breach.

"Busy," Sarah sighed, sinking into a chair. "But we managed."

"I can't thank you enough..."

"Don't thank me. Emma would have my head on a platter if we didn't keep things running," Sarah admitted with a wry smile. "Besides, it seems my entire family has become invested in this 'who killed Luke Devin' mystery."

"Entire?" Lily raised an eyebrow.

A knowing glance at the doorway confirmed Sarah's suspicions. Emma entered, a mischievous glint in her eye, and Pixie trotted behind, her tail wagging excitedly.

"Don't even pretend you weren't researching police procedures all afternoon, Emma," Sarah said, a hint of amusement in her voice. "And as for you, Pixie..."

The tiny dog whined and nuzzled Sarah's hand, maneuvering her head so Sarah's fingers ended up scratching behind her ears.

"Pixie sniffed every solid item in the store and a few more," Sarah explained. "Seems she smelled something odd on Luke when he was... taken away. So, she took it upon herself to check everything."

And it was definitely not in the store, so I am assuming the murderer brought it with him. It's a clue.

"And she thinks it is something the murderer had on him," Sarah repeated Pixie's opinion and buried her face in her hands, a reluctant smile pulling at the corners of her lips.

"Fine then," she conceded. "Goodbye, peaceful Christmas traditions. Looks like the Andersons have a murderer to catch."

"Besides," Emma said, braiding her hair into a thick braid. "I think the ghosts' idea of a quiet Christmas is a little different from yours anyway."

Sarah folded her arms. She wasn't quite ready to give up on the image of a quiet, beautiful family Christmas with all of the trimmings quite yet, even if Matthew had his nose buried in his tablet, Cory looked over his shoulder, pointing at things, Lily looked like she wanted to run away hard and fast, and Emma stared into the corner by the fireplace.

Don't be mad at them. They are trying to help.

So am I, and I wanted a beautiful Christmas—the kind I haven't had in years.

The moment you saw Amelia for the first time, discovered the attic, and started speaking to me, did you ever think this was going to be a normal family?'

Sarah said nothing. She poured herself something to drink and stood by the window, where soft, fat snowflakes began to fall quietly and softly. The kind of snowy late night you could watch on Hallmark movies. With a fireplace and a happy, well-adjusted, normal family.

"I'm sorry." That was Lily by her side, holding out her glass of wine. "I didn't mean to ruin your Christmas."

"You didn't," Sarah said automatically.

"Just say the word. I can go back to my apartment tomorrow," Lily now said, sensing the unspoken anger. "Get a hotshot lawyer, maybe hire my own investigator. Though I've never hired a PI before..." Lily's voice trailed off. "No, you're right. I will go pack."

"You will do no such thing." Sarah turned and made a fist with her right hand, pursing her lips. "I... you're right. This is not what I wanted our family Christmas to be—but you're my best friend."

"Still...."

"Emma and I are having a blast running your store, aren't we, Emma?"

"You bet," Emma said, grinning. "It's the best. I love being at the store, and once this is all over, I actually want you to teach me about running a bookstore. I want to learn, and maybe..."

"Guys..." Sarah raised her hands and turned again to look into the yard, where the snow was starting to pile on the sidewalk. "Somebody is going to have to shovel the sidewalk."

"Mom, but..."

"Emma, I'd rather not have my own children remind me of the meaning of Christmas and family and friends, okay? So, if you want to come help me, go get your boots and coat. If not, that's fine, too. I probably need the workout."

"No, I was going to say Cory and Matthew already got dressed to do it, that's all."

Sarah pressed her lips together. Indeed, out there in the front yard, Matthew and Cory appeared, bundled in thick coats, holding shovels in front of them like weapons. Cory hauled out and threw a massive load of snow at Matthew, who retaliated with a shovel full of his own.

Cory then abandoned his snow shovel and formed a massive snowball in his gloved hands. Cory was a master basketballer. Watch out, Sarah thought.

At that moment, a flurry of white exploded into the air, momentarily blinding her as laughter erupted from the driveway. Matthew, cheeks flushed red from exertion, was under siege by a giggling Cory, armed with a load of snowballs the size of his head.

Sarah watched, a familiar warmth blooming in her chest, as Matthew retaliated with a snowball that sailed wide, smattering harmlessly onto their car's hood. The scene, bathed in the soft glow of the porch light, transported her back to childhood snowball fights, the sting of cold air forgotten in the pure joy of the moment. It felt like Christmas morning all over again, the magic rekindled not by presents, but by the simple pleasure of togetherness. This... this was what she had wanted. Not tinsel and carols and food, not presents or Hallmark moments, but togetherness. Family life.

"Fine then." She swiped the wine glass out of Lily's hand and settled into the most comfortable chair by the fire, putting up her feet and patting her hand on the chair so Pixie would hop up to sit with her. "So, what do we have so far?"

"Penny Harding is convinced Lily is her only and best suspect," Emma said, sitting beside her on the couch curling under her feet. "Just because her aunt Tami can't positively confirm without a doubt she was at the house all night."

"She is very old, and if I remember correctly... it's quite a drive out there, even on a good day," Sarah said, picking up her phone.

"True, but they've done a few simulations, and they think I could have gone to Tami's, waited for her to go to sleep, drove out here to kill Luke, and drove back again," Lily said, looking for a blanket. "They showed me about three models that said it was possible and I could have done it."

"And I have three models that say they are wrong, and you had no reason to do that..." Sarah held out a hand to Pixie, who jumped into her lap. "I do wish you had phoned me that night."

Lily only shrugged. "I got there, realized Tami only wanted attention, and after a bit, went to a pub there. I had a few drinks and decided to stay the night..."

"And then locked your phone and keys in the car." Sarah nodded. "You told me. Now all we have to do is explain to these millennial investigators that you do have the kind of car where that is actually still a possibility."

"Hey, my bug—"

"Is from the seventies, Lily. Nowadays, you have key fobs and safeguards, so that is no longer possible."

Lily raised her hands. "Now, what about that smell Pixie said she detected."

Sarah closed her eyes and folded her hands behind her head.

"Pixie said she smelled something... weird on Luke. Other than..."

Other than death.

She flashed a look at Pixie.

"Something?"

Something warm feeling... and tingly. Like freshly cut grass with a bit of bite, but earthy, with a little bit of lemon that happens when you're cleaning.

Sarah repeated what she had heard from Pixie, and they all stared into the fireplace for a moment.

"It's a spice."

Sarah snapped her head up and found Amelia floating into the room from her favorite corner of the fireplace. At the same time, she felt chilled and pulled her blanket a little tighter.

"Amelia, you just about frightened me to..."

"What?"

"Nothing." Sarah kept her arms wrapped around Pixie and made sure Emma was still on the sofa with her. Lily merely stared open-mouthed.

"What are you talking about—this is a spice? Do you know what kind?"

"No, but it sounds like a spice."

"Amelia, I'm tired." Sarah pulled the hair back from her head and counted to five quietly. "If you know something, would you just tell me? I am just not in the frame of mind to start guessing."

Amelia glowered at her for a moment, and her spectral form shimmered in shades of orange in the curious way she had when she was upset or extremely angry with someone.

"Simon and I decided to pay a visit to the local police station," she said and glided up close to Lily. "Perhaps it is because of Christmas time, but these constables there are very lazy. If they treated my own demise with as much disdain and loafing, no wonder it took one hundred years for the true story to come out."

Lily brought her arms close to her body and seemed to shrink in her chair. Her lips became a pale white line, and Sarah thought she could see her tremble.

"Why? What do you mean?" Lily asked softly.

"Firstly, they are having a Christmas party there at the police station," Amelia scoffed. "This is not the right place for such a celebration of traditions, and they should concentrate on the job. Inappropriate."

"Yes, yes," Sarah spun her hand in circles. With Amelia, she found, you had to keep her moving on. Since discovering the true story of her death, she could easily have moved on to the other side and been with Simon, doing whatever it is ghosts do. But no, now that she was no longer bound to this house, she enjoyed moving around, poking her pert little 1900s nose into the homes and businesses of the living and causing chaos now and then.

Chaos...

Her head snapped up for the second time in the last ten minutes, and she brought her hands to her lips.

"You didn't... did you? Tell me you did not do anything... foolish at the police station."

"Of course not." Amelia sparkled again. "But from their conversations, I gathered they are quite certain that Lily here is, in fact, guilty. They intend to close the case before Christmas."

She moved her spectral, glowing hands as if washing them, eliciting a shower of sparks with each movement.

"No," Lily groaned. "Why won't anybody believe me? I did not hurt Luke."

"Of course not." Amelia glided a little closer again. "One of the benefits of being a specter is that it is nearly impossible to lie to us. We have our ways to see the truth."

Her hand pointed at her chest and disappeared into infinity—another one of her little displays.

"And?"

Sarah got to her feet and advanced on Amelia. There was more. There was always more when Amelia smirked like this.

"We prevented this for the moment," she said haughtily, letting a sparks shower rain from her hands.

"And exactly... how did you prevent this, Amelia?" Sarah took another step, but at that very moment, her phone rang, and simultaneously, she could hear the front door open. Having finished their snow battle and possibly the sidewalk, Matthew and Cory had come back in.

"Sarah Anderson," she said, picking up the phone without looking.

For a moment, she was met with only a static crackle and hiss and thought her phone might be broken. Finally, she heard a voice.

"Sarah? Sarah, are you there? It is Penny Harding."

"Officer Harding? What's going on? This line sounds like you're somewhere in Siberia."

Another horrible crackle and static hiss assaulted her ears and she held the phone a few inches away from her head.

"Officer?"

"...Can't... Electronic troubles at the station... ...mystery..."

Sarah slowly raised her eyes just to catch the tail end of Amelia melting into the corner by the fireplace. She pressed her lips together and bit down hard to keep from chuckling.

"Come again?"

Emma and Lily crowded in close now, even though Sarah waved them away.

"We will... to postpone our investigation... we have... trouble sorted. Can you tell Lily... keep herself available."

"I think I got that. And officer?"

She did not receive an answer, and the line went dead. Whatever Penny Harding might or might not have said was swallowed up in a burst of static hissing and crackle, accompanied by a strangled whistling sound now, just for good measure, and then silence.

Sarah carefully ended the call and finally allowed herself to burst out laughing.

"Amelia, if you were one of my kids, I would give you what they call a grade-A lesson right now, do you hear?"

"Uh oh, that doesn't sound good..."

Cory and Matthew had finally shed their layers of winter clothing and stepped into the den, sweaty, damp, and red-cheeked from their outdoor battle.

"What happened?" Matthew wanted to know. "And what is a grade-A lesson?"

"It's when you've done something really harebrained," Cory supplied helpfully. "And you knew better and did it anyway. Usually, mom makes you perform some sort of service act or chore so you don't forget anytime soon."

"Sounds like you've been there before."

"Oh yeah," Cory rolled his eyes. "Just not in a few years. Last time, I think... Never mind. What's Amelia done this time?"

Sarah put her arm around Lily's shoulders. She could feel Lily trembling through her sweater's thick material and squeezed her shoulder hard. Pixie jumped into her lap and licked Lily's cheek until she managed a thin smile.

"It seems our two ghosts decided to drop in down at the police station," Sarah said. "Apparently, they felt the officers were jumping to conclusions in a hurry to close their case before Christmas... without looking at the whole picture."

"Pfft," Cory rolled his eyes again and threw up his hands.

"And they still think I killed Luke," Lily said. Her hands trembled as she desperately searched for a tissue in her many pockets.

"We all know you didn't. Ghost logic," Sarah continued to Matthew. "Amelia thought for sure she could spot if Lily was lying; hence... she must be innocent. So, she and Simon disrupted, err... the everyday workflow at the station."

"Oh dear," Matthew hid his chuckle, pretending to wipe his nose with an oversized tissue. "And, uhh... how do you know...?"

"You know Amelia and electronics." Sarah closed her eyes for a moment and shook her head.

Matthew dropped into what had become his favorite wingback chair by the fire and reached for the tea Emma had made.

"That doesn't really change the facts or Officer Harding's opinion of Lily's guilt."

"No... but it gives us a tiny reprieve." Sarah squeezed Lily's shoulder again. "A few days to get an idea of what really happened. And perhaps, just perhaps, have a beautiful Christmas after all."

Unlike Cory and Emma, whose laughter echoed through the room, Lily found little humor in the ghost's shenanigans. Lost in thought, she stared into the hypnotic dance of the flames in the fireplace. Her mind churned, no doubt grappling with the surreal turn of events: a successful entrepreneur one day, a murder suspect the next, all while still grieving the loss of Luke...

Lily went to bed when Emma and Cory headed upstairs, and Sarah found herself nodding off in the warm den, listening to the crackling fire.

A spice, she thought as she drifted off to sleep. Amelia thought what Pixie smelled sounded like a spice. Isn't that curious?

Chapter Nine

Sarah didn't have a chance to worry about that curious scent for the next little while, as her day at Lily's bookstore started with chaos and went downhill from there.

She arrived early, dreaming of a quiet morning with coffee and soft jazz, advising a few shoppers with last-minute gift ideas. Instead, she discovered a huge delivery Lily had neglected to warn her about, not only of books but also little reading-related knickknacks that had no official 'home' amongst the store shelves.

With every new box unpacked, "Where does this go?" became a guessing game. Phone calls to Lily flew back and forth until Lily's voice became choked with tears, and Sarah decided the heck with it. She was in charge for the moment and would make the store look nice according to her own ideas. Considering the circumstances, that was not always an easy feat, either.

The store felt busier than it usually was early in the morning. Most of the customers were probably Christmas shopping, but Sarah could see the curiosity that brought many of them out on a bitterly cold day. Wanting to see the place where an actual murder had happened, and speculating on the why and the who of it all.

An hour ago, Rosie and Anne Marie, the directors of the local ladies' club, had snuck past the barrier toward the office and storage area and craned their necks this way and that, trying to catch a glimpse of anything beyond the pink police seal at the door.

They'd been startled when Sarah politely asked if she could help and muttered something about looking for a washroom.

Tony, who ran Grandpa Becker's hardware store when Walter could not, came up to the register holding a few issues of Field and Stream. He frowned and looked at Sarah for a long moment, rubbing his chin.

"Now, you're a levelheaded woman there, right?" he said slowly, wagging his head. No hint of what he thought a levelheaded woman might be.

"What do you think of all of this? She lives at your house now. Do you think Lily did it?"

Just hoping for a thrill.

Small-town living, she told herself and counted to ten. Charming at the best of times, but in large doses, entirely irritating.

She'd given Emma the day off, and halfway into the morning, she fought the impulse to call her daughter. It was Christmas, after all.

∞

Penny Harding found her with her blonde hair tied up in a messy, loose ponytail, her cheeks bright red, and her face glistening with perspiration, up on a ladder a few hours later.

"Whoa there," Penny said, automatically holding onto the library ladder. "You okay up there? You look... beat, actually."

"I feel it."

Sarah clambered down and frantically looked around for her cardigan, which she had discarded an hour ago.

Just as she reached the bottom of the ladder, a massive crash and thump echoed through the aisles of the store. Sarah winced as her elbow caught a stack of boxes, and the uppermost one tumbled precariously, threatening to unleash a cascade of mysteries upon her feet and the floor.

"Penny!" she called out, throwing out an arm and unleashing a shower of packing peanuts. "A little help here?"

The ever-reliable Detective Penny emerged from a cloud of dust motes dancing in a sunbeam, a lopsided smirk on her face.

"I'm not entirely sure you should be handling this store all by yourself, Sarah. Not to criticize your methods, but, safety first."

"Sorry. It was an accident," Sarah muttered, shoving a stray copy of "Knitting for Beginners" back into its box. "Lily had this grand idea of a restock, bless her heart, but apparently forgot to mention the sheer volume of it all."

A shadow flickered across Penny's gaze, a flicker Sarah knew all too well. If she'd had her way, Penny would have issued a warrant for Lily right then and there instead of merely asking her to stay in town and be available for the time being. Sarah came prepared to defend Lily's innocence to the death. But with each passing unpacked box, a tiny voice in the back of Sarah's own head whispered, *What if Penny is on to something? What if there's something I am not seeing...?*

"So," Penny began, her voice adopting a casual tone that Sarah knew masked a sharper inquiry, "any interesting finds in these literary mountains?"

Sarah shot her a wary glance.

"Just the usual suspects, Penny. Agatha Christie rubbing shoulders with Jane Austen. A Hemingway hiding behind a shelf of self-help guides. Anything in particular you are looking for?"

Penny raised an eyebrow, a playful glint in her eye. "No ancient artifacts mysteriously misplaced, then? No suspicious crystals or sapphires demanding rescue?"

Sarah shivered, despite the flush in her cheeks. Not so stupid, this detective. She knew there was more to Sarah's excuses for the strange occurrences in Rosewood Hollow lately. Finally, she spread her arms with what she hoped was a winning smile.

"Officer Harding, the closest Lily gets to archaeology is digging through her purse for a forgotten store receipt. This is just a massive store restock, nothing else."

Penny hummed noncommittally, her gaze lingering a beat too long on a travel guide featuring the Acropolis that peeked out from a half-unpacked box. "Lily's still at your house then?"

"Yup. She and my kids. Probably wrapping presents or baking or making snow forts in the yard for all I know!" Sarah forced a smile, the playful banter suddenly feeling strained.

The jovial mood instantly evaporated, replaced by a tense silence punctuated only by the crinkle of packing paper.

"As long as she stays there," Penny sighed, running a hand through her hair, "This is one of the reasons why I'm here. Back at the station, it's like a scene out of a blackout novel. Computers kaput, phones on the fritz. Nothing is responding. Can't get a decent cup of coffee out of the machine. Can't retrieve a record or even issue a parking ticket."

A small, secret smile played on Sarah's lips.

"Don't let the tourists know that, they'll be parking everywhere."

Amelia and Simon. For once, their playful antics with electronics bought some much-needed time. If the Rosewood Hollow police had thought to solve this case by Christmas, they would not get far. The mere thought made Sarah grin, a reminder that even amidst the mystery, a touch of the otherworldly made their little town all the more charming.

"It's not entirely funny," Penny Harding said, handing Sarah a box of coffee mugs with exaggerated care. "We're not getting any help from the Claremont station until after Christmas, and IT support—forget about it. They're backed up until god knows when. I'm relying on you to make sure Lily doesn't, uhh... do anything ill-advised for now, like jetting off to Greece, if you catch my drift."

"Lily is innocent," Sarah stabbed a pair of scissors into an empty box with more force than needed to break it down and flatten it. "And I can't believe you, who's known her for years, could doubt that."

"Sarah..." Officer Harding ticked items off on her fingers. "Lily was in a relationship with the victim; she had no idea of his criminal past and time in jail, and she loaned him a significant amount of money. That's quite a load in my book."

"Money?" The word slipped out involuntarily. Sarah's heart sank, and a sick feeling spread in her stomach. Lily hadn't said anything about loaning or giving money to Luke. Lily didn't loan money. Never. Half the time, she complained about how broke she was. Sarah clenched her jaws and forced a smile she didn't feel.

"Didn't you know about that?"

"Of course," Sarah lied. "Just a temporary loan, no big deal."

Inside, she prayed it wouldn't turn out to be a massive and ridiculous amount of money. Dear god, Lily, what have you got yourself into this time, she thought, all the while keeping that silly fake grin on her face.

"Then there is the fact that Luke Devin was found here inside Lily's store."

"With the door locked from the inside," Sarah fired back, but Penny Harding only shook her head slowly.

"There's no way to prove that, Sarah. Your, uhh, Dr. Turner and Walter Becker messed with that door enough that our technicians couldn't tell if it was locked or not."

"Sorry." Sarah looked down at her hand, holding the scissors like a weapon, and put them down carefully. Penny Harding put her hand over Sarah's and leaned in a bit closer.

"I'm sure you're just being a good friend, Sarah. All I'm saying, is don't be too sure about this one way or another, okay?"

The little bell above the entrance door relieved Sarah from having to answer, and she smiled again and patted Penny on the shoulder.

"I'll keep that in mind. Hold on. I have a customer."

With all of her heart, she hoped the officer would leave. Alas, Penny Harding did not.

She reached across the counter to help herself to a cappuccino Sarah had prepared and settled into one of the many deep reading chairs Lily had installed with a good view of the entrance and the store proper, sipping coffee, watching customers come and go, and Sarah unpack boxes in between wrapping presents and taking charges.

"Are you having a good time," she finally asked, brushing a sweaty strand of blonde hair from her face. "Because if you are going to be a permanent fixture, you might as well help with this delivery."

"I am a police officer."

"You are. But right now, you are sitting in the middle of my... of Lily's bookstore, watching and making our customers nervous. I understand that your police station isn't really... working right now..."

"Are you asking me to leave?"

Yes, we are, Sarah heard and hugged her arms closer to her body.

The ghosts. Apparently, Amelia or Simon had come to visit the store and make their opinion known.

Pixie, napping at Penny's feet as if she wanted to keep an eye on the woman, lifted her head and growled briefly.

Penny automatically reached down and patted Pixie's head while narrowing a level gaze at Sarah.

"There's something that happens with you now and then I can't put my finger on, you know what I mean?"

"Yup." Sarah stabbed her scissors into another cardboard box and flattened it. "It's called anxiety. Sometimes referred to as nerves. It happens when your best friend is under suspicion while completely innocent, and you are trying to keep things together."

"I see..." Penny nodded sagely into her empty cup, which Sarah promptly took away from her without offering another. "Happened to you just recently, did it not?"

"What? Oh, you mean Katelyn? Yes, fortunately, the real thieves confessed, and the sapphire was found. Given the size of Rosewood Hollow..." Sarah smiled broadly and swept an arm encompassing the store, the street beyond, and the entire village. "Chances are, if someone is under suspicion, you will know them, right?"

"I suppose." Penny stared at her hands. "What about the Johnsons."

"The who? Oh... Our former neighbors. Couldn't rightly tell."

No, because if I did, I'd have to tell you one of them has been turned into a small pile of ashes, and the other one ran at the sight of it.

"Probably living it up in Florida," she said with a giggle that, even to her own ears, came out way too bright. "My ex has a timeshare in

Florida. Loves it. Of course, he golfs, so I suppose that's natural. How about you? Ever think of retiring down south?"

"Not on a cop's pension."

The smile vanished from her face as abruptly as a snuffed candle. Her brows descended, etching two deep lines into her forehead. The corners of her mouth dipped downwards, pulling her lips taut into a thin line.

"Well then."

"Well then," Sarah answered, forcing the brightest smile she could muster. "Nice seeing you."

"I'm sure. Remember now. Lily—"

"Should not leave town. I will make sure she is completely aware and tucked in safely at my house tonight. Anything else?"

"Sarah." Penny shook her head and stared down at the tips of her highly polished black boots. "For a newcomer..."

"Relative newcomer."

"Relative newcomer then, you are strangely clued in in this town. People tell you things. You are aware of things... that I could never figure out."

"I guess." Sarah shrugged and grinned at the officer again. "Maybe people think it's cute that I'm from Baltimore. Couldn't really tell you why."

"No, I don't think it has anything to do with Baltimore." Penny shoved her hands into her pockets and fixed Pixie in a hard, long stare. "I don't know what it is, but please promise me you will tell me if anything... um... comes to you regarding this crime."

"Sure... I think."

"Not just sure, Sarah. Not just, I think. You found a home here in Rosewood Hollow—at a difficult time in your life. We don't get many murders here. The good people of this town deserve an answer if it does happen, do you understand."

Now it was Sarah's turn to look down at her shoes and lick suddenly dry lips.

"I will," she finally said softly, knowing this one was a promise she had to keep, even if she had no idea how.

She stood shuffling her feet as Penny walked out and other customers came in.

Chapter Ten

After Penny left, Sarah mechanically smiled and repeatedly wished people a Merry Christmas until Matthew walked in.

"Excuse me," he said. "I am looking for the extremely good-looking, kind woman who runs this store. Any idea where I might be able to find her?"

Sarah looked up and forced a smile.

"Matthew. Thanks for stopping by."

"Thanks for stopping by?" Matthew put both hands over his heart. "Thanks for stopping by?? Put me in a casket right now; there's an arrow through my heart."

With a flourish worthy of Shakespeare, he raised his hands and put them over his heart again.

"Matt..."

"What's wrong?" With two giant steps, he was by her side and put his arm around her shoulder. "You look troubled. Something happen?"

"Penny Harding was here."

"Oh..."

"And... she's more than ever convinced Lily did it."

"But, there's no real—"

"No evidence, no. But Lily loaned the fellow money. A large amount of money, as far as I can discern."

"Oh…" Matthew's hands dropped to his side. He lifted them again, trying to formulate an answer, and finally shook his head.

"That indeed does not look good. And why on earth did Lily not tell you? I'm sorry."

"Not your fault." She squeezed his hand and made that smile appear on her face again, the one she'd reserved for customers all afternoon. "Now, what brings you here?"

"I thought we might take a wander over to the Christmas market. But if you're not in the mood."

"No, no, I am… I totally am. I need something normal; I need Christmas. Thank you for suggesting it. I'll be just a minute."

Sarah checked her register tapes against cash in the drawer, bagged up the cash that needed to go to the bank, and made the required notes in Lily's ledger, all the while keeping Matthew and Pixie within view.

Pixie sat straight up, ears perked, coat ruffled and ordered, tail wrapped around her feet, keeping an eye on Matthew as if she meant to berate him for something only she understood.

Matthew finally got up and wandered to one of the bookshelves, randomly pulling out books and putting them back.

"Lily was the first friend I made in Rosewood Hollow," Sarah finally said softly. "My best friend. I can't believe—I won't believe…"

"Then don't." Matthew put a hand over hers, stilling her jerky movements with the bank deposit bag and the credit card terminal. "Don't think about it tonight. Let's just walk over to the Christmas market, have some spiced cider, and listen to the carols. You'll feel better."

Sarah nodded and dumped the deposit bag into her tote.

"I just want to know..." she said, faltering again.

"And you will. Maybe not now, not right away, but you will. Promise."

Pixie jumped from the chair she'd been on and wrapped around Sarah's legs a few times.

That cop lady doesn't know her right from her left today, Sarah. Don't let her frazzle you.

And why is that? Oh... because Simon and Amelia are messing with the entire station and the electronics. Maybe that's not exactly wise.'

They know you worry about Lily, and they will keep her here and at home for Christmas.

"Thank you... everybody."

She didn't realize she had spoken aloud until she saw Matthew's face light up.

"For taking you to the Christmas market? Please! It's a privilege to walk with a talented, beautiful, and hard-working lady."

He offered his arm; Sarah grinned broadly and hooked her arm through his to leave. They lingered an extra beat at the lock of the heavy, weathered oak door as it sighed shut behind them with a solid finality.

∾

A fierce wind, the kind that whispered of approaching winter, whipped down Rosewood Hollow's main street, rattling the holly and evergreen boughs strung cheerfully across the storefronts. The festive decorations seemed like a cruel mockery in the face of everything that was going on.

Sarah tucked her hands deep into the pockets of her coat and tried to ward off the dark thoughts crowding into her mind until a familiar comforting scent tickled her nose.

That scent, a heady mix of spices and citrus, was a familiar comfort, a reminder of countless cozy nights spent curled at the fireplace, a mug of steaming cider warming their hands. Tonight, the scent only served to intensify the hollowness Sarah felt.

The Christmas market, a kaleidoscope of sights, sounds, and smells, promised a welcome distraction, a chance to forget, even for a little while, the weight of suspicion that hung heavy in the air. When they turned into the Rosewood Hollow common, Sarah found herself in the center of a riot of twinkling lights and cheerful decorations.

The decorating committees of various churches and service clubs had outdone themselves this year. Wooden booths overflowed with local crafts: hand-knitted mittens in vibrant reds and forest greens, glistening ornaments shaped like snowflakes and rosy-cheeked snowmen, and trays piled high with gingerbread houses that looked like they belonged in a fairytale. Laughter mingled with carols sung by a group of carolers dressed in Dickensian attire. Hot chocolate vendors clanged their steaming mugs, their scent a rich, inviting wave that promised warmth against the crisp New England evening. The joyous chaos was exactly what Sarah needed: a temporary escape from the gnawing worry inside her.

She took Matthew's hand and squinted at the softly falling snow. Golden light spilled from the ornately carved market stalls, casting long shadows that danced with the snowflakes swirling in the air. The scent of roasted chestnuts and gingerbread cookies hung heavy in the crisp air, mingling with the fragrant smoke curling from steaming mugs of mulled wine. Sarah pulled her scarf tighter, the cold air nipping at her cheeks, but a warmth bloomed in her chest, a warmth fueled by the festive spirit around them.

"Look at this." Sarah lifted a hand-knitted scarf from a display and held it up to Matthew to confirm that it was the exact color of his coat.

"But I don't need another…"

Before he could finish his protest, she had bought it for him, along with a pink felt beret for Emma and fingerless skater gloves for Cory.

Taking the paper bag with her purchases, Sarah laughed, spread her arms, and spun around in a circle before tucking tight against Matthew again.

"Thank you," she whispered. "This was exactly what I needed tonight."

Matthew handed her a cup of cider and a pointy paper bag of spiced almonds and put his arm around her waist.

"You are so very welcome."

Suddenly, Pixie, who always walked beside Sarah, came to an abrupt halt in front of a brightly colored stall unlike any other. Its awning boasted a hand-painted picture of a grinning genie rising from a swirling pot, and the air around it shimmered with an exotic mix of aromas. Cinnamon, ginger, and something rich, citrusy, and enticing Sarah couldn't quite place. A strange, musky scent that beckoned her closer and sent a shiver down her back at the same time. Sarah's chest tightened, and she automatically reached down to let Pixie jump into her arm.

Pixie?

Pixie whined and pawed at her arm.

This, she said urgently. *This scent. This is what I smelled at the shop.*

Sarah's breath caught in her throat, remembering Amelia's words: "It's a spice."

Could this unassuming spice stall hold the key to Lily's innocence? She exchanged a worried glance with Matthew, a silent question hanging in the air. The festive atmosphere seemed to dim around them as a determined glint replaced the worry in Sarah's eyes.

She had to investigate for Lily and the truth that seemed to be hiding among the Christmas Market's warm spices and twinkling lights.

"What is it?" Matthew asked and pulled them away a few steps. He wasn't privy to Sarah and Pixie's conversations, but he knew enough to realize something outside of his awareness was going on.

"The scent," Sarah whispered, her eyes pointing toward the spice stall. "Pixie said she smelled the same scent she had at the crime scene."

"And you think...?"

"Amelia thought it was a spice. It's been bugging me all day, and I didn't know why." Sarah made a fist. "Perhaps that merchant knows something. Come on, we have to find out."

Sarah took a few steps closer to the spice merchant again until Pixie stopped her with a desperate yelp and began struggling in her arms.

No... wait. Too much. The little Papillon withdrew and buried her head inside Sarah's coat, sneezing again and again.

Painful. Too much, Sarah heard.

"She's overwhelmed," Sarah shook her head and quickly withdrew a few cautious steps away from the spice merchant's booth. She wrinkled her nose, torn between her desire to explore and the assault on her and Pixie's senses.

The spice merchant's booth loomed before them, a riot of color against the crisp New England night. Tangled like festive cobwebs, strings of fairy lights cast a warm glow on towering stacks of woven baskets overflowing with exotic treasures. Cinnamon sticks, thick as her thumb, curled invitingly. Star anise pods resembled miniature, eight-pointed suns. Heaps of saffron threads gleamed like spun gold.

The air hung heavy with a dizzying symphony of aromas. Pungent ginger wrestled with the warm earthiness of turmeric, while the citrusy brightness of lemongrass cut through the heady sweetness of vanilla. Sarah instinctively backed away, Pixie withdrawing further into her coat, mirroring her movement with a whine.

Beside her, ever the explorer, Matthew plunged right in and approached the first row of baskets, boxes, and jars.

The spice merchant, a gnarled figure shrouded in a thick, black wool coat, materialized from behind a mountain of burlap sacks. His face, obscured by a bushy beard the color of weathered driftwood, was creased with a perpetual grin that didn't quite reach his eyes.

"Ah, welcome!" he boomed, his voice crackling like dry leaves. "Intoxicating scents, are they not? A symphony for the senses!"

Matthew leaned closer, breathing in deeply. "They are incredible," he agreed, eyes wide. "What's this one?" he asked, pointing to a jar filled with what appeared to be rough beads in various sizes, ranging from the size of a pea to a small hazelnut. Their color varied from reddish-brown to light brown; some had a slightly flattened shape.

The merchant's grin widened.

"Ah, those, my friend," he rasped, lowering his voice to a conspiratorial whisper. They are Szechuan peppercorns. They don't deliver a direct heat like black pepper. Instead, they have a unique, citrusy, and floral aroma with a numbing or tingling sensation on the tongue, often described as a prickling or electric feeling. The numbing effect comes from a compound called sanshool."

Matthew instantly let go of the jar.

"Perfect for stir-fries, noodle dishes, marinades, and spice rubs," the merchant said, reaching into the jar to pick a bead for Matthew.

Sarah watched, a knot of unease tightening in her stomach. The man exuded an aura of mystery that bordered on the unsettling. Matthew, however, seemed captivated. He bent close, his brow furrowed in concentration, as the merchant rattled off the provenance of Szechuan peppercorns.

Finally, Matthew straightened, a triumphant glint in his eyes.

"Thank you," he said politely. "I will definitely come back."

He accepted a worn business card, its edges softened by time, with a satisfied nod. As they turned to leave, Matthew bumped into a display of ginger roots, sending a flurry of fat brown knobs skittering across the wooden counter. The merchant's smile widened, revealing a flash of gold beneath where a tooth should have been. Sarah felt a shiver crawl up her spine, and the festive cheer suddenly felt strained.

With a muttered thanks, they hurried away from the booth, the scent of spices trailing after them like a fragrant, lingering question mark.

"Weird fellow," Matthew still studied the card he had taken, steering Sarah toward the women's league stand for a cup of hot cider.

Finally, even Pixie lifted her head again.

I am sorry. My nose could not handle the assault.

No doubt. And you thought…?

No, I know, Sarah. Whatever I smelled at the crime scene. And I have never smelled it before.

"Exotic spices," Sarah said softly, wrapping her hands around the mug Matthew brought her. "What would that have been doing in Lily's bookstore? Let's finish this and go ask her."

"Now?" Matthew blew on his cup of cider. "I thought you wanted to enjoy the Christmas market."

"I do." Sarah turned back with longing and looked at the many displays and booths they had yet to visit. "But I want to ask Lily about this, and..."

"And none of this is going anywhere," Matthew said, wrapping his arm around her waist again. "Tomorrow we can..."

He met Sarah's eyes and sighed. "And this concerns your best friend, Lily, so you're not going to relax anyway."

Sarah looked down at her mug and shook her head.

"You're preparing a spectacular Christmas for all of us, running Lily's bookstore at peak season, and trying to solve the murder of her boyfriend. I'm a little concerned this is getting to be too much for you."

Not really, you have the strength of ten if you put your mind to it, Sarah heard from Pixie and ruffled the little Papillon's long ear fringes.

"But I am here for you if you need anything at all." Matthew squeezed her hand hard.

"Thank you... for understanding and... for being there for us, in all our craziness."

Sarah bent closer and touched her cheek to Pixie's head.

You okay again, girl?

Pixie raised her head and pointed her nose toward the spice merchant's stall. *I can still smell it, you know. It is very predominant.*

"If we just knew what it was."

"What? That spice Pixie smelled? One of hundreds there, maybe even those peppercorns." Matthew collected their mugs and turned them back in at the cider stand. "Needle in a haystack. It reminds me of those game shows on TV where the contestants have to complete impossible tasks. Find one spice among a thousand." Matthew chuckled. "I suppose you could wander by every restaurant in the area until she finds it again."

"Not really practical," Sarah giggled. The cold fingers of the December wind crawled right inside her coat, and she tightened it a little, letting Pixie hop on the ground again.

The little Papillon stood, her nose still pointed in the direction they had come from, her head cocked. Finally, she shook and gave Sarah a mischievous glance.

"If you weren't a dog, I'd say you're up to no good," Sarah said and hooked her arm through Matthew's, walking in the direction of their car.

Chapter Eleven

"Did Luke do any cooking?" Sarah asked at home, breaking the tranquil atmosphere of their cozy gathering by the fire. Lily and Emma, curled up together in one of the deep couches, looked up from their books, their attention piqued by the sudden question.

"Luke? Not really. Unless you call shoving a hungry man dinner into the microwave when he got home cooking. Is this about that odd scent Pixie smelled?" Lily asked, setting her book aside and giving Sarah her full attention.

Sarah recounted the events at the Christmas market, Pixie's reaction to the mysterious scent, and their encounter with the enigmatic spice merchant.

"I doubt it means anything, sorry. I had a catered event there a few weeks ago, and when the store next door was an art gallery, they had those all the time. Who knows what was left behind?" Lily shrugged, dismissing the possibility with a wave of her hand.

Sarah opened her mouth to argue, but her attention was drawn to a stack of intricate drawings and pictures on the coffee table.

"Locks?" she asked, picking up the top drawing. "Why locks?"

"Because..." Lily hesitated, her expression growing solemn as she selected another drawing from the stack. After a moment of contemplation, she placed it back with care. "We know the door was locked from the inside when we arrived in the morning. I know, you know, but Penny Harding insists that Matt and Walter broke the mechanism when they tried to get in. I'm trying to figure out if there's any way at all to prove..."

"Sorry," Sarah murmured, realizing how much Lily was struggling with the troubling circumstances surrounding Luke's death.

"It's alright," Lily replied with a small, understanding smile. "We're all just trying to make sense of it in our own way."

The room fell into silence, broken only by the crackling of the fire and the occasional turn of a page. Sarah couldn't shake the feeling of unease that lingered in the air, but she also couldn't deny the comfort of being surrounded by friends who were willing to face the darkness together, even as they searched for the light.

"So how did he get out," Sarah said, picking up a drawing again.

"He?"

"Oh, Simon thinks he saw the energetic imprint of a male leaving the store right after the murder."

Lily wiped her hands over her face and rolled her eyes dramatically.

"I don't know how you do it, living with those two?"

"Matthew keeps asking the same thing. It's challenging at times." Sarah picked up the drawing again. "But how did he get out? The windows were intact, and the door locked. Do you have a back door?"

"Kind of," Lily shrugged. "It was added later, fire code and all that. But I was worried about burglaries, so it's heavily alarmed. The entire town would have known it if anyone touched it."

"Sure?"

"Yep. The alarm goes directly to the fire department and police. This being an old building filled with books..."

"I understand, but could he not have...."

"Sarah, don't you think that was one of the first things we checked? And I asked Penny Harding to check, and I asked one of her techs to double-check. That damned back door has not been opened since it was installed. Because if it had I would be in my bookstore, grieving Luke, and not sitting here under suspicion."

The weight of Lily's words landed heavily between the two friends, and Lily looked away. Sarah moved over to her friend, placing a comforting hand on Lily's shoulder.

"I keep forgetting..." Sarah began, trying to offer solace, but Lily waved her away dismissively, her movements sharp with emotion.

Sarah saw it: the glitter of unshed tears in the corner of Lily's eyes. Lily was definitely not okay, despite her attempts to brush off the concern.

Pretending she hadn't noticed, Sarah turned away from Lily, pacing over to the Christmas tree and fussing over its ornaments. She needed a moment to let go of the heaviness of the conversation.

"So, our perp goes into your bookstore," Sarah mused aloud, trying to shift the focus away from the somber atmosphere. "How did he get in there anyway?"

"Luke..." Lily's voice trailed off as she shrugged. "I'd given him the keys so he could fix the furnace. It kept..."

"Cutting out, I know," Sarah finished for her. "I remember. And Luke would not have locked the door behind him?"

"I put the keys on the counter. He might have forgotten, or thought it would only take a minute... I don't know." Lily's tone was desperate now, and she yanked her hair out of her face with a stiff jerk.

"I'm sorry, I shouldn't have snapped," she apologized, her voice softer now. "It's a tough situation."

"No shit," Sarah replied automatically, a hint of frustration slipping into her words before she could stop it. She winced at her slip of the tongue, but before she could backtrack, her son bounded down the stairs, interrupting their conversation.

"Hey. Before you criticize me again about Murderpedia...." Cory began, his voice filled with a mix of apprehension and excitement.

"You didn't go there again, did you?" Sarah asked, a dozen alarm bells ringing in her head as Lily reached for the tablet.

"I used to check that site all the time," Lily confessed with a wry smile. "I just never thought I'd know somebody on it."

"You wouldn't, and this isn't about Murderpedia. Mom just got... squirrelly when I told her about it." Cory said. "You see, Mom? Nothing weird about it."

"Maybe you're a bit young to be..."

"Aunt Lily, I'm seventeen," Cory argued, making it sound like twenty-seven. "I was looking for Luke," he continued, redirecting the conversation. "I was thinking, what if the reason why he got stabbed had something to do with why he was in jail?"

"Matthew suggested that, and I'm sure the police checked the people in question," Sarah replied automatically, her mind racing with a mix of concern and curiosity.

Cory rolled his eyes dramatically. "Another person who says I'm sure the police did their job perfectly. Anyway, I didn't find anything. Then I came across this."

He showed them the screen of his tablet, displaying an image of two men and a woman sitting around a podcasting microphone.

"It's an anti-bullying, anti-violence podcast," Cory explained, his tone serious. "We discuss it in the sports youth group sometimes."

"Seriously?" Lily pulled the tablet closer and frowned.

"Luke spoke on that podcast," Cory announced flatly, his gaze fixed on Sarah, waiting for her reaction.

"Talked about his time in jail, and his issues getting back out. And how he wanted his life to mean something because he had taken a life. How he wanted to inspire people to do better. He spoke to youth groups and community centers. He... he really was a great guy."

The silence between them settled like a heavy blanket. Lily sat in one of the deep chairs again, pulling her red curls back from her face, focusing on her breathing. Sarah put her hand on Cory's shoulder and even Emma closed her book and looked at her brother.

"Everything he said was about avoiding where he went," Cory continued until Sarah put her hand on his elbow and shook her head. Lily had turned chalk white.

"Anyway," Cory mumbled and looked down at his tablet. "He got out early because he made a real effort on the... inside. That doesn't sound like the kind of guy somebody would track all the way to Rosewood."

Lily put a hand over her mouth. Tears rolled down her cheeks, and she turned away, facing into the corner by the fireplace so she wouldn't have to look at anyone. Her shoulders twitched with the silent sobs she tried to hide.

"Sounds like I finally fell for a great guy," she said, her voice trembling.

"But Luke was..." Cory began, his voice trailing off as Sarah shushed him with a finger to her lips. She moved closer to Lily, who was visibly struggling with emotions, though Pixie had already begun comforting her in her own way, showering her with affectionate kisses.

"He sounds like a great guy," Sarah said softly, trying to offer some comfort. It was clear that Lily needed it, now more than ever.

Lily held Pixie close, burying her face in the little papillon's fur, seeking solace in her warmth and presence. Sarah watched, her heart physically aching with concern for her friend.

Just then, the doorbell rang, shattering the fragile moment. Pixie raised her head, her ears perking up, but she remained silent. Matthew's voice drifted from the kitchen, announcing that he would answer the door.

Sarah hesitated, torn between wanting to comfort Lily and addressing the visitor at the door. Moments later, Matthew entered the room, holding a thick pack of coupons.

"You know the Lethbridge's? Moved in on the other side of the Jensen house a couple of months ago?" Matthew asked, his tone curious.

"Vaguely," Sarah replied, still keeping her eyes on Lily. "Cassie, I think the woman's name is. Does she need anything?"

In response, Matthew held out the pack of coupons to Sarah. "You tell me. She said they subscribe to some sort of coupon network; who knows? But this month, they got twice the number of restaurant and fine dining coupons they usually get. In case we had use for them."

Sarah nodded and accepted the coupons. Her mind was already racing with thoughts of how she could help Lily and unravel the mystery surrounding Luke's death. For now, she focused on the simple task of accepting the unexpected gift from their new neighbors, a reminder of the everyday moments amidst the turmoil.

She went to the kitchen for the wine, and when she came back, Lily sat cross-legged on the sofa with Emma and Cory, flipping through the coupon pack.

"Hey, these are great," she said. "Not the usual stuff you get in those packs at all, you know a free drink at a fast-food place or something like that." She handed a few to Sarah. "They are two for one or free dinner at some great restaurants in town. I have to ask her what network they use. This is really local... and targeted. Be great for my..."

She flipped through the stack and handed one to Sarah. "Look."

Sarah felt an immediate tingle in her fingers when she took the little postcard-style flyer Lily held out to her. Something inside her connected with the ad. Even as she turned it in her hands, a familiar tingle crawled down her spine.

The coupon for The Jewel of Agra, a local restaurant she'd admired from afar, boasted a mesmerizing image. Against a backdrop of burnt orange, reminiscent of a Tandoor sunset, a jeweled chicken kabob dripped with vibrant red chutney. Next to it, a platter overflowing with fluffy basmati rice and emerald green dolmas sparkled with dewdrops. Bold, saffron-hued lettering proclaimed, Two Can Dine for the Price of One! on a background of intricate paisley swirls in deep blues and purples. Spice... restaurants... dining. A wave of anticipation fizzed in Sarah's stomach.

"They are doing this at Christmas," she wondered, turning the coupon over and over again. "I've been wanting to go to this place with Matthew forever, but they are in the, uhh, expensive category."

"Or try this one," Lily looked up and held out another coupon to her. This one featured a glistening steak amidst a mound of potatoes and vegetables.

Sarah dropped the coupons to the table as if they had burned her fingers.

"We were just talking about spices, and the scent Pixie smelled at the... in the store, with Luke. Now, here's another spice hint? You don't think that's odd?"

"It's just marketing." Lily shrugged and put the remaining coupons down on the coffee table. "What are you thinking? Maybe the guy with the spice booth had something to do with it?"

"It wouldn't surprise me. He gave me the creeps for some reason," Sarah mused. Finally, she swept all the coupons into a little pile and put them into a ceramic dish in the hall that held all sorts of odds and ends.

"It's been a long day. I, for one, can't think anymore. How about we pick this up tomorrow."

"Day in retail catching up with you," Lily said with a faint smile, and Sarah gently cuffed her in the shoulder.

"Don't get smart with me. But get some rest, and try not to spiral into disaster, and tomorrow, we will think about the odd spice man and the rest."

"The spice man, yes, that is the clue that will help," Lily declared, her chin jutting out in a show of determination. "There's no point in sitting around here worrying. If I can't run my store, maybe I will pay a visit to this Exotic Spice Emporium."

A flicker of hope ignited in Sarah's eyes. Maybe, just maybe, Lily was on her way to regain composure. Or perhaps she was about to walk straight into something far more dangerous than a bad case of indigestion.

Chapter Twelve

Sarah's fingers brushed the stack of coupons in the ceramic dish the next morning, as she and Emma gathered their coats and keys for another day at the bookstore. Cory stood digging through his backpack on a hunt for his phone charger. Briefly, Sarah picked up the coupons and dropped them again.

"Is there something weird about these? Or am I just seeing... I don't know...?"

"Mom," Cory rolled his eyes and triumphantly held his charger aloft. "Can you just take the gift, take Matthew to a few really nice restaurants, and not see something strange behind every corner?"

"Look who's all grown up."

But as Cory thundered up the stairs, her eyes met Emma's, and she saw a similar doubt in her daughter's face.

A little while later, Lily tiptoed down the creaky stairs, a dark tote slung over her shoulder. Sarah's oversized, charcoal coat hung loosely on her petite frame; the collar swallowed half her face. A thick scarf, smelling faintly of cinnamon and woodsmoke, muffled the usual sparkle of her smile. Gone were the vibrant scarves, flamboyant coats, and hats Lily usually favored. Today, one would not have spotted her in a crowd.

Dark circles etched beneath her eyes betrayed the weight of her somber thoughts, mirroring the chill that clung to the air despite the impending holiday cheer.

"Ready for the Christmas market, to see what's what," she declared bravely, though her words faltered under Sarah's scrutinizing gaze.

"I want to see if I recognize that spice merchant you call creepy. Maybe I've seen him with Luke. That would help. I didn't think you'd mind my borrowing your coat," Lily ventured, her voice tinged with uncertainty.

"I don't. It's just not you," Sarah remarked softly, her concern palpable.

"Right now, I don't want anybody to recognize me and ask about Luke. Maybe that's something I'll have to get used to. Who knows how this case will turn out," Lily mused, her tone heavy with resignation.

"Stop. Nobody has been convicted yet. Just accused. That's what lawyers are for," Sarah reminded her gently.

"Mine said to lay low and not say or do anything... rash," Lily confessed, her resolve wavering beneath the weight of uncertainty. "There is nothing they can do until after Christmas anyway, so don't blow it now is what they said."

Adjusting the borrowed hat, Lily concealed her fiery locks beneath its brim, ready to vanish into the crowd of tourists milling about the market—no longer Lily, the vibrant bookseller, but a mere spectator in a sea of faces.

"Check out the market, see if there's anything about that spice merchant that strikes you or you can remember, and come right back to the house, okay," Sarah instructed, pressing a spare key into Lily's hand. "Here, in case Matthew and Cory are gone when you get back. They want to..."

Her words trailed off, the unspoken desire hanging heavy in the air. Lily understood without Sarah needing to finish her sentence.

They wanted to go Christmas shopping. Sarah held her tongue, not wanting to add to Lily's pain.

∾

She didn't miss the longing glance Lily cast at her bookstore when they parked behind the building.

"You're going to be okay?"

"I will be, thanks." Lily nodded and slipped out of the car and into an alley between the neighboring buildings.

∾

She and Emma had barely unlocked the store and heated the coffee maker when the bell above the door announced the first visitor with a bright jingle.

"Penny," Sarah said with a sigh, holding out a cup of cappuccino for the police officer. "You're starting to be a regular in here. Any news?"

"Just wanted to use your WiFi," Penny Harding grumbled. "As if our computer troubles and electrical issues were not enough, now the WiFi is down for no discernable reason. It's like the place is haunted."

Sarah's fingers twitched, and the cup and saucer she'd been holding clattered to the floor. The cheerful store music was momentarily drowned out by the discordant crash of the porcelain shattering into a thousand pieces.

Emma rushed over with a broom, her eyes wide and concerned. Sarah couldn't tear her gaze from the shattered cup and saucer, balling her hand into a fist.

Penny Caldwell's casual remark had sent shivers down her spine.

"You alright?"

"Fine, just clumsy. Haunted, huh?" Sarah wiped her hands on a towel and picked up a new cup. "You believe in that sort of thing?"

"Of course not. Just an expression. Is there something I should know about?"

"Nope." This time, Sarah managed to pour another coffee and nodded toward one of the many cozy nooks where Pixie snoozed in a plush armchair.

"Have a seat, use the WiFi. Just watch out for Pixie, she does curl up in these chairs."

Penny Harding gave Sarah a long look and finally shrugged. "Sure thing."

Pixie, I need you to keep an eye on her, Sarah thought. *And if you hear or see anything...*

Pixie barely opened an eye and sighed with contentment.

Always on the job for you.

Despite the bustling morning filled with customers, cheerful Christmas carols, and endless requests for gift wrapping, Sarah and Emma finally found themselves with a momentary break in the midday lull. Even Officer Harding had left her temporary post in the cooking section in pursuit of other police business.

"Whew," Sarah sighed, stretching her arms behind her back. "I need to remember to tell Lily how hard she works."

"You seemed to be enjoying yourself," Emma teased with a grin. "I don't know who enjoyed your gift wrapping more, you or the customers who will get to give those gifts. Go, Mom."

"You'll get yours in a store-bought gift bag," Sarah joked back, feeling the strain of the day's work. "Have you heard anything from Lily?"

Emma shook her head. "No, Cory just texted me that she was back home. But no news beyond that."

Sarah's hope wavered. If Lily had made any breakthroughs, surely she would have come in or at least let them know, wouldn't she?

"Working all morning under the eyes of that policewoman sure gave me the creeps," Emma remarked, trying to find some reassurance. "Like she was looking for something. I felt guilty just walking past her."

Sarah managed a smile, though it felt forced. "Must be something they teach at the police academy. I don't know what we'll do if Lily..."

"You said it wouldn't come to that," Emma reminded her gently.

"No," Sarah agreed, trying to hold onto optimism. "And Matthew said she has a good lawyer, but... things happen."

"And innocent people go to jail," Emma added softly, her expression solemn.

Nobody is going to jail. I still have a few tricks up my sleeve.

Pixie shook, her collar tags tinkling, as she stretched her back in a deep bow and glanced from Emma to Sarah and back.

"Are you up for a stroll outside?" Emma asked.

"I'll just let her out for a quick break," Sarah replied, reaching for her coat and the little pink leash. "Are you going to be okay minding the store for a minute?"

Emma gestured toward the empty store. "I'll be able to manage, don't you think?"

Sarah and Pixie darted into a quiet side street behind the bookstore, and Pixie took care of business in record time. She immediately put her paws back on Sarah's knee to be picked up.

That ground is icy, Sarah heard.

Did you hear anything from Officer Harding while she was sitting there? she asked.

Yes, and it's not good. Pixie cocked her head slightly and snuggled deeply into Sarah's oversized collar, hiding her paws. *She was talking to another officer at the station... whispering.*

Her large fringed ears moved back and forth like little antenna dishes, the long reddish fringe dancing. *Whispering!*

Sarah stroked Pixie's little chin, eliciting a groan. *And?*

She thought it was time to get an arrest warrant ready. Any evidence that points at somebody other than Lily, she said she can explain away.

Like the locked door.

Matthew did it.

And the fact she was at Tami's place.

Enough time to race back and do the deed. She was cussing out the IT techs because she wants to hurry up with that warrant and close the case.

"Oh, Pixie," Sarah murmured, holding the little papillon a little tighter. "What are we going to do?"

For starters, you need to follow the spice clue. I know I smelled it, and I know it's not something common or something Luke brought with him.

What if he bought it for Lily? For Christmas?

Sarah, Pixie said, straightening a bit in her arms. *He went there to fix the furnace, not to carry around exotic spices.*

Yeah, I know. Sarah sighed. She saw a car pull into the bookstore parking lot and started walking toward the door again. *Customers. I just wish...*

You wish there were something you could do, yet you keep overlooking the best shot you've got: your own powers.

Sarah opened the front door and let Pixie run into the store again.

While the ghosts are busy over at the police station, figure out where that spice came from, she heard, and Pixie shook herself before going in search of another chair for a nap. *That's when we will find the killer.*

Chapter Thirteen

B ack home, the mood was equally somber. Lily had locked herself in her room, and Cory sat munching tortilla chips in the kitchen, staring at his tablet.

"What did Lily say?" Sarah asked, plunking her purse on the sideboard in the hall. "Did she check out the spice merchant? Any idea?"

"You're not going to like it," Cory said, brushing the hair out of his face and pushing back from the kitchen table.

Sarah thought he needed a haircut, especially now, for Christmas. She also needed to clean the kitchen, make plans for dinner, and...

"What am I not going to like?" she asked instead, pushing her to-do list to the back of her mind.

"Lily saw the spice merchant and didn't recognize anything familiar about him."

"But he looks..."

"Yeah, he looks creepy," Cory interrupted, swiping the tortilla crumbs from his mouth and taking his tablet. "Very creepy, but I checked him out online. That's just part of his gig."

"His gig?"

"He makes himself look creepy, like the old-style merchants, traveled all over the world, seen all sorts of stuff, had lots of adventures."

"Yes, yes, I understand that, but he could still be involved."

"Mm, I don't think so," Cory said, swiping his finger up the side of his tablet, faster and faster, until he had found what he was looking for. "His real name is Andre Meyer, pretty harmless guy."

"That's not for us to say."

"Plus, he got into the Rosewood Hollow Christmas Market on a cancellation two days ago. He was minding his own store in New York City before that, the night Luke was... you know."

"So? You know what..." Sarah finally flung her coat over the back of a chair and went to wash her hands in the kitchen sink, desperate for better news. "I'm tired of this. Lily was at her aunt Tami's, and Penny Harding says, 'Oh, but she could have driven back, stabbed Luke, and gone back to Tami's,' when I know she didn't. Who's to say this... this Meyer dude couldn't have done the same thing, huh?"

Upstairs, a door opened and closed again, and out in the driveway, she could see Matthew sweeping in on his bike. Emma, who'd brought her things upstairs first, came back down and stopped in the doorway, looking from Cory to her mother.

"YouTube does," Cory finally said, and Sarah cocked her head.

"What?"

"Dude does a lot of online live videos showing people how to pick the right spices, and store them and treat them and whatnot," Cory said with an eye roll. "I wouldn't watch it, but he's got like ten thousand followers."

"So?"

"So, he was doing a YouTube live the night Luke was stabbed. The link is right on his website. He was there, Mom."

"Oh." Sarah brought her hands to her face and sat down hard. "I didn't know you could check stuff like that."

"Hmm," Cory shrugged. "I am not saying you can't cheat on it either, but you've got to think, if he deals with spices, wouldn't Pixie have smelled more than one if he were the one in the bookstore stabbing Luke?"

"True."

"Good evening, family."

The front door slammed, and Matthew breezed in on a cloud of chilly air and snow. "Geez, it's brisk outside today. Should have gone into town in the car with you..."

He stopped, looking from Sarah to Cory and back.

"Everything okay?"

"You know you're a little scary when you do that," Sarah said to Cory. "I get the suspicion you can find anybody anywhere as long as they have a website."

"It's a skill. And the website is optional." Cory grinned. "But that still doesn't give us much. We're back to square one."

"Anybody care to clue me in?"

Matthew took off his coat and gingerly picked up Sarah's, clearly wondering why the usually tidy and careful Sarah had discarded it on a kitchen chair.

"Nothing. The spice merchant clue is a total bust. He was on a live show when Luke got stabbed," she grumbled and heard a gasp from the door.

"So he's in the clear, and I am still—"

"Lily." Sarah snapped around and saw her friend in the doorway with Emma.

"I didn't know you were there..." Sarah felt a pang of guilt at the stricken look on Lily's face. She hadn't meant to keep anything from her friend, but she hadn't had the time to digest what Cory had found, never mind sharing it with Lily.

"We've been trying to piece together everything we can, and we all thought the clue about the spice merchant might lead somewhere. But Cory found out that the guy was doing a live video the night Luke was... you know."

Lily's expression softened slightly, but the hurt still lingered in her eyes. "I know you're trying."

Sarah sighed, feeling the weight of the situation pressing down on her. "I just wish there was something more concrete we could go on. It's like chasing shadows sometimes."

Matthew, who had been listening quietly, stepped forward and placed a comforting hand on Lily's shoulder. "Then we will chase them. Chasing shadows is something we all excel at. Remember that."

"Thanks, Matt."

Lily tried her best to manage a little smile, but in the end, she turned away, wiping the corner of her eyes with the heels of her hands.

Pixie sat regally by her food dish, long fluffy tail wrapped around her paws like a stole.

It might not be the creepy spice merchant, but I still say that smell is the right clue, she said, and Sarah swiped her bowl from the floor.

Then, help me figure it out was all she could answer.

Lily grabbed a glass of water, turned on her heel, and headed back upstairs to the guest room. No one spoke for a long minute. Cory turned off his tablet with exaggerated care and shrugged into his jacket. The discarded hockey bag by the front door spoke of his plans.

"I'm gonna go out with some friends," he mumbled, his voice barely audible as he shuffled out the front door. Emma, ever the quiet observer, cast a sympathetic glance at Sarah before making a beeline for the stairs herself.

Sarah sighed, the tension finally leaving her shoulders. "Well, that went well," she muttered to Matthew, who was already opening his tin can of exotic teas. "I wasn't trying to lie to her, but I would have softened the blow had I known..."

"She's scared," Matthew offered with a shrug and closed his box of teas again. "Understandable. Want to grab some dinner? Maybe a change of scenery will help all of us."

Sarah's stomach grumbled in agreement.

"Perfect timing, actually. We have all those coupons kicking around Cassie Lethbridge gave us."

Chapter Fourteen

Over steaming plates of pasta, Sarah recounted the afternoon's events. Matthew listened patiently, nodding occasionally.

"You know," he finally said, swirling his wine. "I know a guy at the city archives."

"You mean you know every guy at the city archives," Sarah responded with an eye roll. "How is this going to help Lily?"

Matthew put down his fork and leaned back in his chair, bringing his hands together. He stared off into the distance.

"Rosewood Hollow has a pretty small police station," he mused. "And Penny Harding is a lovely person, but completely overwhelmed with a murder investigation. I know she wants to be the one to solve this, but it is a bit above her pay grade."

"Then they should have brought someone with experience, or at least someone who has seen a murder before," Sarah snapped.

"True, but next week is Christmas, and I'm sure Penny is telling people she has everything under control and the murder solved. Her first ever murder—solved within days."

"So far, this doesn't sound encouraging. Your point?"

"My point is that she makes assumptions, gets hung up on the murder happening at Lily's store, and she had, maybe, a motive." He drew air quotes around the word motive. "Completely ignoring the locked door."

"She thinks you and Grandpa Becker broke it."

"I just want to see if there are any old connecting doors into the next-door building, that's all. Then, the murderer could have gotten out that way. Voila, alternate theory and explanation."

"Matthew." Sarah put her hand over his, stilling the sweeping motions he always made when he fell into professor mode. "Can you at least try not to make it worse right now? If you go ahead and prove that there is another exit, I can just see Penny feeling confirmed in her theory that Lily and only Lily could have done it. Because... who else knows that building and all its exits? You see, your honor, it had to be someone who works there and is familiar with everything."

Dramatically, she swept a hand as she imagined a courtroom judge would do.

"I'm just looking for a clue—any clue—that will point at someone else. It may or may not exonerate Lily." Matthew frowned and took a bit of pasta, chewing for an extraordinarily long time. "Whoever did, in fact, kill Luke still had to get out of that building somehow. And I want to know how... maybe that will lead me to the who."

Sarah squeezed his hand. "Fine. Keep digging, keep looking, but promise me not to incriminate Lily any further."

Matthew sighed, his gaze drifting to the window where snowflakes danced in the evening light. "I hate feeling so helpless in all of this. I only met Luke a few times and I didn't know about his past. But you want to know what my first awful reaction was? I judged him for it. He did have a good reason not to tell anyone he'd been in prison. According to Cory's research, he was a kind man, and he deserves justice."

Sarah stabbed at her own food, her heart heavy with the weight of their task. "He was there to fix the furnace," she said softly. "Doing something to help Lily."

Dinner tasted like cardboard after that. Matthew speared a piece of pasta with his fork, poking it listlessly.

"Any other ideas?" he finally asked, breaking the silence that had stretched between them since.

Pushing away her plate, Sarah sighed. "Not really. Let's get the check and take a little walk around the block before we head home."

Outside, Matthew linked his arm through hers.

"That must have been the most inexpensive dinner out we've had in a long time. I mean, I appreciate it, but if the local BIA came up with the idea for that coupon action, they wouldn't be doing the merchants any favors. Nobody's making money on this."

"Maybe banking on return customers, who knows," Sarah said, glancing across the street where the Rosewood Hollow Police Station resembled a disco in meltdown.

The normally stoic brick building was pulsating with a chaotic symphony of flashing lights. The once-proud Open 24/7 sign sputtered on and off in a strobe effect, casting jerky shadows across the manicured lawn.

Sarah snorted. "Looks like Amelia and Simon are throwing a rave for the night shift. Maybe they're taking it a bit far."

Matthew popped up his collar to hide the silly grin on his face. "Sort of reminds me of a time not too long ago when all of the electronics at the museum went haywire. That's when we found the stolen sapphire finally."

Sarah only stared down at the ground, saying nothing.

"Never had a problem since, either."

"Isn't that something," Sarah chuckled, a nervous tremor in the sound. "Do you think they'll keep it up long enough for us to find something, some clue that exonerates Lily?".

∞

When they returned, all was quiet at the house, and Sarah sat by the fire, staring into the dancing flames for a long time while Matthew answered a few emails in the next room.

Pixie hopped up on Sarah's lap and proceeded to sniff her hands, arms, and clothes thoroughly until Sarah giggled.

You're tickling.

Hold still. Well, you didn't eat it tonight.

It was tasty, but I didn't need a lot.

That's not what I mean. The spice I smelled. You did not have it tonight.

Sarah gathered her arms around the little papillon. *Thank you, but I don't think this will help. We can't find one spice amongst thousands when we don't know its name or what it's used for.*

Pixie lowered her head onto her paws. *I'm trying.*

Chapter Fifteen

The next morning, Sarah rushed once again to open the bookstore, Emma by her side.

"We've been almost sold out of gift wrap since yesterday," she explained to Emma, ticking tasks off her fingers. I think we have a new shipment coming today, books need to be sorted and organized, and it's going to be a busy day."

As they passed the building, she gave a sideways glance at the police station, not daring to stop and gawk. In the chilly early morning, all was quiet, and the lights were off as they should be. Or was that just the quiet before round two?

"You think Officer Harding is going to join us in the bookstore again today?" Emma asked with a grin and a little giggle, catching her mother's look. "Amelia and Simon are doing a fantastic job over there," she added.

"I know it seems funny right now, but maybe I should talk to them," Sarah said, fishing in her pocket for the slim, modern key that came with the new lock at the store door. "They might be going a bit too far."

"No, Mom! The longer the police are busy..."

"That's not a long-term solution, Emma."

Sarah reached around and disengaged the new alarm, letting the peace of Lily's bookstore envelop her for a moment. The first day she lived in Rosewood Hollow, she had come in here, talking to the quirky, friendly bookseller and felt at home immediately.

Morning sunlight slanted through the tall, arched windows, casting a warm glow on the polished Rosewood floorboards and the books they'd left in a stack yesterday, waiting to be put away.

Before she knew it, the store was busy as always, and the air buzzed with a low murmur—a comforting soundtrack formed by the rustle of turning pages and the quiet conversations of patrons. A group of teenagers huddled in a corner, excitedly discussing the latest fantasy release. A retired gentleman, a regular with a penchant for historical non-fiction, perched on a velvet armchair, engrossed in a weighty tome, and Pixie, walking around with the air of a celebrity greeting customers.

Despite the somber mood hanging over the town, the bookstore offered a refuge, a place where normalcy, albeit a fragile one, persisted. Every shelf and nook held a piece of Lily's spirit, making the current situation all the more heartbreaking. Sarah found herself choking up every time she discovered one of her friend's sweet, quirky touches.

Just as she hefted a stack of books that needed shelving, a couple browsing the romance section approached, followed by a woman tapping her cane on the floor, and crowded in close.

"Such a shame about poor Lily," the woman murmured, her voice laced with morbid curiosity. "Do you think they'll convict her?"

Sarah opened her mouth, but no answer was forthcoming. With a little smile, the woman continued as if nothing had happened. "It's so wonderful to see you and Emma have the bookstore running like a charm. You should think about taking over. Rosewood needs this little gem."

Sarah's smile felt brittle as she hung on to politeness with all her might.

"We're just here to help Lily through this," she said tightly. "This is a difficult time for everyone. I'm sure it will all be resolved soon."

Across the room, Emma, sporting a bright Santa hat that seemed a touch too cheerful under the circumstances, was helping another customer. Sarah could almost hear Emma's forced enthusiasm as she wrapped a shiny, red-ribboned copy of *A Christmas Carol*. The irony was not lost on her. The idea of running the bookstore would have been a reason to celebrate for Emma a mere week ago; now, the beautiful store felt shrouded in suspicion.

Her best friend was trapped in a nightmare, and Sarah felt powerless to wake her. Glancing at Pixie, curled up contentedly in one of the reading chairs again, Sarah silently pleaded.

Come on, girl. Show me something, anything, that can help Lily. Even the customers think she did it.

Pixie's eye cracked open for a fleeting moment before closing again. Not the response she'd been hoping for. Clearly, even Pixie was struggling this time.

The cheery jingle of the bookstore door shattered the tense quiet. Sarah whirled around, expecting another curious customer, only to be met by the sight of Officer Penny Harding. She automatically grimaced and went to the coffee machine to prepare a cup.

Penny, a kind woman in her fifties with a perpetually worried crease between her brows, looked even more flustered than usual. Her normally crisp uniform seemed rumpled, and wayward strands of hair escaped her efficient, tight bun.

"Good morning, Penny. When I didn't see you first thing, I thought surely everything at the station was working well again, but you seem… flustered."

"I didn't know it was that obvious," Penny sighed dramatically. "It's still a disaster at the station! Today, the power's been out all morning. Forensics are backed up, and the copy machine decided to take a permanent holiday. It's mayhem, absolute mayhem."

Sarah turned away to hide her smile.

"Oh dear, that sounds even worse than yesterday," she offered sympathetically. "Hopefully, they'll get it all sorted soon."

Penny shot her a suspicious glance. "You sound awfully chipper considering the circumstances," she said just as Sarah handed her a cup.

"I find I do enjoy running Lily's store." Emphasis on Lily's, Sarah thought. Might as well make it clear that she was only holding down the fort until the case was solved.

"It is a little busy today, but there's a quiet corner in the gardening section where you can spread out your laptop and work for a while if that's what you are looking for."

"Another thing that refused to boot up this morning." Penny rolled her eyes. "But that's not why I am here."

She reached into a police-issue messenger bag hanging at her shoulder and extracted a small, worn manila envelope.

"I wanted to drop off this," she said, pushing it across the counter towards Sarah. "These are the keys to Luke Devin's apartment on Elm Street. We're done combing the place for evidence. Would you mind?"

Relief flickered across Sarah's face, momentarily overshadowed by a pang of sympathy for the life cut tragically short.

"Of course not," she said, automatically reaching for the envelope. "Should I give these to Lily?"

Penny nodded grimly. "If you don't mind. You'll save me driving out to your place this morning. It's snowing again, and who knows when my cruiser will join in the electronic mess we face. By the way, the landlord wants to know when he can rent the place again. Maybe arrangements can be made with Luke's family to collect his belongings. I haven't been able to get in touch with any of them. This whole thing is just..." Penny trailed off, shaking her head. "Between Christmas holidays and the problems in our building, we're all at a standstill, so perhaps Lily could take care of that."

Sarah offered a tight smile. "Of course. Best of luck to you," she said, the weight of the envelope a physical reminder of the case's grim reality. As Officer Harding bid her farewell, Sarah quickly put the envelope into a drawer under the counter. Not right now. She would deal with it another time.

A tinkle of collar tags alerted her to Pixie standing by her right foot.

Come on, we should go check that out.

Check what out? She bent down, scratching Pixie under the chin. *Luke's apartment? But Penny said they—*

Looked for evidence. Pixie shook and went down into a deep stretch. *I think we both know how thorough they were.*

After closing, Sarah thought, ruffling the soft fur again. *Rest up, I expect you to work that nose of yours.*

※

The afternoon wore on. More than once, a customer would crowd in close and ask if they were taking over, settling in, or had any news. This was gossip at its finest, and Sarah tired quickly of saying, 'We're just helping out.'

The shadows lengthened, and finally, the jingle of the bell brought a welcome customer. Relief flooded Sarah as she spotted Matthew. Clad head-to-toe in black, a turtleneck hugging his lanky frame, he looked like a misplaced crow amidst the festive decorations. His shaggy brown hair, desperately in need of a trim, flopped over his forehead. He gave Sarah a crooked smile as he knocked the snow off his black wool coat.

"Ready for a Dickensian escape from this whole mess?" he asked, his voice a soothing rumble.

Sarah nodded gratefully, the warmth in his eyes a balm to her weary spirit. "More than you know," she replied, finally allowing her shoulders to drop and her mind to relax.

How had she never realized how much silent, quiet strength Matthew was giving her? Thank you for leading him into my life, she thought and winked at him.

"Do you know how many people have asked me today if we were taking over the store," she asked aloud.

"Probably as many as asked me whether the historical society had any interest in taking over the store or the building," Matthew deadpanned.

"No," Sarah grabbed his hand. "Really? Has this entire village condemned Lily already? She's lived here forever. They know her, and now..."

"Hush," Matthew squeezed her hand, grinning at the last of the customers lining up at the register. "it's just gossip. You know how that works."

"Please do not give me the talk about things that are sometimes not fair. I know they are not. I – just need to be angry at that for a minute."

"Wouldn't dream of it," Matthew said with a crooked smile. "You do what you need to do to close up, I'll be over here checking out what's new in the history section."

Frustration crackled in the air and flared in Sarah's blue eyes. She slammed a display copy of *A Christmas Carol* shut a little too forcefully.

"Honestly," she muttered, shoving the book onto a shelf with more vigor than necessary, "you'd think they'd have better things to do than gossip about Lily."

Emma, perched on a stepladder, carefully replaced a stack of travel guides. "Mom," she said gently, her voice laced with concern, "are you okay?"

Sarah took a deep breath, forcing a smile. Between the constant questions from well-meaning customers, the weight of the murder investigation, and the never-ending to-do list, her nerves were frayed.

"Just peachy," she said, her voice a touch strained. "Let's get out of here. Matthew must be getting impatient."

As Sarah shoved the last stray receipt into the drawer of the checkout counter, her fingers brushed against the worn manila envelope containing Luke's apartment keys. A low growl rumbled from beneath the counter, followed by two sharp barks. Pixie had abandoned her napping chair and now tilted her head and stared intently at the envelope.

An idea sparked in Sarah's mind, a mischievous glint replacing the frustration in her eyes.

"Pixie, you clever girl, I had almost forgotten," she murmured, a sly smile playing on her lips. Maybe a visit to Luke's apartment, with a bit of spectral help from Amelia and Simon, was exactly what they needed to find a clue the police had missed.

A plan was already taking shape in Sarah's mind as she turned around and faced Matthew and Emma.

"Penny Harding brought me the keys to Luke's apartment today. For Lily. What if we go check the place out ourselves?" she suggested, her voice barely a whisper above the rhythmic jingle of the closing register. "Penny said they were done combing the place, but who knows, do you think they might have missed something?

Emma brushed the dust off her hands and looked up at Sarah with a mischievous little grin.

"Do I ever. You want to go on a little investigation of our own? What are we waiting for? I'm in."

Matthew, leaning against the counter, his arms folded across his chest, chuckled thoughtfully.

"Count me in, too, ladies. Penny Harding suffers from a bit of tunnel vision just now. A fresh perspective, especially aided by a perceptive canine," he glanced down at Pixie, who wagged her tail enthusiastically, "could be just what we need."

Sarah grinned, her earlier frustration giving way to a tiny spark of determination.

"Then let's go! I haven't been to that part of town, but Cory should be able to find the address online in about two minutes." With a decisive nod, she grabbed her phone and dialed his number. "Hey Cory," she said when her son answered, "I need a quick favor. Can you look up an address for us?"

Moments later, she input the information Cory had unearthed into the maps app on her phone. Thirty-one Elm Street, she announced. "Apparently, it's on the other side of town."

Sarah glanced out the store window at the near-deserted street. The snow had morphed into a full-blown blizzard, the streetlamps casting a hazy glow through the swirling white.

"Well, this is festive," she muttered, a nervous laugh escaping her lips.

Matthew, ever the gentleman, rose and held Sarah's coat for her. "Let's go find this elusive apartment then," he said, a reassuring warmth in his voice. "Just promise you won't make me drive through a blizzard again next time."

Chapter Sixteen

T he drive to Elm Street turned into a white-knuckled affair. Visibility was near zero, and the only signs of life were the occasional flicker of warm light from a nearby window. The festive glow of Christmas trees, a stark contrast to the harsh winter landscape, tugged at Sarah's heart. She couldn't help but picture cozy family gatherings and shared laughter, a world away from the unsettling circumstances that had drawn them out on this snowy night. Maybe, just maybe, they would finally find the clue that had eluded them until now.

After what seemed like an eternity, the GPS announced they had arrived at their destination. The apartment building where Luke had lived until his death loomed before them, a hulking silhouette against the snow-laden sky.

"Well, dilapidated would be putting it mildly," Sarah said and craned her neck.

Peeling paint clung precariously to the facade, and several windows were boarded up with plywood. A lone Christmas wreath hung crookedly above the entrance, its once-vibrant red now a faded echo of the holiday spirit.

The worn wooden stairs groaned under their weight as they climbed towards apartment 415. The building's interior reeked of stale cigarette smoke and something vaguely sour. Muffled sounds of a heated argument filtered through a nearby door, punctuated by a sickening slap. Sarah winced, her grip tightening on Matthew's hand.

"Sounds like a lovely bunch of neighbors," she muttered, her voice barely audible over the creaking floorboards, and she automatically gathered Emma a bit closer.

A tense silence hung heavy in the air as they reached the fourth floor. Sarah's gaze darted nervously between the identical apartment doors until it landed on number 415, identified by a faded number scrawled on a chipped green plaque. It looked no different from its neighbors.

Taking a deep breath to steady her trembling hands, Sarah fumbled with the envelope, the keys inside jangling like anxious whispers. She cast a questioning glance at Matthew, her eyes reflecting the unease churning in her gut. With a resolute nod, she unlocked the door.

A wave of stale air, tinged with the faint scent of pine needles and disinfectant, washed over them. The interior of Luke's apartment defied Sarah's expectations. The space, though modest, was surprisingly neat and tidy. The light from the street lamp outside filtered through a thin layer of grime on the windowpanes, casting an uneven glow on worn but well-maintained furniture. A bookshelf, crammed with an eclectic mix of novels and biographies, stood sentinel in one corner. A half-finished crossword puzzle lay abandoned on a small coffee table, a testament to a life abruptly cut short.

Matthew quietly closed the door. They all stood in the tiny one-room space for a moment, their silence a heavy weight in the air. Sarah ran a hand through her hair, pushing back a stray strand that clung to her damp forehead.

"Feels kind of wrong to be here," she said, her voice barely a whisper. She knelt down and released Pixie from her carrier. "Small as it is, this was Luke's private space."

Pixie immediately darted towards the tiny utility kitchen space, her nose twitching inquisitively.

Calling it a kitchen was generous; it was no more than a hot plate and a fridge with a few ancient plywood cabinets, but Pixie sniffed the air, her ears perked up with alert curiosity.

I am trying to see if that spice came out of this kitchen, Pixie said to Sarah. *Not having much luck right now. Salt, pepper, a bit of cayenne, and Italian Seasoning. Lots and lots of Italian Seasoning.*

"Are you still on the spice?" Sarah asked, a hint of exasperation creeping into her voice. "Nothing came out of this so-called kitchen except microwave dinners and ramen noodles."

Pixie ignored her question and pressed her nose against the lower cupboards one by one.

"Interest in automotive repair and mechanics," Matthew said, running his finger along the spines of the books on the shelf. His brow furrowed in concentration as he scanned the titles. "Appliance repair and... oh, a few history books."

He pulled out a few books and flipped through them quickly, and his lips pursed in disappointment.

Sarah wandered over to the bed couch, drawn by the meticulous folds of the blankets and sheets. They hinted at someone's recent presence, but a subtle disarray suggested a careless search. She reached out, her fingertips grazing the soft fabric as if hoping to glean traces of Luke's essence lingering amidst the folds.

A wave of sadness washed over her. Regret and a powerful, glowing feeling above all of that. She felt energy, positive energy, and a drive to make the best out of what he had and... hope. A tear welled up in Sarah's eye. Hope, because he had met Lily and had another job interview and a new perspective.

Quickly, she pulled her hand away, breaking the energy link. Only Emma, who possessed many of the same talents, realized what had just happened.

"He really loved Lily, didn't he?" Emma asked softly, her voice laced with sympathy. Sarah nodded gently, unable to speak past the lump in her throat.

"Lily gave him... hope," she finally said, her voice thick with emotion. "That he could start over here."

The final piece of furniture in the room was an old writing desk. They hadn't found anything useful so far, and disappointment gnawed at Sarah. The writing desk, though old, held a certain charm with its lovingly restored wood. But instead of personal letters or photos, the drawers yielded only stacks of neatly organized legal documents—court papers, it seemed. No glimpse into Luke's life, no hints of the person he might have been beyond his incarceration. A pang of sadness echoed within her. Was there no one waiting for him, no family mourning his loss? Didn't he get into an argument with his brother-in-law? Where was his sister then in all of this?

Carefully, Sarah replaced the files, a sense of duty urging her to leave the apartment undisturbed. Just as she straightened the final document, a sharp bark startled her. Pixie, who had been unusually quiet throughout the exploration, stood by the kitchen cabinets, her head tilted, barking insistently.

Three sharp barks pierced the tense silence, pulling Sarah's gaze back to Pixie. The dog's tail thumped a frantic rhythm against the worn linoleum floor. It wasn't just any bark; it was a message, a clear "get over here and look at what I found" explicitly directed at Sarah.

Curiosity momentarily flickered back to life, sparking a glimmer in Sarah's eyes. "What is it?" she whispered for Emma and Matt's benefit, crouching down to Pixie's level.

Pixie rolled onto her side, her paw pawing impatiently at the bottom drawer of a kitchen cabinet, swelled long ago with the moisture of a forgotten flood.

That smell, that smell, Pixie said, her paws still working frantically at the drawer. *There's the tiniest trace of it right here. Hurry.*

A thrill shot through Sarah. Could this be what they were looking for? A hidden clue the police might have missed? With renewed purpose, she reached for the handle and pulled on the worn brass knob. It was stuck.

Some flood had swelled these cheap plywood cabinets a long time ago, and the drawer no longer fit easily into its space. Probably, no one had opened it in ages.

"Pixie is smelling that scent from the crime scene," Sarah said to the others, renewing her efforts with the drawer. "If I could just get this darn thing open."

"If she's smelling that odd spice in here, then that means Luke brought it with him after all," Matt added. "I didn't think that would take us very far."

Pixie shook her fur out dramatically, her posture radiating supreme confidence. It was clear the tiny little dog considered herself to be in charge of this investigation, and the tip of her tail began to glow a subtle shade of gold.

"Well, what have you got?" Matt asked, his curiosity piqued. "Is that drawer stuck? I can..."

The question died on his lips as the drawer popped open with a groan, revealing... nothing.

Disappointment washed over Sarah's face as she peered into the empty drawer. "Nothing, absolutely nothing," she said, her voice heavy with defeat. "Dammit."

She struck the drawer once, trying to force it back into the proper place.

Pixie whined, nudging Sarah's hand with her nose.

It can't be, Pixie insisted, crowding in close again. *It is there. You can't fool my nose. Look again.*

"Wait, Mom, wait..." Emma knelt down beside Sarah and swept her hand around the bottom and in behind the dark space once again. Her fingers brushed against something thin and papery. Wrestling it from its hiding place, she revealed five or six old newspaper clippings and a few tightly bound typed sheets, all held together with a cheerful yellow paperclip, the kind Lily used at the bookstore.

Confusion clouded the faces of Sarah, Matthew, and Emma as they stared at the meager contents of the drawer. Emma furrowed her brow, flipping quickly through the stack of worn papers.

"These are... articles about a prison break?" she muttered, her voice barely a whisper.

Sarah snatched the papers, her eyes scanning the dates. The clippings were indeed old, news reports from Jackson, Georgia, five years ago, detailing the audacious escape of an inmate from a medium-security prison. "Convicted murderer escapes," screamed the bold headlines, and Sarah felt a jolt of fear mixed with curiosity course through her.

"Why would Luke have these?" she mumbled, her voice laced with unease.

Matthew leaned in to get a better look at the articles. "Nothing to do with him at all. It says here..." His finger followed a printed line. "Convicted murderer Vincent Carlisle escaped the Georgia State prison in Jackson, Georgia. What does this even have to do with him?"

Other than the fact that Luke had been in prison as well? The unspoken question hung heavy in the air, reflected in Matthew's tense expression. He shook his head slowly and took the papers from Emma.

Underneath the newspaper clippings sat a crumpled list, written in neat handwriting, of restaurants located in various cities across the United States.

"What in the Dickens?" Matthew muttered, picking up the list. "Fine dining and an escaped convict?"

Sarah shook her head, a growing unease gnawing at her stomach. This wasn't leading them to a murder weapon or a confession note. This was... bizarre. As if sensing her frustration, Pixie let out a sharp bark, her tail wagging exc*itedly.*

That smell from the crime scene is on there, Pixie said. I'd know it anywhere. It's very faint, but I'm positive it is the same.

Matthew only stared in disbelief when Sarah brought the stack of papers and the list to her nose, inhaling deeply.

"I don't smell anything," she said.

If Pixie could have rolled her eyes, she would have. Instead, she settled back on her haunches and stared with an expression that could only be described as unimpressed.

You didn't just say that.

"We should go," Sarah said finally, a sense of urgency creeping into her voice. "This place is starting to feel..."

Her sentence was cut short by a sharp rap on the door. Sarah, Emma, and Matthew exchanged startled glances. Before anyone could react, the flimsy door flew open, revealing a disheveled man standing in the doorway. He looked to be in his late fifties, overweight, with a receding hairline and a rumpled shirt clinging to his unkempt frame. His eyes narrowed with suspicion and darted between them.

"You folks from the police again?" he rasped, his voice gruff. "I told them there's nothin' here to see!"

Matthew, ever the diplomat, stepped forward with a placating smile and his hand raised. "Easy there, good man," he said calmly. "We're not with the police. We're here on behalf of Luke's girlfriend, Lily, to collect a few of his belongings."

The man's face contorted in a mixture of anger and confusion.

"Belongings? In the middle of a freakin' blizzard?" he bellowed, his voice echoing in the cramped apartment. "And I never heard of any Lily. This isn't some five-star hotel, you know! There'll be plenty of time during normal hours. Besides, the tenant's dead! You can't just come waltzing in here like you own the place! This is an honest, decent place."

A sarcastic chuckle escaped Sarah's lips. This gruff individual clearly wasn't aware of the irony dripping from his words. Here he was, berating them for 'sneaking around' in a dilapidated apartment building, a place he deemed a 'good decent house.'

"Look," Sarah said, her voice firm but laced with a touch of weariness. "We just want to take a few things and get out of your hair. We understand it's late, and frankly, the weather isn't ideal." Her gaze flicked pointedly towards the window, where snowflakes danced wildly in the streetlight's glow. "We'll be out of your way right now and come back."

Pixie, sensing the rising tension, let out a low growl. Sarah reached down and stroked the dog's head reassuringly.

"See?" the man scoffed, his anger seemingly abating a touch. "Even the mutt knows you should be home on a night like this. Come back during the day, take your stuff, and let a decent tenant rent the place. That's what I say."

The man's words, though gruff, held a certain logic. Pushing their luck in this weather, and with a clearly disgruntled landlord, wouldn't be wise. Sharing a resigned glance with Matthew and Emma, Sarah knew it was time to retreat.

"Alright," she conceded, her shoulders slumping slightly. "We'll be back tomorrow. Thank you for your time."

With a final, suspicious look at them, the landlord grunted and slammed the door shut, pushing them out into the dimly lit hallway. Disappointment gnawed at Sarah. They'd left empty-handed, the mystery of the newspaper clippings and the restaurant list swirling unanswered.

"That was a bust," she muttered, cradling Pixie in her arms. "What are you grinning about?"

Matthew shrugged and reached into the roomy pocket of his overcoat, coming up with the folded sheaf of papers.

"You took them..." Sarah started, surprised. "Matthew, for God's sake, if that man finds out... But thank you."

"Hush." Matthew put a finger to his lips and turned toward the closed door of Luke's apartment. "He's probably in there seeing if there's anything he has use for. But I didn't want him to have these. Now, let's go before this blizzard gets any worse."

The windshield wipers battled a losing war against the relentless snow as Matthew navigated the treacherous roads back to their Victorian home. Inside the car, a heavy silence settled, punctuated only by the heater's rhythmic hum and the blizzard's fierce howl.

Sarah stared out the window, her mind replaying the events of the evening. The cryptic newspaper clippings, the restaurant list, the unsettling encounter with the landlord all felt like pieces of a puzzle that didn't quite fit. Her hand rhythmically massaged the back of Pixie's neck, who joyfully leaned into the touch.

What if... Sarah heard Pixie thinking. *What if Luke got killed because of that scent?*

We don't even know what it is yet. Sarah hugged Pixie a bit tighter and buried her face in the dog's fur. *I wish I had your nose; I could probably figure it out.*

You'd look funny.

Matthew reached over and squeezed Sarah's hand.

"I know right now it doesn't make much sense." he said gently. "But with a little time and some luck, we'll figure it out."

Sarah offered a weak smile, her heart heavy with doubt.

The moment they walked through the front door, a gust of warm air engulfed them, a welcome relief from the biting cold. Cory hovered in the hallway, his face etched with concern that deepened as he saw their glum expressions.

"How'd it go?" he wanted to know, his voice laced with trepidation.

Before Sarah could answer, a mischievous glint sparked in Pixie's eyes. With a playful yip, she leaped from Sarah's arms and dropped the crumpled list of restaurants at Cory's feet.

"Looks like Pixie wants you to see the only thing we found," Sarah said, a hint of amusement creeping into her voice despite the weight on her shoulders. "I'm just warning you, it's not much."

Cory's eyes widened with excitement, mirroring the investigative spirit Sarah had nurtured in him. He scooped up the papers, a playful grin replacing his earlier worry.

"Let me guess," he said, his voice tinged with a playful challenge, "you need a research rabbit hole to dive down?"

Sarah chuckled, a welcome sound in the tense atmosphere. "You got it," she admitted.

With the promise of hot cocoa and a roaring fireplace, Sarah, Matthew, and Emma settled into the living room, recounting their strange encounter with Luke's landlord and their frustrating search. Cory, meanwhile, had disappeared into his room, the newspaper clippings and restaurant list clutched tightly in his hands.

As Sarah sipped her cocoa, a faint but persistent flicker of hope warmed her heart. The warmth of the den became a distant memory as Lily came downstairs, her face etched with exhaustion and worry. Deep shadows hung beneath her eyes, starkly contrasting the festive twinkle lights adorning the bookshelves and the Christmas tree. The sight of Sarah, Matthew, and Emma huddled on the couch, the air thick with unspoken concern, did little to ease the burden on Lily's shoulders.

Sarah rose, her heart heavy with empathy, and reached out to offer Lily the little brown envelope.

"Luke's keys. Penny Harding gave them to me... for you," she said softly, her voice barely a whisper above the crackling fire.

"Maybe... you know his family... his sister? They're hoping you would..."

Sarah's voice trailed off when Lily only nodded.

"We went to the apartment," she added.

Lily's fingers tightened around the envelope, a single tear tracing a glistening path down her cheek. The key, a cold metal object, seemed incongruous in her trembling hand, a stark symbol of a life cut short. The festive decorations—the plump red Santa Claus nestled in the corner, the Christmas tree adorned with glittery ornaments—all felt woefully out of place against the backdrop of her grief.

Taking a deep, shuddering breath, Lily wiped her tears with the back of her hand.

"Thank you," she only murmured, her voice choked. "Thank you. What... what did you find at his place? I haven't been there."

Sarah squeezed her hand gently, a silent promise of support hanging heavy in the air. Then, with a tentative voice, she broached the subject that had been gnawing at her since their clandestine visit to Luke's apartment.

"Lily," she began, choosing her words carefully, "did Luke ever mention anything about a prison break? Maybe in Jackson, Georgia?"

Lily's head snapped up, a flicker of surprise crossing her features. The question, seemingly out of place amidst the Christmas cheer, hung heavy in the air. Her brow furrowed in concentration, her pale fingers tightening around the key.

"I told you, I didn't even know he'd been to prison, let alone released," she whispered. "No, I am absolutely certain he never mentioned anything about a prison break, of all things. Why do you ask?"

Sarah gnawed on her lower lip, unsure how much to reveal. "We found some old news clippings at Luke's place," she explained, her gaze flitting between Lily and Matthew.

"Articles about a prison break in Atlanta from a few years ago."

Lily's brow furrowed further, a crease appearing between her eyes. Though seemingly random, the prison break had sparked a flicker of unease within her. She didn't understand the connection, but a strange sense of foreboding gnawed at her.

"That's... weird," she said slowly, her voice barely above a whisper. "Luke wasn't even into true crime or anything like that. I can't imagine why he'd have those clippings."

"Vincent Carlisle? The name tell you anything?"

Lily only shook her head.

Sarah nodded; her own curiosity piqued. "We'll figure it out, Lily," she promised, her voice firm with conviction. "Are you in touch with Luke's family at all? To collect his things so the landlord can..."

Lily shook her head. "No. I only knew him. We always would joke that we were all alone in the world."

Pixie let out a little bark and put her paws on Lily's knee. *Not alone,* she said, and Sarah repeated for everyone.

"You have us," she said, squeezing Lily's hand again. "No, how about some cocoa?"

Chapter Seventeen

The pre-dawn light cast long shadows across the kitchen as Sarah tiptoed through the house, a steaming mug warming her hands. The only sounds were the soft ticking of the clock and the rhythmic tap-tap-tap of Pixie's tail against the floor. The little papillon fixated on the forgotten toast in Sarah's hand, her brown eyes gleaming with an almost uncanny intelligence.

Sarah sighed, settling at the kitchen table with the newspaper clippings spread out before her. She glanced down at Pixie, nestled at her feet, and murmured a question, her voice barely a whisper, "What does it all mean, girl?"

Pixie whined softly, tilting her head in silent inquiry.

Just then, footsteps thumped down the stairs. Cory entered the kitchen, backpack slung over his shoulder, his hair a mess of sleep-tousled curls.

"Early bird, Mom?" he mumbled, grabbing a granola bar with a yawn.

Sarah, her eyes heavy with worry, attempted a little smile.

"Couldn't sleep. Too much on my mind."

Cory offered a sympathetic nod. "Anything new with Lily?"

Sarah shook her head, feeling the heavy weariness of the moment again.

"Still asleep, I hope. We're waiting on news from your research, though."

A familiar glint of mischief sparkled in Cory's eyes as he grinned.

"Actually," he said, taking a bite of his granola bar, "I have something. Not sure how important it is. Shouldn't you be prepping for your bookstore shift surrounded by festive cheer, fruitcakes, and nosy neighbors?"

Sarah grimaced. "Don't remind me. But spill it, what did you find?"

Cory pulled out his phone, his fingers flying across the screen before a dramatic tap.

"Okay, so, bad news first..." He paused for effect, watching his mom lean in. Sarah inched closer, her eyes glued to Cory's phone screen. The playful glint in his eyes had been replaced by a newfound seriousness, mirroring the knot of tension coiling in her gut.

"The prison break in the articles," Cory continued, his voice low and measured. "It happened at the same prison Luke was in."

Sarah's breath hitched. So, it wasn't a random detail. There was a connection, a chilling tendril reaching out from the past. A sense of foreboding washed over her, prickling the hairs on her arms.

"But..." Cory said, his voice lightening a touch. "There's a good side too." He tapped the screen again, scrolling down the page screwing up his face as he looked.

"Apparently, the break happened right after Luke arrived. Like a rude welcome, you know?" His smile never quite reached his eyes. "And more importantly," he continued, his voice firm. "It seems Luke didn't serve his entire sentence. No conduct violations, matter of fact he got early parole because of excellent conduct. If they suspected him of anything connected to the break, I don't think that would have happened."

Relief flooded Sarah's face, a wave that momentarily dissipated the tension gripping her shoulders.

"So, no direct link between Luke and the fellow who broke out? Nothing?" she asked, her voice laced with a hint of disbelief.

Cory only shrugged and pursed his lips. His eyes became unfocused, staring at something beyond the kitchen window.

"Not unless there's something else at play," he said, shaking his head. "Maybe someone involved knew Luke, or he wanted to say something, or maybe..." His voice trailed off, his brow furrowed in concentration as he tapped away at his phone, a silent conversation with the device in his hand.

"Maybe what?" Sarah prompted, her curiosity piqued. The unanswered question hung heavy in the air, a weight pressing down on them both.

Cory glanced up from his phone, his gaze locking with Sarah's.

"I don't know. None of this makes sense," he said slowly, making a first with one hand. "Why keep those articles? And why hide them in the back of a drawer unless he knew the guy, whoever it was, knew the case? Do you think he could be involved after all? Maybe he helped with this escape after all, and it just never came out?"

A cold dread settled in Sarah's stomach. The seemingly insignificant detail—the hidden newspaper clippings—now loomed large, a puzzle piece that didn't quite fit but hinted at a darker picture.

"Even the police missed those clippings," she said, her voice barely a whisper. The weight of a terrible realization pressed down on her.

"The police..." Sarah thought you could have caught the sarcasm in his voice with a bucket.

"Still, we might have removed important evidence..." Her voice trailed off, the accusation hanging heavy in the air.

"Get real. Even if you'd called them right away," Cory said, his voice gentle but firm, "If you'd presented those clippings on a little platter, I doubt Officer Harding would have cared much. She would have found some other excuse why that's there. She's got tunnel vision, focused only on Lily."

Despite his sarcasm, Sarah winced, only because she knew how right her son was. Disappointment and a flicker of anger rose inside her.

"You know, you're awfully cynical for someone who can't even drive yet," she teased, a feeble attempt to lighten the mood.

Cory smirked. "Maybe," he admitted with a playful wink. He hoisted his backpack onto his shoulder and adjusted it with a sigh. A car horn blared from outside, shattering the tense silence.

"That's Trevor's mom," Cory said, shoving his phone into his back pocket. "We'll be at hockey practice."

Sarah nodded, offering a weak smile.

"Have fun," she managed, the words heavy on her tongue. She watched as Cory dashed out the door, and drove off with his friend. Christmas cheer seemed a world away as she stared at the forgotten toast in her hand, the mystery of Luke's death a cold knot in her gut. Another day stretched before her, filled with forced smiles and the pretense that everything was sparkling and bright.

⁕

A bitter wind whipped itself into a frenzy outside, flinging icy pellets of snow against the windows with a relentless beat that mimicked the disquiet, tapping a frantic rhythm against Sarah's ribs. Getting ready, she fumbled with a stubborn necklace clasp, yanking at the little metal chains repeatedly until her common sense told her she'd break them if she kept going. A moment later, Emma, already dressed in plain jeans and a festive sweater, came downstairs to grab some breakfast.

Sarah debated whether she should tell Emma to stay home and prepare their own Christmas today when the bedroom door opened upstairs, then closed again. Matthew appeared in the doorway, his jaw firm, a hard glint of determination in his eyes.

"Change of plans," he declared suddenly, his tone hard and unyielding. He marched into the kitchen with determined strides, his eyes locked on Sarah.

"I'm coming with you to the bookstore."

It wasn't a request but a resolute statement, leaving no room for argument.

Sarah opened her mouth to protest, but Matthew raised his hand, halting her words.

"I just received the old building plans for that street from my contact at the hall of records. Something's not adding up, and I want to investigate what that is."

His jaw set hard, and his eyes narrowed with a resentment and suspicion Sarah had never seen in his normally friendly and open face. Even Emma cocked her head, surprise flickering across her face.

"But didn't the police already..." she began, her voice trailing off.

"Right," Matthew growled. "The police. They still insist that the bookstore door was never locked in the first place, that Walter and I forced it open. But I know better..." He paused, knuckles whitening as fists clenched, a hot flicker of anger dancing in his eyes. "It was definitely locked—from the inside."

Sarah's heart lurched. Matthew's anger mirrored the simmering unease in her own gut. Here was another piece of the puzzle, a detail that didn't quite fit the picture the police were painting.

"They're not listening to Lily or me," Matthew continued, his voice softening slightly. "What sense would it make for Lily to lock her own door from the inside if she were going to commit a crime? What? I am determined to figure out exactly how the real killer got out of that building."

A wave of gratitude washed over Sarah. Matthew's unwavering belief in Lily's innocence was a beacon of hope in a time of doubt and suspicion.

"Thank you," Sarah murmured, her voice thick with emotion.

A hint of a smile played on Matthew's lips.

"Any time," he replied, his gaze meeting hers. "I have no intentions of letting them pin this on our friend because it's an easy, quick explanation. Besides," he added, a playful glint returning to his eyes. "I want to watch you and Emma in action at the bookstore. I only ever come to pick you up or drop you off."

A genuine smile now broke through Sarah's worry, a welcome flicker of warmth in the face of the mystery that loomed. She put her arms around Matthew and leaned into him for a moment, smelling his clean scent of soap and shaving cream.

"I know there was a reason I fell in love with you," she whispered, and Matthew hugged her a little tighter.

"Other than my rugged good looks and talents in the kitchen, you mean," he said with a wink.

"All right, let's go then," Emma shrugged into her coat and stood by the front door. "Honestly, watching the two of you…"

And Matthew and Sarah followed, holding hands all the way out to the car.

Chapter Eighteen

At the store, Sarah wrestled with the industrial-sized coffee machine, its imposing copper presence still making her feel like a hobbit wrangling a dragon, even after a week of using it. Emma, meanwhile, fussed with a Christmas display of local cards and wrapping paper setting them up just so to please her critical eye.

With a satisfying hiss, the machine finally came to life, promising the comforting aroma of fresh coffee to fill the bookstore soon.

Across the room, Matthew, transformed into a one-man construction crew, swiping across the old blueprint of the building on his tablet while eyeing the walls critically. He paced meticulously, measuring tape dangling from his hand, a frown etching lines on his forehead. Every few steps, he'd rap his knuckles against a wall, his ear pressed close, listening intently for any telltale echoes.

The silence stretched, punctuated only by the rhythmic hum and hiss of the coffee machine. A strange sense of unease settled over Sarah. She glanced out the window, where the police station across the street loomed in unexpected darkness. Was it closed today? Had the antics of the ghosts proved to be too much for the local force?

A shiver danced down her spine, a feeling that intensified as a familiar coldness pricked at her skin. The telltale tingling sensation, a precursor to Amelia's ghostly appearances, started at her fingertips and crawled up her arms.

Sarah exchanged a worried glance with Emma. Their day had started with unease, and with the police station mysteriously dark and a spectral presence about to materialize in the store—it was about to get a whole lot more interesting and possibly a whole lot more complicated.

Sarah noticed a lone figure browsing the new releases section. "Customer!" she whispered to Emma.

Emma put down the cards she was arranging, a practiced smile plastered on her face.

"Hey there! Welcome to the Rosewood Hollow Bookstore! Can I help you find anything specific today?" she chirped, her voice radiating enthusiasm.

Sarah melted back into the shadows and darted towards the back room. The air grew colder as she neared the doorway, the unmistakable prickle of Amelia's presence intensifying. Taking a deep breath, Sarah flung open the door, hoping to catch the ghost off guard.

But Amelia, as always, seemed to defy expectations. She quite suddenly materialized beside Matthew, her translucent form shimmering faintly in the dim light.

Matthew, in the midst of meticulously measuring a utility shelf, gaped at her, his mouth hanging open like a landed fish.

Amelia, seemingly oblivious to his astonishment, pointed a spectral finger towards a corner of the room. A section of the wall, unlike the rest of the smooth plaster, was constructed from rough-hewn fieldstones. A shiver danced down Sarah's spine. That wall, an anomaly in the otherwise modern bookstore, had always felt out of place.

"There," Amelia rasped, her voice a faint echo in the silent room. She gestured towards the fieldstones, her spectral hand leaving no impression on the rough surface.

Just then, a loud laugh came from the front of the store. Amelia flinched, her form flickering faintly. She turned to Sarah, a reassuring smile gracing her translucent features.

"Do not be concerned. I know your customers are not quite ready for the sight of me," she whispered, her voice fading into a sigh on the last word.

Before Sarah could respond, Amelia shimmered and dissolved into nothingness, leaving behind a faint chill and a lingering sense of anticipation. Sarah stepped fully into the back room; her curiosity piqued.

"What was that all about?" she asked, her voice barely a whisper.

Matthew straightened up, his eyes wide with a mix of excitement and apprehension.

"Of course, how'd I miss it? I knew there was something odd about this wall," he said, gesturing towards the fieldstones, "Amelia confirmed my suspicions. It's hollow." His gaze flickered towards the empty space where Amelia had stood moments ago.

"If I'm correct in my assumptions, we may have just figured out how the murderer got out."

Sarah heard the cash register's ring out front, and moments later, Emma appeared in the doorway.

"What's going on back here? Was that Amelia?"

Matthew nodded and shook his head like a dog coming out of the water. "I still can't get used to her, but look here."

He enlarged the old blueprint on his tablet. "See this?" With a pen, he pointed to a section corresponding to the corner with the fieldstones. "This used to be a fireplace."

Sarah and Emma leaned in, their eyes widening in understanding.

"A fireplace?" Emma echoed, tracing the faded outline with a finger. "But why would there be a fireplace in the back room?"

Matthew grinned, a glint of triumph in his eyes. "Because this part of the building," he tapped another section of the blueprint, "used to be one large home with a fireplace, strategically placed in the dividing wall. It could be enjoyed from both sides and heat both sides of the ground floor."

"One side now being Lily's bookstore," Sarah murmured, piecing together the puzzle.

"Exactly," Matthew confirmed. "And the other side..." he pointed towards a blank space on the blueprint, "the empty store next door."

A flicker of comprehension dawned on Sarah. "And the two sides are potentially connected? By, oh, let's say, a small passage of some sort?"

Matthew grinned broadly and snapped his fingers.

"You got it! Likely an access hatch for cleaning and maintenance. I'm thinking a simple sliding panel, maybe hidden amongst the fieldstones. Over time, with the building being remodeled and the stores separated, the passage would have been shut off and forgotten."

His gaze darted back to the fieldstone wall, a renewed sense of purpose in his eyes.

"That could be what that hollow sound means. A hidden passage, right behind this wall, leading to the empty space next door."

The discovery sent a jolt of adrenaline through Sarah. The locked front door, the cryptic newspaper clippings, and now a hidden passage—each piece of the puzzle seemed to point towards a secret Lily wasn't privy to. Had Luke stumbled upon this hidden passage? And if so, what secrets did it hold?

The revelation hung heavy in the air—a hidden passage tucked away behind the unassuming fieldstone wall. Another puzzle piece had clicked into place, but the overall picture remained frustratingly blurry.

"So," Emma finally broke the silence, her voice tinged with a mix of awe and trepidation, "there really is a secret passage in Lily's store."

Sarah nodded, her gaze lingering on the wall.

"It seems so. But the question is, who knew about it?"

Matthew tapped his finger thoughtfully against the blueprint. "I doubt Lily did," he mused. "Or she would have told us about it right away. Considering the state of the passage, it's likely been hidden for a long time."

"Exactly," Sarah chimed in, a frown creasing her brow. "Lily is in this building almost every day. If even she wasn't aware of it, then who was?"

A cold dread settled in Sarah's stomach. This could work for or against them. The hidden passage wasn't just some architectural quirk. It was a secret, and whoever knew about it was likely the same person who murdered Luke.

"And why?" Emma added, voicing the question that echoed in all their minds. "Why kill Luke over a dusty old passage?"

The room sank into a heavy silence. No matter how thrilling, this discovery now cast a long shadow of doubt. The more they learned, the more complex the mystery became. Was the passage the key or simply another layer of obfuscation?

⚭

The warm glow of the Christmas tree cast a festive light on Sarah's living room that evening, a stark contrast to the heavy weight of the secret they carried. Lily, perched on the edge of the sofa, her face drawn with worry, listened intently as Sarah spoke.

"We... uhh, found something at the bookstore today," Sarah began, her voice hesitant. "A hidden passage behind the fieldstone wall in the back room."

Lily shook her head and blinked a couple of.

"A passage? From my store?" she trailed off, her voice laced with uncertainty. "I do remember hearing something about the two stores being one big house a long time ago. But a passage? I would have known about that, wouldn't I?"

Her brows drew together even more.

"Wouldn't I?" She didn't trust her own mind any longer.

"We were hoping you might have heard something about it when you rented the store," Sarah said softly. "For sheer curiosity's sake. But if even you didn't..."

The sentence hung unfinished, the unspoken question heavy in the air. It was Lily's store and had been for many years now. Who could have known about that passage and make use of it so easily?

Just then, the front door creaked open, and Cory burst in, a gust of cold air swirling around him. He shrugged off his jacket, his eyes sparkling with youthful enthusiasm.

"Hey, I'm back! Did you guys figure anything out at the bookstore?"

Sarah gave him a quick hug and launched into a brief explanation detailing the discovery of the hidden passage.

Cory listened, his initial excitement morphing into a thoughtful frown.

"Wow," he finally breathed, processing the information. "That's... huge. But that's not something you would expect to find in a regular rental contract, is it? Includes hidden passage. So, how would you even know...?"

He didn't need to finish the sentence. Without waiting for a response, Cory's eyes darted toward the bookshelf, landing on his laptop. With a determined glint in his eyes, he grabbed it, opening the lid in one smooth motion.

"Alright, let's see what our old friend, the search engine, has to say. Old fireplaces with hidden passages, that's gotta be a thing, right?"

Before anyone could respond, Cory had opened a browser and his favorite research portal, fingers flying across the keyboard. The festive cheer of the Christmas decorations seemed to mock the seriousness of their situation, but Sarah couldn't help but feel proud of Cory's unwavering enthusiasm.

Cory scanned article after article and finally looked up.

"Do I even want to know? What did our Officer Harding have to say about all of this?" he asked, his voice barely a whisper above the click-clack of his keyboard.

Sarah, perched on the couch beside Lily, shook her head. "We haven't actually seen her all day."

Lily wiped the exhaustion and stress off her face with both hands and pulled the hair back from her head, untangling the limp, dull strands.

"Penny came by the house earlier," she said softly. "Apparently, all of the electrical and IT issues at the station have become unmanageable for the moment."

"Unmanageable," Sarah asked with a flicker of concern. "What does that mean in concrete terms?"

Lily shrugged one shoulder. "Penny said the station will be closed until after Christmas. Claremont PD will be taking over patrols and preliminary investigations until a proper assessment of the building can be made."

A beat of silence followed, then Sarah finally voiced the question that hung heavily in the air. "What about you, Lily? Did she say anything about...”?

Lily's eyes welled up with fresh tears.

"She said not to get my hopes up. Claremont will be following the same investigation thread. I need to cooperate further if required and definitely not leave Rosewood for any reason," she choked out, her voice tight with emotion.

"But, technically, I could run the bookstore again if I want."

A flicker of anger sparked in Cory's eyes. "Run the bookstore? Like nothing happened? Like they never pointed more than one finger at you, made all of Rosewood gossip about your involvement?"

He drew air quotes around the last two words.

Lily's shoulders slumped. "She said if anybody even... well, you don't need me to finish that sentence, do you?"

The unspoken words filled the room, a suffocating weight. Customers. The public. Even after everything, whispers would linger, suspicion hanging over Lily like a shroud: what that would do to her business was unknown.

Sarah reached out, gently squeezing Lily's hand. "We won't let that happen," she promised, her voice firm with determination. We'll clear your name, Lily. Watch and learn; we've done it before."

Lily offered a watery smile, a flicker of hope battling the weariness in her eyes.

"I found a couple of articles," Cory chimed in from his tablet. "Unfortunately, there really is not much. They did exist, these fireplaces with two access sides. As to how common they were, I don't know."

Lily rubbed her temple with her fingers.

"But," Cory insisted. "The person who stabbed Luke, they still would have to be an expert of some kind to know about it. Someone who maybe recognized the design, had some knowledge, like a builder or..."

"Let it go, Cory." Her voice was tired and papery, and Lily let her hands drop into her lap again. "You all are trying to help—so much—just because of me."

"You didn't do it," Cory said with conviction, finally eliciting the ghost of a smile from Lily.

"Besides," Matthew said. "Sarah's ghost pointed me toward this double fireplace—"

"My ghost?"

"She's definitely your ghost." Matthew held a glass of wine out to Lily. Usually, he was the first one to subtly steer her toward water or one of his many teas. This was serious.

"Amelia made a point of... coming around—manifesting or whatever—to show me that passage in the wall. I would have to think there's a purpose to that."

Pixie abandoned her seat by the fire and hopped up on Lily's lap, cuddling close to her and putting her paws on Lily's arm.

Then there's still that smell. Sarah heard and rolled her eyes.

Pixie, unless you are willing to go back into that spice merchant's booth at the Christmas market, I don't think there's anything there we can use... as much as we want to.

Not likely. Pixie shook her head, ear fringe flying, and settled back in. *If I did, my nose would probably go blind for weeks, and I'd be no use at all. And we still wouldn't find anything.*

Disheartened silence settled over the little group. The crackling fire in the hearth cast long shadows on the walls, mirroring the gloom that had descended upon them. Cory's vague few resources struck a blow to their latest discovery, leaving them with limited resources and facing a public that might still see Lily as a suspect.

"Well," Matthew finally broke the silence, his voice tinged with forced optimism, "since tonight's a bust, how about we order some takeout? We've still got those coupons thanks to the generosity of our neighbors, right?"

"About that," Sarah said, wrinkling her brow. "Cassie Lethbridge was in the store yesterday. I wanted to thank her, but it was like she knew nothing about it. Could you have maybe confused her with one of the neighbors?"

"Maybe..." Matthew hunched his shoulders. "Could be. I mean I thought it was, but..."

"Never mind, I'll work out who the generous giver was." Sarah, lost in thought, offered a half-hearted nod. She rose and headed toward the hallway where the bowl overflowing with restaurant coupons sat on her little mahogany hall table. That graceful little table had been there when she moved in and was one of her favorites. Reaching for the bowl, a chill ran down her spine.

Scrawled in the dust beside the bowl, two words glared back at her: "USE THEM."

Sarah ground her teeth, battling the frustration welling up inside her.

"Seriously?" she muttered, her voice tight with annoyance. "Who in the dickens thought this was a good idea? This is the last thing I need right now."

The last few days had been a whirlwind of activity, sleep a distant memory. The idea of someone criticizing her housekeeping, especially with everything on her plate, was infuriating.

"Whoa, what's wrong?" Lily asked, the lines on her forehead deepening now.

Sarah held up the bowl, the accusatory message stark against the dust. "Someone felt the need to remind me to use these coupons and, I gather, to step up my dusting game," she said, her voice low with sarcasm. "Any ideas?"

Cory, Emma, and Matthew exchanged bewildered glances.

"Definitely not me," Cory protested, both hands raised. "I never go near that table because I know I'll break it, and you'll have my head."

The others echoed his sentiment, all denying any involvement in the dusty message.

Matthew reached out to wipe it and the dust off the hall table, but Pixie, who had been curled up with Lily, perked up at the commotion.

She hopped off the couch and trotted toward the hallway, sniffing the air curiously. She examined the inscription in the dust, then trotted back to Sarah, a knowing glint in her eyes.

It shimmers just the tiniest bit, don't you see? Magic dust, it was Amelia, she declared and shook, her comment on the situation.

Sarah blinked and peered closer at the message.

"Amelia, why?"

Pixie tilted her head. *Who knows with that ghost. Your ghost.*

A slow smile spread across Sarah's face. Amelia, with her ghostly meddling, was indeed the only logical explanation. Even amidst their serious situation, the willful spirit couldn't resist a little nudge. Besides, every now and then, Amelia still considered this 'her' house.

"So, pick your favorite," Lily said.

Sarah stared into the overflowing coupon bowl and riffled with her fingers. Takeout sounded like the perfect comfort food after the day she'd had. She reached in, her fingers brushing against the paper edges. Suddenly, a familiar burst of bright orange caught her eye.

It was the Indian restaurant coupon that had caught her eye the night they had received the package. The bright orange background starkly contrasted with the muted tones of the others.

Suddenly, a jolt of energy surged through her—the color, the restaurant—it drew her almost magically. Before she could think twice, her fingers had closed around the orange rectangle.

The bright and mouthwatering images of the food made her feel doubly hungry. But the lettering said two for one, and this wasn't about her. This was about a quiet family dinner.

She'd take Matthew to that Indian restaurant if they ever had more than ten minutes for a date night, she decided. Taking a deep breath, she forced her hand open and let the orange coupon slip back into the pile. Instead, she fished out a much simpler voucher for a local burger joint, a place known for its greasy goodness and bottomless fries.

"Alright," she announced, a hint of a smile playing on her lips, "who's up for some burgers and onion rings?"

Matthew's eyes lit up. "You read my mind, Sarah. Burgers sound fantastic right now."

Lily and Emma chimed in with their agreement, and Cory, with the bottomless appetite of a seventeen-year-old, couldn't resist the siren call of perfectly greasy fries. As Sarah placed the order, she tucked the bright orange coupon into her phone cover. Date night with Matthew sounded perfect.

Chapter Nineteen

Date night arrived sooner than Sarah anticipated. The whirlwind of activity surrounding Lily's case had pushed thoughts of romance to the back of her mind. But two days later, Cory and Emma were whisked away to a Christmas movie marathon by a classmate. Lily was off to answer a few more questions at the Claremont PD, and a rare lull settled over the house. Sarah felt as if she could breathe for the first time in days and grinned at Matthew, a question hanging in the air.

"So," she began, a hint of a blush creeping up her cheeks. "There is one of these coupons in our collection I have been saving for a special occasion..."

"Oh?" A slow smile spread across Matthew's face. "Would it be the one I saw you tucking into your phone the other day? How could I forget? It would be an honor to take you there, my lady."

Sarah's heart did a little skip. "You don't mind eating out again?"

"Absolutely not," Matthew confirmed, his voice warm and inviting. "Anything to take your mind off things, even if it involves questionable levels of spice. And, in this case, I am all for obeying your ghost."

With the decision made, Sarah busied herself getting ready, a nervous flutter in her stomach that wasn't entirely unpleasant. She got dressed in a chic little dress she hadn't worn in ages, added high heels and just the right jewelry, and spent time on her hair and makeup. It would be a magical evening.

As she headed for the door, a pang of guilt tugged at her heart. Leaving Pixie home alone wasn't her perfect idea for an evening this close to Christmas. The little papillon wouldn't complain, but her expectant, hopeful eyes...

With a sigh, Sarah detoured to the living room, where Pixie sat on the couch, fluffy tail wagging cautiously. Scooping up the little Papillon, Sarah gently placed her into the black and white purse carrier Lily had bought for her a while ago. Ever adaptable, Pixie simply blinked at her once before curling up comfortably for the ride.

You'll have to be very quiet, okay?

Trust me; I know how to behave on date nights.

Pixie actually winked. Maybe this wouldn't be just any ordinary date night. With a mischievous glint in her eye, Sarah locked the door behind them, ready for a night of good food, good company, and perhaps a touch of magic courtesy of the tiny stowaway in her purse.

∞

The air in The Jewel of Agra shimmered with an intoxicating blend of exotic aromas from Northern Indian cuisine. Cardamom, saffron, and the heady musk of roasted cumin danced with the rich warmth of sandalwood incense, weaving a spell that transported Sarah and Matthew to a world far removed from Rosewood Hollow.

Dimmed lighting filtered through ornately carved amber sconces, casting a soft, golden glow on the plush ruby-red booths that lined the restaurant's perimeter. Intricate tapestries depicting scenes from Indian mythology adorned the walls, their vibrant hues punctuated by gleaming brass lamps that cast flickering patterns on the tablecloth.

A symphony of gentle sounds filled the air. The rhythmic clinking of silverware mingled with the soft murmur of conversation, punctuated by the occasional melodic strains of a sitar playing a traditional raga. A gentle breeze, seemingly infused with the scent of jasmine, rustled the silk curtains that draped the large picture windows, offering glimpses of a bustling city street transformed into a shimmering dreamscape by the amber glow of streetlights.

Matthew leaned back and sighed with contentment as he sipped his drink.

"This place opened before you moved to Rosewood Hollow, maybe five years ago? Caused quite a stir back then. Most people in town were used to the diner or Mrs. Henderson's meatloaf. Nobody gave them more than three months in Rosewood."

"I think I remember hearing about it," Sarah said, furrowing her brow. "Isn't it also owned by—"

"A guy from NYC without any Indian ancestry at all," Matthew finished, laughing. "He's all about shaking things up. Takes the classic Indian dishes and adds his own twist. My assistant at the museum told me it's like he's playing culinary jazz with flavors and tastes you won't find anywhere else."

"Well, bring it on. Tonight, I am more than ready for that."

Sarah looked around, her brow furrowing slightly. The name, Jewel of Agra, seemed to tug at a forgotten memory, a half-formed thought buzzing at the edge of her consciousness. She tried to grasp it, but it remained frustratingly elusive.

Just then, a soft whine emanated from beneath the table. Sarah glanced down at her purse, a faint bulge betraying Pixie's presence. The little Papillon, used to the hustle and bustle of the bookstore, was suddenly restless in the confines of her carrier for some reason.

Sarah reached down and surreptitiously unzipped the compartment a crack, offering Pixie a reassuring pat through the fabric. A tiny pink tongue darted out, licking Sarah's finger in thanks before Pixie settled back down, soothed by the familiar touch.

Sarah watched, mesmerized, as the waiter placed a steaming dish of Saag Paneer in front of her. Vibrant green spinach formed the base, dotted with pillowy cubes of paneer cheese, all bathed in a creamy, fragrant sauce. The aroma itself was a poem—a symphony of ginger, turmeric, and a hint of something warm and earthy that sent her taste buds tingling.

Just as Sarah was about to spear a piece of paneer, another disgruntled whine erupted from beneath the table. Her gaze darted downwards, where her purse carrier began to wobble precariously. A frantic snuffling sound filled the air, followed by a series of frantic tugs at the zipper. Then, with a triumphant squeak, the zipper budged open a fraction, revealing a tiny black nose pushing its way out.

Panic seized Sarah. Pixie's escape act, usually a source of amusement, now threatened to derail the entire evening. But what truly sent a jolt through her was the disembodied voice that echoed faintly in her mind amidst the soft murmurs of the restaurant.

The spice...Sarah, that spice... It's right here.

The voice was laced with urgency. Before Matthew could question the sudden furrow in her brow, Sarah shot up from her seat, her heart pounding in her chest.

"Excuse me!" she blurted out, her voice a touch too loud in the otherwise hushed restaurant.

With a mumbled apology to Matthew and a desperate yank on the purse strap, Sarah practically bolted toward the ladies' room. Clutching the now-heaving purse close to her chest, she hurried into a stall, locking the door behind her with a trembling hand.

Once inside, she carefully unzipped the carrier, her eyes wide with apprehension. Pixie, her tiny pink tongue lolling out in a panting grin, looked up at Sarah with a mischievous glint in her eyes.

"What in the world, Pixie?" Sarah whispered, her voice barely a breath. "And what was that about the spice?"

Pixie tilted her head, her brown eyes reflecting Sarah's concern. She shook her head a few times and sneezed so hard that her chin hit the top of the purse.

It's the spice I smelled... At the crime scene.

Sarah's world slowed down and seemed to tilt at the same time. The mysterious spice they'd been searching for, here at this Indian restaurant? But the bathroom door creaked open a crack before Sarah could decipher Pixie's cryptic message.

"Sarah? Is everything alright?" Matthew's worried voice filtered through the gap.

Sarah glanced down at Pixie, a dilemma flashing across her mind.

There are so many different spices here, Sarah. We need to hurry.

The little dog's eyes seemed to water, and she ducked back down in her carrier.

"Just a little... incident with my lipstick," she said. "I'll be right out!"

Inside the cramped stall, Sarah knelt before Pixie, her voice a hushed whisper.

Pixie, are you sure?

Pixie's ears drooped, her tail tucked between her legs. She let out a soft whine that sounded suspiciously like an apology.

Yes, even if it ruins your date night. Sarah couldn't help but smile. Despite the near disaster, a newfound warmth bloomed in her chest.

"Alright, alright," she soothed, scratching Pixie behind the ears. "You didn't ruin the date. You helped us get a clue."

Taking another deep breath, Sarah zipped up the carrier and straightened her clothes. Emerging from the stall, she rejoined Matthew at the table, a weak smile on her face.

Matthew studied her intently.

"Everything alright? You look a little flustered."

"Just fine," Sarah mumbled, avoiding his gaze and looking around to see if anyone was listening in. The lie felt heavy on her tongue, but she wasn't sure if she should come out with her discovery in the middle of the restaurant.

Matthew didn't seem entirely convinced. He opened his mouth to speak, but Sarah cut him off.

"So, how's the food?" she asked brightly, forcing a cheerfulness she didn't quite feel.

"Delicious," Matthew replied, taking a bite of his chicken tikka masala. "Though, you haven't touched yours yet. Is everything alright with the curry?"

Just then, the waiter, a man with a neatly trimmed mustache and a welcoming smile, approached their table.

"Everything alright with your meal, madam?" he inquired, his voice polite.

Sarah's mind raced. Could she use this opportunity to her advantage? Taking a deep breath, she decided to gamble.

"Actually," she began, her voice calm and measured, "there is something very interesting about this dish."

The waiter's smile widened. "Interesting? How so?"

Sarah pointed towards her Saag Paneer. "There's a particular spice," she said, her voice barely a murmur. "It has a unique... peppery quality, with a hint of citrus."

The waiter's eyes gleamed with recognition. "Ah, yes! That would be the grains of paradise. A somewhat unorthodox choice in Indian cuisine, but our chef has a penchant for fusion cuisine and rare spices."

"Grains of paradise?" Sarah repeated, the name echoing in her mind.

A jolt of excitement surged through her. Now she had a name. The spice, the message, the hidden passage—all they needed to do now was connect it all to create a trail that led straight to the killer. A newfound determination set in Sarah's eyes. This date night, with all its twists and turns, had given her an idea.

"Could we take the rest of our food to go, please?" she asked with a broad smile, without offering any explanation. Their waiter looked at Matthew, who merely shrugged, his mouth in a tight line.

"Fine," he said with a curt nod. "I'll get the check."

Matthew's body language was stiff with anger as they exited the restaurant. Thin and heavy silence stretched between them. The walk to the car was punctuated only by the click of their heels on the sidewalk, each step echoing the growing tension between them.

Matthew finally turned to Sarah in the car, his voice tight with frustration.

"Alright then," he said, his jaw clenched. "What was that all about in there? If you didn't want to go out, you could have said so. And what on earth is going on with Pixie? Bringing her to a restaurant was clearly..."

Sarah, her own heart hammering in her chest, met his gaze head-on. But unlike Matthew, her eyes sparkled with a newfound excitement. She waited until he was finished, letting the silence hang in the air for a beat longer before a slow smile spread across her face.

Slowly, she unzipped the carrier and let Pixie pop her head out.

"Pixie smelled it again," she declared triumphantly. "In the restaurant, Pixie figured out what kind of spice it was."

"Spice..." Matthew said, confused for a moment. "Oh, the stuff she thought she smelled at the crime scene?"

"The very same." Sarah nodded. "She smelled it in there."

"If you want to search every curry shop in the area..." Then the penny dropped. "Grains of Paradise. 'A somewhat unorthodox choice in Indian cuisine,'" he repeated the waiter's words. "'But our chef has a penchant for fusion cuisine and rare spices.'"

For a moment, neither spoke.

"I've honestly never heard of it," Matthew said slowly.

"Neither have I., but I believe in this case... that is a very, very good thing." Sarah grinned broadly now. "Tomorrow, I am going back to that spice merchant and getting some of those grains of paradise. So that Pixie can be sure... and us. But for now, well, the suspect pool is ever shrinking."

Chapter Twenty

T he front door slammed with an echoing bang, announcing Cory and Emma's return. Sarah, practically vibrating with barely contained excitement, shot up from the couch the moment the door had closed.

"Guys!" she exclaimed, her voice bubbling with urgency. "Cory, I need you to look up something for me...again, sorry."

Cory, laden with popcorn bags and movie theater memorabilia, blinked at her in surprise.

"Research? Now?"

"It's important," Sarah insisted, putting as much charm into her request as possible. "Look into the Jewel of Agra restaurant. Everything you can find about it its history, the owner, anything."

Cory, sensing the seriousness in her voice, readily agreed. He deposited his spoils on the coffee table and disappeared into his room, the rhythmic click-clack of his keyboard soon filling the air.

Emma, perched on the armrest of the couch, raised a skeptical eyebrow. "That trendy Indian restaurant in the east end? What does that have to do with anything?"

Sarah gently ruffled the back of Pixie's head and offered a cryptic explanation. "Maybe something, maybe nothing, but for the moment, it's all that we have. Just wait for your brother to do his magic on the internet."

The sound of that sentence alone made her shiver.

Moments later, Cory reappeared, his brow furrowed in concentration. "Alright," he announced, "here's what I found. The Jewel of Agra was founded three years ago by a guy named Travis Harrington. Apparently, he's a culinary whiz, known for his Indian fusion cuisine and creative use of rare spices."

A triumphant smile bloomed on Sarah's face. She scooped Pixie up from the floor, burying her face in the tiny papillon's fur. "You're the one who found it, Pixie!" she whispered, her voice thick with emotion.

The others, however, remained unconvinced. Matthew, who had been listening intently from the doorway, chimed in with a voice laced with doubt.

"It's still only a spice. Not exactly a smoking gun, as it were. I mean, it could be a coincidence. It's thin."

Disappointment flickered across Sarah's face, but she quickly squashed it. There was more to this than just a spice. She just had to figure out how to explain it to the others, or at least part of it.

"It's not just any spice. It's very unusual," she argued. "Grains of paradise. You and I had never heard of it. I doubt it's a staple in the kitchens of Rosewood Hollow."

A thoughtful silence descended upon the group. Emma, ever the pragmatist, finally broke the quiet.

"Okay, so there might be a connection," she conceded. "But a connection to what? And how does it help us find Luke's killer?"

Sarah set her jaw. The spice was just a piece of the puzzle, but it was a new piece, and a big one at that.

"We need to dig deeper, find out everything we can about the Jewel of Agra, about this Travis Harrington. Maybe there's something else, something that will truly connect the dots. I'm going to see that spice merchant tomorrow. Pixie smelled that spice at his stall; he had it there. We'll have her compare it; maybe he'd be willing to tell us if there are any regular customers of this spice at his store. Is he not the expert on spices on YouTube?"

The playful ambiance of the evening had been replaced by a tense urgency. Sarah cradled a mug of tea in her hands, the warmth doing little to dispel the chill of unease that crept down her spine.

The name, Jewel of Agra, still echoed in her head, a mantra on repeat, each syllable thrumming with a hypnotic power she couldn't explain. Her fingertips tingled with a strange energy, and a knot of frustration tightened in her stomach. The connection was there—she could feel it—but the missing piece refused to click into place.

"How does it all tie together?" she murmured, her voice barely a whisper. "The spice, the restaurant... what do they have to do with Luke's murder?"

Matthew, his gaze fixed on the flickering flames in the fireplace, offered no immediate response. He seemed lost in his own thoughts, his brow furrowed in a contemplative frown.

Suddenly, a memory jolted Sarah, a fragment of the past breaking through the fog of confusion. It was the day they had checked Luke's tiny apartment, but now, a detail surfaced, one that she hadn't considered before.

"The list," she gasped, her voice breaking the silence. "Luke's list!"

Matthew's head snapped towards her, a flicker of interest sparking in his eyes. "What list?"

Sarah scrambled to her feet, her mind racing. "Remember the list we found at Luke's," she explained, her voice laced with newfound urgency. "A list of restaurants, all in different states."

A wave of realization washed over Matthew. "Restaurants? Could that be the connection? Was the Jewel of Agra on that list?"

"Not the one here in Rosewood, but I'm almost certain I've seen the name before."

Matthew made a face. "Could be," he muttered. "It's not that common a name, but do you really think...?"

Sarah didn't need to answer. A surge of certainty coursed through her. The memory of the list was hazy, but the name Jewel of Agra burned bright in her mind. It had to be on there.

"We need to check that list," she declared, her voice firm with resolve. "Maybe it holds the key to everything. Maybe it tells us why Luke was investigating the restaurant, why he was murdered, and a connection is hiding to a restaurant by the same name right here in Rosewood."

Just then, the front door opened and closed again, and relief washed over Sarah, momentarily chased away by the icy gust that sneaked in behind Lily.

Emma was already on her feet, a steaming mug held out with a smile.

"Mulled cider, Lily? You look about ready to melt into a snowdrift."

Lily took the mug with a shaky hand, her usually vibrant emerald eyes dull. The festive fairy lights strung across the living room seemed to mock her misery.

"Thanks, Em. You won't believe the interrogation I've been through. The Detective in Claremont is like a bloodhound with a bad case of the sniffles."

Sarah watched concern war with a flicker of something else in Lily's eyes. "They think you did it, too?"

Lily sank into the worn armchair, the faded floral print seeming to swallow her whole. "Penny warned me they'd be following the same investigative thread…" she hesitated, taking a tentative sip of cider. "Like I'm going to say anything else when they asked for the fifteenth time."

Pixie hopped onto Lily's lap, her fur shimmering with an other-worldly luminescence.

"Well, Matthew and I found something," Sarah said with a grin.

Lily's head snapped up, surprise momentarily banishing the shadows from her face.

"I'll take it… anything. What did you find?"

A flicker of recognition ignited in Lily's eyes as Sarah caught her up about the scent Pixie had discovered and rediscovered at the restaurant. A flicker of cautious hope dared to show on her face.

"The Jewel of Agra?" Lily echoed, the name rolling thoughtfully off her tongue. "That Indian place with the beautiful tapestries? I know it. Hmm…" she trailed off, her brow furrowing in thought as she replayed Sarah's words in her mind.

Silence stretched between them, punctuated only by the rhythmic crackle of the fireplace.

"Actually," she continued, her voice gaining a newfound strength, "I think I might even know the man who is running it at the moment if I remember correctly. His name's Travis Harrington, right? Used to do some catering for the Gallery that was next door before they moved out. Nice guy, always friendly. He'd sometimes come to the bookstore with sample trays, offering us a taste of his latest creations." Lily's smile faltered slightly, the memory casting a long shadow.

"I didn't know him really well, but… He doesn't strike me as a guy who'd kill anyone."

"Do you think Luke and Travis knew each other," Sarah asked, and Lily shook her head.

"You've been to that restaurant," she finally whispered, disbelief lacing her tone. "That's an expensive place. Luke barely had enough for rent, let alone overpriced fusion restaurants."

Sarah furrowed her brow, mirroring Lily's confusion. "That's what we were thinking, too. We only went because of those coupons the Lethbridge's gave us, which they didn't even remember."

Lily's head shot up, eyes widening.

"You know what... Amelia had to be the one who left that message in the dust pointing us that way?"

"Amelia," Sarah asked in the direction of the fireplace corner. "Did you have anything to do with this? Is there something you want us to find?"

She listened for a moment, but all remained silent except for a sudden chill draft that softly made the Christmas tree's glass ornaments tinkle.

With a sigh, Sarah turned back to the worn leather armchair where Matthew was settling in, a sheaf of papers clutched in his hand.

"Is that the list from Luke's apartment?" she asked, a sliver of hope flickering within her.

Matthew peered over the top of the papers, his dark eyes twinkling. "It is. And guess what? The Jewel of Agra is right there at the top." A slow smile spread across his face, mirroring Sarah's own growing sense of anticipation.

Sarah and Matthew were just about to dissect the cryptic clue further when Cory burst into the room, his tablet clutched in his hand like a lifeline.

"Mom, check this out!" he exclaimed, his voice brimming with teenage excitement. He shoved the tablet towards her, momentarily blocking the flickering flames that had sprung to life in the fireplace. Amelia? A prickle of unease crawled up Sarah's spine.

Chapter Twenty-One

"What? What did you find?" Sarah asked, forcing her attention back to her son.

Cory, oblivious to his mother's internal debate, tapped the screen impatiently.

"Here, look. It's an article about an art show opening a couple of months ago! Right next door to Lily's bookstore!"

The tablet displayed a brightly lit storefront bathed in the warm glow of fairy lights. A colorful banner proclaiming "Grand Opening" stretched across the windows, adorned with a whimsical paintbrush and palette. The caption below identified the location as "The Muse," a new art gallery in Rosewood Hollow.

Sarah's mind raced, trying to slot all the puzzle pieces into the correct position. For a moment, she didn't know what she was looking at; the image of Lily's bookstore and a brightly lit art gallery side by side brought back memories from earlier, happier times.

But if Cory had found something about this art gallery, "The Muse," in his searches, she'd take it.

Sarah leaned closer to the tablet, scrutinizing the image of the bustling art gallery opening. The vibrant paintings lining the walls and the excited chatter of the crowd seemed a world away from the tense atmosphere gripping their own living room. Yet, a tiny detail snagged her attention, pulling her back to their mystery.

"Not so fast," Cory said, his voice tinged with impatience. "You almost missed it. See?" He zoomed in on the picture, his finger tracing a specific spot on the screen. "Right there, do you see?"

Sarah followed his gaze. A section of the back wall, where The Muse presumably met Lily's bookstore, was obscured by a velvet rope, cordoning off an area from the celebratory crowd. But, beyond the velvet barrier, a flicker of orange light caught Sarah's eye. There, nestled within the shared wall, the fireplace was crackling merrily, spreading cozy warmth.

"The fireplace!" Cory exclaimed, his voice brimming with excitement. "It's lit in that picture! That chef, Travis, catered the event, am I right? He must have seen it then. And if he knew there was a fireplace, maybe he knew there was a passage!"

A sudden chill washed over Sarah, and she zoomed in on that image as far as she could.

"That's a lot of maybes," she muttered, but the seemingly insignificant detail of a shared fireplace now took on a whole new meaning. What if they were looking at the secret passage the killer had used to enter and exit the bookstore undetected?

"Let me see that." Lily pushed in between Cory and Sarah and put her finger on the image. "That is so against fire code having it lit."

"I don't think that's your biggest worry right now," Cory said with an eye roll.

"We have to see this man Harrington right now." Lily threw up her hands and made tight, hard fists. "If you are right, I want to nail him. Ask him why he would stab Luke and why, of all places, inside my store."

Fury vibrated off Lily like a live wire. Her cheeks were flushed a deep crimson, her eyes blazing with a storm of hurt and betrayal. She snatched a heavy wool coat from the rack by the door, her movements jerky and tense.

"I can't just sit here," she spat, shoving her arms into the coat. "If Travis killed Luke, then I need to confront him, make him understand what he's done, make him confess so I can have my life back!"

Sarah and Matthew exchanged a quick glance. Lily's normally bright eyes were clouded with a raw grief that threatened to consume her. The urge to lash out, to seek immediate vengeance, was understandable but also incredibly dangerous.

"Lily, wait!" Sarah reached out, her voice firm but gentle. "Just storming over there, flinging around accusations, won't solve anything. On the contrary, he will be warned. We need a plan."

Lily whirled around, her coat flaring dramatically. "What plan? He's a murderer! He deserves to rot in jail!"

Matthew stepped forward, his hand resting placatingly on her shoulder. "I know, Lily," he said quietly. "I understand your anger. But trust me on this one, a well-thought-out approach will be far more effective."

Sarah took over, trying to put as much calm and reason as possible into her voice. "Think about it, Lily. There has to be a reason Travis did this. Maybe they had some kind of history, a past connection. Were they ever friends? Enemies, even?"

Lily faltered, her fiery defiance momentarily flickering. She chewed on her lip, brows furrowed in concentration.

"I... I don't know. Luke never talked much about his past. You were there..."

"Exactly!" Sarah seized on the opening. "There could be a hidden motive, something deeper at play. If we can figure that out, we can use it to build a case against him. Something we can show to Officer Harding, something she won't be able to dismiss. Going in there without a plan, fueled by anger, isn't going to make him confess. He'll shut down, and you're the one who looks guilty... again."

Lily slumped back against the coat rack, the fight seeming to drain out of her. She looked at Sarah and Matthew, a flicker of hope sparking in her eyes. "So, what do we do?"

Matthew's eyes crinkled at the corners and glinted with quiet confidence. "We start by digging. We talk to people who knew Travis and see if anyone can shed light on his past. Maybe there's a connection between him and Luke, some kind of history that explains this tragedy."

Sarah nodded in agreement. "And then, once we have some concrete information, some leads, we go to the police. Armed with some real evidence they can't ignore, we can help them bring Travis to justice."

Lily took a deep breath, trying to steady her trembling hands. Her mind could see the logic, offering a path forward where blind rage couldn't, but her heart was still furious.

"Alright," she finally conceded, her voice hoarse. "Let's do this."

The anger didn't vanish entirely, but a steely resolve took its place.

The tension that had crackled in the air like static electricity finally dissipated with Lily's retreat upstairs. Sarah sank back onto the worn armchair, letting out a long sigh. The weight of the situation, the weight of Lily's grief, pressed down on her. A comforting paw patted her leg gently, and Sarah looked down to see Pixie nuzzling her hand.

"Another mystery on our hands, isn't it, girl?" Sarah murmured, scratching Pixie behind the ears.

Matthew joined her on the worn rug in front of the fireplace, the dying embers casting dancing shadows across his face. He held up the crumpled list from Luke's apartment.

"So, I took a closer look at Luke's list," he began, his voice low. "Turns out, the Jewel of Agra is probably not relevant to our case."

Sarah looked up, her curiosity piqued.

"What do you mean?"

"Well," Matthew continued, "according to a quick online search, the Jewel of Agra Luke referenced was actually located in Atlanta. Apparently, it was quite the hot spot back in the day, but it closed down about six years ago."

Surprise flickered across Sarah's face.

"Six years ago?" she echoed. "Another mystery. Why would Luke save the name of a restaurant that's been closed for so long?"

Pixie yipped once, her head tilted inquisitively.

The question hung heavy in the air. A closed restaurant, a cryptic clue, and a connection to Lily—the pieces still didn't quite fit, and every time they found another one, Sarah hoped the picture would become clearer.

"Maybe," she mused, her brow furrowed, "the restaurant itself isn't the point. Maybe it's something else entirely. A name, a location, some kind of inside joke between Luke and..."

Her voice trailed off. Between Luke and who? Was Travis somehow involved? And if so, how? The more Sarah pondered the mystery, the murkier it became.

Chapter Twenty-Two

A sliver of winter sunlight peeked through the lace curtains, casting a dusting of gold across the living room floor. Lily emerged from her room, her eyes still red-rimmed from the previous night's tears, but her chin held high. Defeat wasn't an option. Her bookstore needed her, and she wouldn't let the weight of suspicion keep her from her beloved haven of stories.

Stepping out into the crisp morning air, she straightened her scarf, hooked her arm through Emma's and closed the door behind her with a resolute click. Her customers awaited.

Meanwhile, a covert operation was underway. Armed with a hefty wad of cash and a mischievous glint in his eyes, Matthew whisked Cory away on a shopping mission to the spice merchant at the Christmas market.

∞

Sarah, left to her own devices, had decided a brisk walk through the charming streets of Rosewood Hollow was just what she needed to clear her head.

The historic district buzzed with holiday cheer. Strings of twinkling lights adorned the storefronts, and the air carried the sweet aroma of roasted chestnuts and spiced cider. Sarah wandered down a cobblestone lane, her boots crunching rhythmically on the frosted ground. Ahead of her, a familiar figure emerged from a bakery, a gingerbread latte clutched in her hand.

"Detective Harding!" Sarah called out, a flicker of surprise followed by a surge of determination. Here was her chance, a chance to share the peculiar connection she'd discovered. Penny, looking a little more relaxed today, though still every bit the capable detective in her tailored coat and sharp bob, only offered a curt nod.

"Ms. Anderson. Fancy meeting you here." Her tone held a hint of suspicion, a constant reminder of the cloud hanging over Lily.

"Lily is running her store," Sarah began, plunging right in. "Listen. There's something I need to tell you about the crime scene..." She explained about the scent of an exotic spice Pixie had smelled, a detail she'd initially dismissed as unimportant. Then, she delved deeper, revealing her discovery—the identical aroma Pixie had discovered at the Jewel of Agra restaurant.

Penny listened with a polite but skeptical expression. "Interesting theory, Ms. Anderson," she said finally, her voice laced with a cool indifference. "Perhaps you should try some writing. But it's a bit of a stretch, wouldn't you say? A restaurant using spices, a fireplace in a gallery and a bookstore. Those are hardly leads that point away from Ms. Morrison. When she was dating the victim and had loaned him a significant amount of money."

Sarah bristled. This dismissive attitude was infuriating. Just as she opened her mouth to counter, a tiny head popped out of the canvas tote bag slung over her shoulder. Pixie let out a sharp bark, her dark eyes fixated on the detective.

Penny jumped, startled by the unexpected canine intervention. A flicker of surprise, a momentary crack in the detective's composed facade, crossed her face and Sarah seized the opportunity.

"Pixie seems to think you should listen," she said, a hint of a challenge in her voice.

"This is on Claremont PD's desk now; I'm only going Christmas shopping."

The detective's skepticism remained, but a seed of doubt had been planted. Sarah knew she had to nurture that seed, to make it grow into something that could help Lily.

She watched Penny Harding walk away and patted Pixie in her carry bag.

She doesn't believe us, does she?

No, Pix, she does not, at least, not yet.

I know what I smelled, Simon saw the imprint of a man walking away, Amelia pointed us in the direction of the restaurant...

As if to agree with Pixie, the lit sign above the Rosewood Hollow Police station flickered briefly. Simon and Amelia. Sarah hefted the carry bag a little closer.

Matthew is going to hate me for this... Pixie, I am thinking of going to see that man, Harrington.'

Matthew will hate it because he worries about you. But you and I both know you have powers to rival those of a chef with a rare spice any day.

So you keep saying.

A brief encouraging whine sounded from inside the carrier, and Pixie settled down once again. Sarah adjusted the bag on her shoulder.

You know, you could just walk, Pixie.

No, I couldn't. There's snow on the ground.

A seed of determination grew inside Sarah, getting bigger as she strolled down the street. The dismissive attitude from Detective Harding had only fueled her resolve. The Jewel of Agra held a key, a connection she couldn't ignore, and it was just down the road. A brisk ten-minute walk through beautiful pre-Christmas Rosewood Hollow.

They'd told Lily not to storm in there with questions, but Sarah was not going to do that, she was a calm third party with a harmless inquiry.

With a brisk stride, she set off towards the Indian restaurant, its name painted in elegant script above the darkened doorway. Pushing open the heavy oak door, Sarah was greeted by a wave of cool air and the faint echo of the revelry of busy nights. The place looked far less grandiose and impressive in the bright light of spotlights and daylight streaming through the tall windows. Tables sat empty stripped of all but the base linens and the vast space felt empty and unwelcoming. She should have known the restaurant would be closed until early evening, she thought, should have checked before she made the trip out here.

But just as she considered turning back, a figure emerged from the direction of the back, and behind a towering potted palm. Tall and broad-shouldered, the man exuded a quiet confidence that instantly drew her attention. His dark hair was flecked with grey at the temples, and his eyes, a deep brown, held a hint of weariness. A faint scent of cumin and coriander lingered in the air around him, a whisper of the restaurant's menu. It had to be him.

"Mr. Harrington?" Sarah approached, her voice laced with hopeful inquiry.

The man stopped, a flicker of surprise crossing his features, momentarily breaking the mask of stoicism he seemed to wear.

"Yes," he confirmed, his voice deep and rumbling, a stark contrast to the hushed emptiness of the restaurant. "Travis Harrington at your service. The restaurant is still closed, I'm afraid. We don't open until dinner time. Can I help you in any way?"

Relief washed over Sarah. Finding him here by chance, not ten steps into this empty restaurant, felt like a stroke of good luck.

"I hope so," she replied, stepping forward and extending her hand. "My name is Sarah Anderson. I'm... a friend of Lily Morrison's."

Travis's brow furrowed slightly as he took her hand in a firm, calloused grip.

"Lily Morrison?" His expression remained unreadable, betraying nothing of his emotions. A tense silence stretched between them, punctuated only by the faint creak of the settling building. "A patron who recommended my restaurant perhaps," he finally asked with a curious tilt of his head.

Sarah, determined not to fall for the charming restauranteur's facade, took a deep breath and plunged into the reason for her visit.

"Lily Morrison, the owner of the Rosewood Hollow Bookstore," Sarah clarified. "Her very good friend Luke Devin was murdered there a few days ago. I thought you might have known him."

The utility lights above the food service station between the kitchen and the dining room cast a bright, hard light on Travis's face that found every crease and every reaction to her question.

Travis's expression flickered ever so slightly, a shadow of surprise momentarily replacing his composed demeanor.

"Luke Devin?" he echoed, his voice a low rumble. "Can't say I've heard the name."

"Are you sure? I was certain he mentioned your name at one point."

Not a muscle moved in Travis face, but his hand... his hand clenched tightly all of a sudden.

"Nope. Must have me mixed up with someone," he said and smiled, but the smile never reached his eyes. The lie sat heavy in the air, at the same time his friendly, accommodating demeanor suddenly shifted, and his eyes became shuttered, not betraying a thought. His stance was suddenly straighter, hands flexed at his side, as if ready to defend himself.

A tiny movement suddenly bulged the tote bag hanging on Sarah's shoulder. Pixie, in her comfortable carrier, shifted, letting out a faint yip muffled by the fabric. Travis's gaze darted towards the bag, a flicker of something akin to unease crossing his features.

"Is something wrong with your purse?" he asked, his voice laced with a hint of forced nonchalance.

Sarah's hand instinctively moved to rest protectively over the bag, her eyes narrowing as she scrutinized Travis. The smirk that played on his lips now felt more like a sneer, a mask barely concealing the disquiet she sensed beneath the surface.

"No," she replied curtly, trying to hide the suspicion in her voice. "Pixie just likes to make herself heard sometimes."

Travis held her gaze for a beat longer than necessary, the smirk morphing into a shrug of indifference.

"Dogs in my restaurant," he said, his voice regaining its previous air of nonchalance. "Not something the health department likes to see. Anyway, if you're here to talk about your friend Lily, I'm afraid I don't have much to offer. I do know of her bookstore, of course, everyone in Rosewood Hollow does. But I have to admit, I'm not much of a reader. And now I think it is time..." He nodded at the carrier with Pixie.

Sarah wasn't convinced. His denial rang hollow, the fleeting emotions that flitted across his face betraying his words. There was a connection here, a link between Travis and Luke that he was desperately trying to sever. And Sarah was determined to unravel it.

Frustration gnawed at her. Travis's practiced lies and the guarded look in his eyes offered no answers. She rose to her feet, her interview clearly over.

"Thank you for your time, Mr. Harrington," she said, her voice clipped. Just as she turned to leave, a strange sensation washed over her.

An unexpected energy, almost a jolt, suddenly crackled between her and Travis. The air itself seemed to shimmer, holding them both captive within a ribbon of shared energy for a fleeting moment.

In that split second, a torrent of thoughts flooded Sarah's mind, not her own. Panic, almost—*Walk away, walk away woman, you will not ruin what I have here. Leave now or you will pay for this. I will not let you.* The thoughts, raw and unfiltered, belonged to Travis.

Sarah stumbled back, a gasp escaping her lips. Her gaze darted around the food prep station. Her eyes landed on the polished counter behind Travis. A set of gleaming chef's knives rested there, each one sharp and menacing. A flicker of movement caught her eye: Travis's head snapping towards the knives, his pupils dilating for just a heartbeat before he forced them shut again. *I will not let you.* Then the connection snapped as abruptly as it began, leaving Sarah reeling.

The casual smirk had vanished from Travis's face, replaced by a mask of forced composure. He cleared his throat, the sound unnaturally loud in the sudden silence.

"Is something wrong, Ms. Anderson? You went pale there for second." But the question lacked conviction, his gaze flitting nervously between Sarah and the knife rack.

Sarah's mind raced. The connection, the fury and anger in Travis's thoughts, the knife. It all pointed to a secret he desperately wanted to keep buried. The raw fear in Travis's thoughts hinted at something more sinister than a simple lie. She needed to tread carefully and without raising his suspicions, to investigate further, but to do so she had to leave, at least for now.

With a deep breath, Sarah forced a neutral smile onto her face.

"Just felt a sudden... draft," she lied, gesturing vaguely towards the curtained entrance. "Perhaps another time, Mr. Harrington."

As she turned to leave, she couldn't help but steal a final glance at the knife rack, at Travis, and at the unspoken truth hanging heavy in the air.

Sarah stumbled out of the Jewel of Agra, the brisk winter air a welcome shock after the charged encounter with Travis. She leaned against the cool brick wall, gasping for breath and trying to make sense of what had just happened. The fleeting connection, the intrusion into Travis's thoughts: it was a revelation that defied logic, a superpower she never knew she possessed.

Suddenly, a tiny voice echoed in her mind, clear as day.

I heard him too, it said. Sarah froze, her heart hammering against her ribs. Pixie.

How did I hear him? Sarah whispered, her voice trembling slightly.

You can hear me, silly, Pixie replied, a hint of amusement dancing in her words. *When you need to, you can hear anyone.*

Sarah's mind reeled. Another power she didn't know she had, it was all too much. She clutched her purse tighter. If this new ability was real—and controllable—then it could be a powerful tool in her quest to help Lily.

Adrenaline surged through her as she hailed a cab and instructed the driver to take her downtown, to the heart of bustling Rosewood Hollow. She needed the safety of crowds, the comforting noise of chatter and traffic. She found solace nestled in a cozy corner booth of a brightly lit coffee shop, the aroma of freshly brewed coffee and cinnamon rolls filling the air. The rhythmic hum of conversation and the clatter of cups provided a soothing background symphony, masking the frantic beat of her own heart.

As she sipped her steaming latte, Sarah tried to organize the whirlwind of thoughts and emotions swirling within her. The unexpected connection with Travis, his fear, the glimpse into his mind—it all pointed to a darkness he desperately wanted to conceal. But what was it? And how did it tie into Luke's murder and Lily's predicament?

A shiver ran down her spine. This newfound ability, this telepathic link... it felt both exhilarating and terrifying. Where did it come from, why was it given to her? How did she even control it? She could use this, she suddenly thought, use it to help Lily.

Perhaps it would get her answers. Answers about the cryptic clue of the closed restaurant, about the shared fireplace between the bookstore and the restaurant, and now, most importantly, about the fear that lurked behind Travis Harrington's carefully constructed facade.

Outside, the frosted window displayed a scene straight out of a Christmas postcard. Twinkling lights adorned the snow-dusted trees, families hurried by bundled in scarves and hats, their faces lit with infectious holiday cheer. Yet, the idyllic image offered no comfort.

Her gaze drifted across the bustling crowd, searching for a familiar face. A jolt of surprise shot through her as she spotted Matthew and

Cory walking down the opposite street. Cory, bundled in a bright blue winter coat, bounced excitedly from one store window to another, his laughter carried away by the winter wind. Matthew walked beside him, a canvas tote overflowing with shopping bags, a weary smile etched on his face. They looked so happy, blissfully unaware of the strange turn Sarah's life had taken.

How could she possibly tell Matthew that she could now hear the desperate thoughts of a prime suspect? The very notion seemed out-landish. As Matthew and Cory disappeared around a corner, Sarah sighed, the weight of her secret pressing down on her.

Hailing a cab, she made the familiar journey home. The warmth of the house enveloped her as she stepped inside, a stark contrast to the crisp winter air. In the den, the crackling fire cast flickering shadows across the room. A steaming mug of chamomile tea found its way into her hands, its soothing warmth radiating upwards. Her gaze drifted towards the twinkling Christmas tree, its ornaments casting an ethereal glow on the room. Yet, the festive atmosphere failed to lift the heavy weight that settled on her chest.

Uncertainty gnawed at her. How did she navigate this new reality? Would this newfound power help or hinder her investigation? One question, however, echoed loudest in the quiet of the room – how, oh how, did she tell Matthew about all of this?

Sarah clutched the ceramic mug, it's comforting warmth a stark contrast to the inferno of anger raging within her. Travis Harrington's dismissal, his carefully constructed facade, all fueled a fiery conviction. He was guilty. Every fiber of her being screamed it. The fear in his mind, the connection, it was all a confession in disguise. Frustration morphed into righteous fury, a heat that burned through her veins. She slammed the mug onto the coffee table, the clatter echoing sharply in the quiet den.

"He thinks he can just lie to me," she murmured. "He thinks he can get away with murder!"

Pixie, who had been curled up at her feet, suddenly lifted her head, her dark eyes filled with concern. A tiny voice echoed in Sarah's mind, soft yet firm.

Tone it down, Sarah. When you get angry, unexpected things can happen.

Sarah scoffed. "Unexpected things? Right now, I couldn't care less, Pixie. I want something real. I want to prove Travis Harrington is guilty—for what he did to Luke, and to Lily—and for his self-righteous arrogance!" The words tumbled out, fueled by a potent mix of anger and determination.

Pixie whined softly, the sound a gentle reprimand.

But anger clouds judgment, Sarah. It won't help you find the truth.

There was a hint of wisdom in the tiny voice, a calmness that contrasted sharply with the storm raging within Sarah.

A wave of shame washed over her. Pixie was right. Blind anger wouldn't unmask Travis, wouldn't clear Lily's name. Had she not told Lily just that, last night?

She needed a plan, a clear strategy. Taking a deep breath, Sarah forced her anger down, pushing it to a simmer instead of a boil. The heat retreated, replaced by a steely resolve.

"You're right, Pixie," she said, her voice quieter now but no less determined. "Anger won't help. But maybe... maybe this new ability, this connection, maybe that can help me find the truth. We'll use everything we have—connections, clues, and maybe even a little bit of magic—to uncover what really happened."

As she spoke, a sense of purpose replaced the anger with a focused determination. Travis Harrington might have dismissed her, but Sarah wouldn't be silenced.

There on the couch, looking harmless as could be, was the little tablet Cory used every time she asked him to research something. She reached for the tablet, the cool, unfamiliar surface sending a shiver down her spine. The vibrant, festive living room around her stood in stark contrast to the lit screen in her hand.

Rows of puzzling icons—a chaotic array of squares and circles in every color imaginable—stared back at her, mocking her lack of technological prowess. She was slightly more at home on her laptop, or her phone, but this was where Cory found all of his information.

Menus unfolded like digital origami, each page revealing more indecipherable symbols and cryptic language. This wasn't browsing recipes on her trusty laptop; this was navigating a virtual jungle filled with unfamiliar predators.

Just as frustration threatened to boil over again, a voice, laced with amusement, sliced through the tension.

"Can I help you with something, Mom?"

Sarah spun around, startled. Cory's presence, at once comforting and unsettling, filled the room. He held her gaze for a moment, a playful glint in his eyes, clearly sensing her struggle. Here was the boy who could effortlessly navigate the world of digital research, a world she'd barely dipped a toe into.

"Oh, hey honey," she stammered, the tablet feeling heavy and awkward in her grip. "Just... this thing," she gestured vaguely at the screen. "Your set-up's a bit more complicated than I expected."

A slow grin, wide and knowing, stretched across Cory's face.

"By the time I explain it all to you, we'll both be old and grey, Mom," he said, his voice laced with amusement. "Matthew set it up for me, so it's nothing like your kitchen computer. What exactly are we hunting for today?"

Sarah fidgeted on the couch, torn with the weight of her decision. Cory was her tech-savvy son, while she felt like a novice in the digital world. Yet, something in Travis's eyes and thoughts made her immediately feel the need to protect her son.

"Well," she began, her voice barely above a whisper, "I, uh... I was just curious what the internet had to tell us about Travis Harrington."

Cory's brow furrowed in a momentary lapse of his playful demeanor, but the glint in his eyes remained. "Easy, I set up a search alert earlier," he declared, snatching the tablet from her with the practiced ease of a seasoned navigator. His fingers flew across the screen, a blur of taps and swipes that seemed like an intricate code only he could decipher.

Behind them, a new voice sliced through the tense air, laced with a sharp edge of suspicion that sent shivers down Sarah's spine.

"And why do you suddenly have more questions about Travis?"

Matthew stood framed in the doorway, his arms crossed and a scowl etched into his forehead like a permanent fixture. This wasn't part of the plan. She hadn't anticipated Matthew returning home so early, let alone catching her red-handed with Travis's name on her lips, and Cory readily diving into an online investigation...

Sarah, who always insisted on brutal honesty with her kids, especially when it came to things they'd inevitably uncover anyway, took a deep breath and blurted it out.

"I went to see Travis Harrington."

The playful banter between Cory and the tablet screeched to a halt. Cory's head snapped up, surprise momentarily eclipsing his usual amusement. Matthew, however, erupted. His scowl morphed into a thundercloud, and his voice boomed with a fury that sent shivers down Sarah's spine.

"After we agreed it was a bad idea for Lilly?" he roared. "You went to see that... that creep? Alone?"

His words lashed at her like icy wind. Regret burned in her cheeks, but it was quickly eclipsed by a prickle of defiance.

"Yes, I did," she countered, her voice surprisingly steady. "Penny Harding wouldn't believe my story, and I needed to know the truth."

Matthew threw his hands up in exasperation.

"The truth? What truth, Sarah? That this man might have killed Luke Devin? Might. You could have gotten yourself hurt! Did you even think about Cory and Emma? About me?"

His concern, laced with anger, was a double-edged sword. It warmed a tiny corner of her heart, but the underlying accusation stung.

"Of course, I thought about you," she retorted, her voice rising in pitch. "That's exactly why I had to do something! Penny thinks I'm imagining things, and if Travis is behind this..." Her voice trailed off, the terrifying possibilities hanging heavy in the air.

Cory, with all of his seventeen years, put down the tablet and raised his hands.

"Whoa, whoa, whoa. Mom, I know you have... abilities and all, but you go see a guy like that? Alone? You know that's a bad idea. Have you listened to any true crime?"

"No," Sarah snapped. "And I don't intend to. Besides, I had Pixie with me."

"Pixie," Matthew said, shaking his head. "Pixie is a five-pound papillon dog, Sarah. And I agree she is special, but that man…" He shook his head and pulled Sarah into a rough embrace. "That man, if we are right in our suspicion, then he followed Luke, surprised him when nobody was around and stabbed him. I remember finding the body. I don't ever… Don't you understand? I don't ever—"

"I'm sorry."

Sarah looked down at her shoes and remembered the glinting knife block in the kitchen prep area, Travis's angry thoughts and the menacing glint in his eyes.

"It may not have been the best thing to do."

"Yeah, it probably wasn't."

The tension in the room hung thick enough to slice with a knife. Sarah, cheeks flushed with defiance, stood her ground against Matthew's simmering anger. Just then, the front door slammed, momentarily breaking the charged atmosphere.

Lily, a bright smile plastered across her face, stepped into the den followed by a bright eyed red cheeked Emma. The air crackled with unspoken questions, but Lily remained blissfully oblivious.

"Alright, world, what did I miss?" she chirped, her voice bubbling with unexpected cheer. "I was bracing myself for a public flogging, but believe it or not, half my customers practically ran up to me and squeezed my hand. Apparently, the rumor mill is more concerned with the fact that the Rosewood PD is currently closed." Lily winked. "Incompetence somebody told me," she whispered.

Her words landed with a thud, shattering the tense silence. Sarah and Matthew exchanged a surprised glance.

"That's nice," Matthew managed, never taking his eyes off Sarah.

"Nice? Merry Christmas to you too, Dr. Matthew Turner. What's going on in here?"

She flung off her bright fuchsia coat and sat on a hassock across from Sarah."

Sarah gently shook her head.

"Sarah felt it was a good idea to go see Travis Harrington," Matthew explained, staring out the front window as if he expected an invasion. "And damn the consequences."

"I had Pixie."

"Pixie... Yes, how could I forget."

Lily took her hand. "Thank you, Sarah. Really. For believing in me, for being there for me. This will come out, I am confident. But don't put yourself in danger."

"You didn't..." hear his thoughts, Sarah wanted to say, but bit off the end of the sentence.

Matthew came back and stood in front of the women.

"Travis Harrington," he began.

"Does not exist," Cory finished, waving his tablet, and the room fell silent once again. "Buckle up because this is where it gets weird."

Chapter Twenty-Three

All eyes turned to Cory now. Sarah's apprehension mirrored in Matthew's furrowed brow. Lily, ever the optimist, simply tilted her head, a playful glint in her eyes.

"See, Mom?" Cory continued, gesturing excitedly at the tablet in his hands. "Thanks to the wonders of the internet, I just spent the last five minutes digging into this Travis character. And guess what?" He paused for dramatic effect, a mischievous grin spreading across his face. "He. Doesn't. Exist."

A collective gasp filled the room. Sarah felt a jolt course through her, a mix of disbelief along with a glimmer of hope.

"Okay. But what do you mean by that? I saw him," she stammered, her voice barely a whisper.

Cory, basking in the spotlight, pointed to the tablet screen.

"According to every background check, social media platform, and public record database I could access," he explained, tapping the screen with each point, "Travis Harrington is a ghost. No birth certificate, no driver's license, no social security number. Until five years ago, when like magic, he materialized out of thin air and opened a restaurant here in Rosewood Hollow."

Matthew, initially skeptical, leaned closer to examine the screen. Sarah watched his face morph from anger to confusion. Lily's smile faltered, replaced by a frown of genuine concern.

"But... I certainly saw someone," Sarah insisted, her voice gaining strength despite the tremor in her hands. "At the restaurant, in the kitchen. He said he didn't know Lily, but he'd been to the bookstore."

Matthew looked from one to the other and finally pulled Cory's tablet to himself. With a finger hovering above the screen, he re-read everything Cory had just told them, shook his head, and read it again.

"You know how that Agra place..."

"Jewel of Agra," Sarah replied mechanically.

"Whatever. How it says 'Award-Winning Chef Travis Harrington' in the ads? It also looks like no chef by that name has ever won any award."

"But..."

"I guess it could have been something small, but there's still nothing about it here," Cory said and nodded. "But their website mentions this award all over the place. Without a single link to a culinary institute, or a winner's listing, or a press release, or anything else. I would expect them to flaunt the award for all its worth. Don't you think that's odd?"

"So he's lying."

"He's more than lying, Mom. Something is really, really hinky with that guy."

Just then, with a sparkle and a cold draft that sent shivers down their spines, Amelia materialized in the corner by the fireplace.

Her presence, despite her spectral form, flowed into existence like a painting brought to life. Her gown, a shimmering emerald green that seemed to capture the fading light of day, cascaded around her ankles in layers of lace. Her wispy hair, the color of spun moonlight, was pulled back in a loose bun adorned with a cameo brooch. Her eyes, the only substantial part of her form, were black as coals, sparkling with a mixture of amusement and concern. Emma automatically rose to approach the ghost and reached out for her. Uncharacteristically, Amelia completely ignored her.

"Travis is a scoundrel," she declared, her voice a melodic whisper that echoed through the room. "And you know this better than anyone, don't you, Sarah?"

All eyes swiveled towards Sarah now. Her face, pale in the fire's light, held a mixture of shock and a flicker of something Amelia recognized all too well—a buried truth.

The weight of Amelia's words hung heavy in the air. Sarah seemed to shrink under the collective gaze.

"It's true," she confessed her voice barely a whisper. "I... I do know more about Travis than I let on."

A flicker of understanding crossed Amelia's spectral face. Matthew and Lily watched in stunned silence as Sarah continued, her voice gaining strength with each word.

"When I met him at the restaurant, it was like... I could hear his thoughts. It was a jumble of words, but there was one thing clear as day."

She paused, pressing her lips together for a long moment. Cory leaned forward, his eyes wide with fascination and a hint of fear. Sarah met their gazes, her own filled with a newfound resolve.

"He wanted me to leave," she revealed, her voice dropping to a low tremor. "He was feeling guilty and, at the same time, arrogant because he had gotten away with something, and I–I was not going to destroy everything he had built for himself."

The room erupted in a cacophony of sounds. Matthew let out a frustrated groan. Cory choked on a surprised gasp. Lily's eyes widened in disbelief. Even Amelia seemed momentarily taken aback. Only Emma sat with a serene smile, looking at her mother.

"But... that's crazy!" Cory exclaimed. "How can you hear people's thoughts? Can you hear mine?"

Sarah, her shoulders squared, took a defiant stance.

"I don't know how," she admitted, "but I did. With his words, he denied even knowing Lily and Luke, but his thoughts gave him away."

Sarah's bombshell about hearing the man's thoughts hung heavy in the air. Even Cory, usually a beacon of calm, seemed momentarily overwhelmed.

Just then, Amelia's voice, a melodic whisper that echoed through the room, cut through the tension. "As for the man you encountered, Sarah," she began, her form shimmering with a soft, luminous sparkle. "You are quite correct; his name is not Travis Harrington."

This new revelation sparked another collective gasp. Sarah's confession about hearing thoughts was shocking, but this added another layer of unsettling mystery.

"Then what is it?" Lily blurted, her voice trembling slightly.

Amelia glided closer to Sarah, a hint of melancholy flickering in her violet eyes.

"As ghosts," she explained, her ethereal voice a mere murmur now. "We tend to frequent graveyards. It's a place of solace, a connection to our earthly lives. Years ago, while wandering the cemetery in Willow Creek, the next town over, I met a young boy. His name was Travis Harrington, a bright spark extinguished far too soon in a tragic carriage accident."

A hush fell over the room. The image of a playful child gone too soon painted a heartbreaking picture.

"So, the man who is a chef at the Jewel of Agra," Emma stammered, piecing things together, "is using the name of a dead boy?"

Amelia nodded slowly, a faint wisp of mist curling from her transparent form. "Indeed. But why he has chosen that particular path remains a mystery."

The revelation sank in: a man with a stolen identity and a chilling motive. The air crackled with newfound tension, and the cozy den suddenly felt oppressive under the weight of the truth.

Chapter Twenty-Four

Pre-dawn light filtered through the gaps in the curtains, casting long shadows across Sarah's rumpled bedsheets. Sleep had been a fleeting visitor, chased away by the whirlwind of revelations from the previous day. The man who didn't exist, his angry thoughts—the whole scenario playing on a loop in her mind.

Just as she was about to rise and face the day, a soft clatter from downstairs drew her attention.

Tiptoeing down the wide wooden stairs, she found Lily perched at the kitchen counter, a steaming mug clutched in her hands. Gone was her brief glow of hope; worry etched lines onto her forehead again as she stared intently into the swirling vortex of her teacup.

"Couldn't sleep either, huh?" Sarah asked softly, pulling up a chair across from her friend.

Lily lifted her head, a weary sigh escaping her lips.

"No," she admitted, her voice barely a whisper. "This whole Travis Harrington thing... I can't wrap my mind around it. A man who just appeared one day and opened a restaurant. No history, no connections. And yet, we're pretty sure he killed Luke."

Sarah nodded, a knot of unease tightening in her gut. On top of everything else, there was Amelia's unsettling story about the real Travis Harrington, a child lost to a tragic accident years ago.

As if summoned by the thought, the sound of footsteps on the stairs announced Matthew. He shuffled into the kitchen, dressed in wrinkled joggers, his eyes heavy with exhaustion. He selected one of his teas and ran his fingers through his tangled hair, waiting for the water to boil.

The three sat in tense silence for a moment, each lost in their own labyrinth of thoughts. Finally, Matthew spoke, his voice laced with a newfound urgency.

"What if..." he began, his gaze flickering between Sarah and Lily, "what if this imposter isn't just playing a game of charades with a fake name? What if he's gone a step further?"

Sarah and Lily exchanged a worried glance. Matthew briefly worried his lower lip, his voice dropping to a low, almost conspiratorial murmur.

"Identity theft isn't just about maxing out credit cards or draining bank accounts anymore," he explained. "It can be much more intricate. In some cases, criminals steal the identities of deceased people, especially those who died young, with little to no public record."

He leaned closer, his next words sending a shiver down Sarah's spine. "Think about it," he said. "No birth certificate, no social security number for this fake Travis. But there is a child, a real Travis Harrington, who died decades ago, according to Amelia."

The weight of Matthew's words hung heavy in the air. Sarah and Lily exchanged a worried glance, a flicker of dawning comprehension reflected in their eyes. Sarah, her voice barely a whisper, broke the tense silence.

"So, you're saying this fake Travis, he just basically... stolen a dead person's identity?"

Matthew nodded grimly, swirling the tea in his mug thoughtfully. "It's certainly a possibility. The dark web," he began, his voice taking on an investigative tone. "It's a haven for all sorts of nefarious activities, including identity theft. Criminals can purchase fake social security numbers, passports, even birth certificates for a price."

Lily shuddered, instinctively reaching for Sarah's hand across the table. "But why steal the identity of a dead person?" she asked, her voice trembling slightly.

"That's the clever part," Matthew explained. "Imagine a child who died young, like Amelia mentioned. There wouldn't be a lot of public records on them, no existing credit history, and no real digital footprint. It would be much easier for someone to assume that identity and build a new life from scratch."

He leaned forward, his gaze flickering between them. "Think about it. This fake Travis couldn't pick some random, living person's identity. The risk of getting caught would be too high. But a deceased child? Their records are likely archived, gathering dust somewhere. It could be the perfect way for someone with the right resources to disappear without a trace."

A cold dread settled over the room. The ghost who wasn't a ghost was now a man with a stolen identity, and his motive for targeting Luke remained a chilling mystery. The stolen name and the ability to vanish without a trace all pointed towards a calculated plan, a game with unknown objectives played by a man with a dark secret buried in his past.

Lily's eyes widened in horror as the pieces of the puzzle began to click into place. The mystery of the man Sarah encountered had morphed into something far more sinister—a game of stolen lives and hidden motives played by a man who had probably killed before.

Lily rubbed her hands together. A shudder wracked her slender frame, and her bright eyes dimmed with a flicker of fear.

"This is all just... too much," she mumbled, pushing herself out of the chair. "I think I'll head over to the bookstore and get things prepped for the opening."

With a quick peck on Sarah's cheek and a mumbled goodbye to Matthew, Lily practically floated out of the kitchen, her usual chipper demeanor replaced by a quiet worry and caution. His brow furrowed in thought, Matthew finished his tea in one long gulp.

"I'm going to hit the internet and see what else I can dig up on identity theft and fake documents," he announced, his voice resolute. "The more we know, the better equipped we are to handle this, and I don't want Cory to be tempted to look it up."

He patted Sarah's shoulder reassuringly before climbing the stairs, his steps heavy with the weight of the situation. Sarah was left alone at the kitchen table; the silence punctuated only by the rhythmic tick of the grandfather clock in the hallway. She reached down and absent-mindedly stroked Pixie's soft fur, offering a small measure of comfort.

"Scared, girl?" Sarah murmured, her voice barely a whisper. Pixie tilted her head, her large, expressive eyes reflecting the worry etched on Sarah's face. Sarah sighed, burying her face in the dog's silky fur.

"Well, I am, Pixie," she confessed, her voice thick with emotion. "There's a coldness in that man's eyes, a darkness I can't quite place. And the fact that he's using a dead child's name... it feels so wrong, so twisted."

Be careful, Pixie said, licking Sarah's hand gently. Sarah closed her eyes for a moment and connected with Pixie deep down, drawing strength from the unconditional love radiating from her.

A flurry of fat snowflakes descended outside, blanketing the world in a pristine white. Sarah, lost in the comforting rhythm of Pixie's gentle caress, barely registered the shift in weather. It wasn't until the rhythmic scrape of the snow shovel against the porch steps that she looked up, a jolt of surprise running through her. There, silhouetted against the now-grey sky, stood Cory and Emma. Their hair was dusted with snow, and a thin layer clung to their coats; their cheeks were bright red, and a triumphant grin stretched across their young faces.

"Look what Mother Nature decided to grace us with," Cory announced, stepping inside and shaking the snow off his boots. "Just in time for Christmas."

"Since when do you care about snow for Christmas," Emma asked primly. "All you did so far was complain about having to shovel it."

Sarah managed a weak smile, the weight of their conversation still heavy on her chest. As if sensing the tension, Pixie lifted her head and let out a playful bark, tail wagging furiously.

Sarah, caught momentarily in the whirlwind of their usual teenage banter, felt a pang of love and fierce protectiveness. Here they were, in spite of the darkness lurking on the periphery of their lives, bickering over snowball fights and Christmas decorations. A lump formed in her throat at the image of the lovingly decorated den, a testament to their holiday spirit, a stark contrast to the chilling secret she now harbored.

She squeezed them both tightly, the warmth of their bodies a welcome solace.

"Whoa," Cory said, untangling himself. "What's going on with you today?"

"Nothing." Sarah grinned. "Nothing at all. Would you like some tea?" She hadn't missed Cory's glance, wandering to a plate of Christmas cookies she had meant to bring to Lily's bookstore later.

"You might as well," she said with a wink, and moments later, Cory had two of them in his hands and a third one in his mouth.

"You think any more about this Travis character," he asked around a mouthful of cookie. "Like who he could be and how he could…"

"Can you do me a favor and please drop it? Just for the moment," Sarah said, pushing the plate of cookies closer to her son.

"But why? The guy is obviously a creep and up to no good."

"That's part of the reason." Sarah nodded. And I saw in his heart that he wouldn't hesitate to hurt you, she added in her mind and turned away so Cory wouldn't see her face.

"Mom's just worried," Emma supplied helpfully. "About us, about you. Maybe you should leave it be."

Cory folded his arms and gave them a hard stare.

"Have you forgotten? Claremont PD and Penny Harrington all still think Lily is responsible for Luke's death. They don't even want to look at anybody else. It's still up to us to prove otherwise. Jewel of Agra…" He wagged his head, mocking the name. "What a BS name for a restaurant anyway! And to think there's even two of them."

Two of them.

The beautifully iced Santa cookie Sarah had taken from the plate fell from her fingers and crumbled on the ground, where Pixie snatched the crumbs.

"Jewel of Agra," she said softly, staring off into the falling snow outside, without really seeing it.

"Yeah. What about it?" Cory asked.

"You know how there was a Jewel of Agra on that list we found in Luke's apartment," she said. "And Matthew thought it couldn't have anything to do with Luke's death because it was in Atlanta."

"Yeah, so," Cory shrugged. "He has a point."

"What if he doesn't," Emma said and came to stand beside her mother. "What if it has everything to do with it? What if it is the connection?"

Sarah raised her eyes and looked directly at her daughter. Emma nodded softly. As hard as it had been for Sarah to come to terms with her own unique abilities, it had been even more challenging to understand that her daughter and youngest child shared some of the same skills.

"You think…?" she asked Emma, and her daughter nodded again.

"It's a possibility."

"Cory, I know I said to back off, but…"

"On it." Cory had already pulled his tablet to his knees and began typing furiously.

Cory's fingers tapped away, navigating through search results and archived articles about the Jewel of Agra. Sarah hovered anxiously behind him, her heart pounding with anticipation.

"Okay, here we go," Cory announced, excitement lacing his voice. "According to this online article, the Jewel of Agra closed down about six years ago. It was a super popular spot until then, but there's no explanation for why it shut its doors."

Sarah leaned in closer, her breath catching in her throat. "No explanation at all?" she asked, urgency evident in her voice.

Cory shook his head, his eyes scanning the screen. "Nope, just says it closed suddenly from one day to the next. Some patrons were disappointed, but there wasn't any official statement from the owners or anything. Just a sign that said closed."

Sarah chewed on her lip, her mind racing with possibilities.

"So, if there is a connection between the closure of the Jewel of Agra and Luke's death, what is it?" she mused aloud, her voice barely above a whisper.

Cory's answer was to lean over his tablet again and open search portal after search portal.

"Give me a sec," he muttered without looking at his mother.

Sarah nodded, her determination growing stronger with each passing moment.

Cory nodded in agreement, his fingers flying across the keyboard with renewed vigor. The closure of the Jewel of Agra suddenly seemed too coincidental to ignore.

Following a hunch, Sarah leaned over Cory's shoulder as he typed away on his tablet. "Try this," she began, her voice tentative yet hopeful. "Do you think you could find out the chef's name at the Atlanta Jewel of Agra?"

Cory furrowed his brow, curiosity piqued by his mother's request. "Probably," he replied with a casual shrug.

After a few moments of searching, he glanced up at Sarah. "The name that keeps popping up is George Banner," he said, a hint of disappointment in his voice. "But I don't recognize it, and there's not much else about him online."

Sarah's shoulders slumped slightly, a sense of letdown washing over her.

"George Banner," she repeated, the name feeling unfamiliar and insignificant. Even her intuition barely fluttered at the name. Nothing here. "Any other details about him?"

Cory shook his head, his expression reflecting Sarah's disappointment. "Not really," he admitted. "Seems like a pretty standard chef, worked at a few other restaurants before landing at the Jewel of Agra in Atlanta. Nothing out of the ordinary."

Sarah sighed, her hopes of uncovering a significant lead fading. "It was worth a shot," she said, trying to sound optimistic despite her disappointment. Thanks."

Cory nodded, glaring at his tablet as if the little electronic device were at fault for their strikeout.

"No problem, Mom," he said, reaching over to give her a reassuring pat on the shoulder. "You think of anything else, just fire it at me."

Sarah began pacing up and down in their cozy little den. Every time she passed the Christmas tree she touched the little glass ghost that Emma had hung, just for good luck.

Emma sat on the couch, her knees pulled up to her chest, her face screwed up tight in concentration without saying a word.

Help me out here, ghosts, Sarah thought. *You must know something we are missing, don't you?*

Not really. But that was from Pixie.

They can hear and see things on the other side and mess with electronics, but I doubt they are better than Google.

Sarah said nothing, but neither Amelia nor Simon appeared, so perhaps they agreed with Pixie's assessment.

"Sous-chef must have been a riot, though," Cory snorted suddenly. "Found an old Yelp review here, and it says never order Vince's Curry; it is made by sous chef Vincent Carlisle, and it's hotter than... you know..."

Sarah had just turned away from the big front window when a massive crash brought her out of her reverie. She spun around just in time to see Matthew in the doorway to the hall, his hands frozen in the air, his precious teapot smashed to a thousand bits on the ground, and a puddle of tea slowly spreading across the floor.

"Let me see that!" Matthew said, his expression a mix of shock and urgency. He stomped over the shards of the teapot in two giant steps toward Cory, his hand already outstretched for the tablet.

Matthew scanned the screen frantically. Cory could only watch in stunned silence, his gaze shifting between Matthew and his mother. A dawning realization began to creep over Sarah as a massive pit opened in her stomach.

"Vincent Carlisle," she murmured, her voice barely above a whisper, the puzzle pieces falling into place in her mind. "The man mentioned in all of the newspaper clippings we found at Luke's... Vincent, the man who broke out of the very prison where Luke had been serving his sentence."

Chapter Twenty-Five

The reality of the situation hit Sarah so hard that she dropped onto the couch to sit beside Emma and squeezed her daughter's hand.

Vincent Carlisle, the sous chef with a notorious reputation for his fiery curry, was none other than the escaped convict linked to Luke's past and now here in Rosewood Hollow in the persona of Travis Harrington.

Matthew's hands trembled as he scrolled through the information on the tablet, his jaw clenched with determination. "We need to get this information out," he declared, his voice firm with resolve. "Vincent Carlisle escaped prison just after Luke started his sentence."

"Perhaps they knew one another," Sarah continued. "Met in the yard, in the mess hall..."

Cory's head swiveled from his mother to Matthew and back.

"But how did he find Luke again, and why kill him?"

"Luke probably repaired his boiler," Sarah said, her voice barely above a whisper. "Remember, when he fixed Lily's furnace, he told her he'd fixed the same model in a restaurant in the area. If he met Vincent, if he recognized him…"

"Even if he didn't," Matthew said. "Vincent basically is still on the run; he couldn't take the chance that Luke did recognize him and would turn him in, so he decided…"

Matthew swallowed hard and pressed his lips together.

"Oh, Luke knew who he was, all right," Sarah said. "That's what all of the research in his apartment was about. He wanted to turn him in. He wanted to do the right thing."

Their den was deathly quiet for a moment, and then the big grandfather clock in the hall began chiming, pulling them out of their shared silence.

"Dear god, I have to tell Lily," Sarah whispered, patting her pockets for her phone. "This is the proof we need. She is innocent. Lily is free…"

"Wait." Matthew stopped her with a raised hand. "Police first. If Carlisle—or Harrington—gets the slightest inkling that we're onto him, he will be dangerous. The man has already proven once that he will kill to protect his secret."

"So, what does this mean, then?" Emma asked, nervously fidgeting with a piece of ribbon left over from wrapping presents. Her eyes darted over to the corner of the fireplace, hoping for Amelia. "Can we not just call the police and tell them we found their suspect living under a fake name and have them take care of everything?"

"That is exactly what we will do." Sarah declared, already reaching for her phone. "But first, I want to tell Lily. She needs to hear this. Maybe I should just go there. I so want to see her face when we tell her this whole spooky thing is finally over." She looked over at the corner of the fireplace and winked. "Sorry, Amelia."

Just as her finger hovered over Lily's contact, a loud bang rattled the windows, followed by a sustained howl of wind. Sarah almost dropped the phone. Cory, peering out the window through the swirling snow, let out a groan.

"It was just a branch from the big tree out front," he muttered. "But it looks like that snow flurry has decided to become a full-blown blizzard again. Nobody is going to go anywhere for now."

Disappointment clouded Sarah's features. Peering out the window, she confirmed Cory's words. The once picturesque scene outside was now a battleground of swirling snow and howling wind. A massive branch lay broken across their porch, visibility had dropped to near zero, and the once-innocent snowflakes were now transformed into sharp, icy projectiles. A classic New England blizzard, the kind that shut down entire towns and left people stranded in their homes.

Frustration bubbled up inside Sarah.

"This can't be happening now!" she complained, throwing her hands up."

As if on cue, Sarah's phone buzzed in her hand with a cheerful Christmas carol ringtone. The one that made Cory roll his eyes and mutter about old people. It was Lily.

"Sarah, thank goodness you picked up!" Lily's voice crackled faintly through the receiver, strained against the howling wind. "This storm came out of nowhere. The bookstore is deserted, but I'm pretty much stuck until it blows over. I'll hunker down here for the night. Fortunately, I have a cot in the back. How's everything out there?"

Thank goodness, Sarah thought, but the relief was short-lived. She opened her mouth to share the news about Travis Harrington, but before she could speak, a loud crackle filled the line, followed by dead silence. Frustration turned into full-blown anger. She slammed her phone down on the table and ground her teeth.

"Now the line's gone dead!" she snapped, a frantic edge to her voice. The others exchanged worried glances, and Matthew raised a hand, no doubt to say something calming and comforting she did not need just then. The power flickered, casting an unsettling gloom over the normally cozy den, and did little to ease her mood.

Sarah felt trapped. She had this newfound knowledge of the imposter, but her phone, their only way to get anything to Lily, was now rendered useless by the storm's fury. The blizzard raged outside as if to mock her with its fury.

Just as she opened her mouth to vent her continued frustration, the power went right out, plunging into semi-darkness.

"Hang on, everyone," Matthew said calmly, a hint of authority in his voice.

Using his phone as a flashlight, he pulled a drawer open and emerged with four old-fashioned, chunky flashlights.

With practiced efficiency, he checked the thermostat and peered down the basement stairs.

"Furnace seems to be doing just fine," he reported, a reassuring note in his voice. "Should keep us warm for the duration. All we can do is wait it out."

A faint shimmering glow by the fireplace grew into an orb and from there into a figure, announcing the arrival of Amelia, regal and sparkling with energy, as always. A little blizzard apparently could not touch the ghost in any way.

Sarah slowly turned towards the ghost, whose sparkling glow provided a surreal source of light in the darkness of the den.

"Was that you?" she asked with an edge in her voice, "The power cut?"

Amelia glided closer, her spectral form pulsing with a soft, inner light.

"Certainly not, Sarah," she replied, her voice a gentle whisper. "This storm is quite powerful. I only came to check that you were all right."

"Sorry. And thank you—we are." A flicker of relief crossed Sarah's face. However, a gnawing unease lingered in her gut. "I assume you know what we know by now, that Travis Harrington is the man who killed Luke."

Amelia inclined her head a little, and Sarah thought she saw the faintest hint of a smile.

"You could have just told us instead of playing the game with those coupons."

"Alas, I cannot investigate human hearts as well and as thoroughly as you can, dear Sarah," Amelia said softly. "But I did have my suspicions."

"Don't keep them to yourself next time," Sarah snapped, a hint of desperation creeping into her voice. "That man is dangerous."

A knowing smile touched Amelia's spectral face. "Fear not, Sarah," she assured her. "Simon and I will keep an eye on him," she added, a hint of mischief in her voice. "After all, a ghost couple has its advantages, especially during a blizzard."

Sarah managed a faint smile, a small spark of hope flickering within her. Despite the power outage and the howling wind outside, Amelia's presence offered a strange sense of comfort and light, but the unsettling feeling wouldn't completely disappear.

She felt the gentle pressure of Pixie's paws on her knee and bent down to scoop up the tiny Papillon.

"I still can't shake this feeling," she murmured, snuggling Pixie close, breathing in her doggie scent, and stroking the silky fur. "Like something bad is about to happen."

You're fine. Nothing can happen right now, Pixie said. *Not even a mouse is out there if they have any sense.*

But Sarah hugged her even closer.

"Amelia is here, she will protect us," Emma said, stretching out her hand so it almost touched Amelia's. A little shower of sparks erupted in the tiny space between them, and Sarah fought the impulse to pull her daughter back and close to her. Amelia and Emma had their own connection, and instinctively she knew it was not something she should, or could, disturb.

Cory and Emma finally huddled closer, their faces lit by the warm glow of the flashlights and the merrily dancing fire. Cory produced a deck of cards and began to teach his sister how to play poker.

Matthew gently placed a hand on Sarah's shoulder.

"I can see you are worried," he said. "But as long as we can't go anywhere, nobody else in Rosewood can either. I've been through these storms before."

"I know... but Harrington..." Sarah didn't finish the sentence. She looked around at her family, sweet Pixie in her arms, and finally Amelia, peering curiously at the ornaments on the Christmas tree.

As the blizzard raged outside, the den, illuminated by flickering flashlights and Amelia's spectral glow, became a haven of warmth and comfort. Still, Sarah couldn't completely silence the voice whispering a warning in the back of her mind.

∞

Exhaustion finally overcame them. One by one, Cory and Emma succumbed to sleep, lulled by the rhythmic thrum of the wind against the windows and the flickering warmth of the fireplace.

After tucking them in upstairs, Sarah returned to the den, where Matthew sat by the fire, his brow furrowed in thought. Amelia, sensing the weariness that settled upon them, drifted away with a soft wave. The room plunged into deeper darkness, broken only by the dancing flames.

Sarah snuggled into the couch, the worn leather cool against her skin.

"Do you really think everything is fine?" she murmured, her voice barely a whisper.

Matthew shifted in his chair, leaning closer.

"Of course, it will be," he assured her, his voice warm and comforting.

The conversation flowed on in hushed tones, a quiet symphony of worry and determination. Hours ticked by unnoticed as they strategized their next moves, how to contact Lily, how to deal with the looming threat of Travis Harrington. The weight of the situation, mixed with the fatigue brought on by the sleepless night, eventually won over Sarah. Her eyelids fluttered, and her head lolled against the back of the couch.

Chapter Twenty-Six

Agentle nudge woke her. Sarah blinked and saw the morning sun filtering through the storm-battered windows. A warm blanket was wrapped around her, and a crackling fire still danced merrily in the hearth. Pixie slept snuggled in the crook of her arm, and across from her, Matthew dozed peacefully in the oversized armchair, his brow creased with the remnants of worry.

A surge of gratitude and love washed over Sarah. She reached out and gently squeezed his hand, a silent thank you for his unwavering presence.

Matthew's eyes fluttered open, blinking away sleep. A flicker of surprise crossed his face before a warm smile softened his features.

"Morning, sleepyhead," he said, his voice raspy.

"You didn't stay up all night, did you?" Sarah asked, her own voice thick with sleep.

"Couldn't really sleep anyway," he admitted sheepishly. "Someone had to keep watch in case the storm got worse or something... else happened." He winked at her, the worry momentarily replaced by a playful glint in his eyes.

Sarah returned his smile, her heart full.

A sliver of curiosity, mixed with a bit of trepidation, pulled her towards the large bay window at the front of the den. Gently, she pulled back the heavy drapes, a wave of cool air greeting her chilled skin. Mounds of snow, sculpted by the wind into swirling drifts, stretched as far as the eye could see. The fence, usually a clear demarcation line, was now a buried memory, swallowed whole by the relentless white tide.

The street beyond was a mere suggestion, its asphalt surface replaced by a seemingly endless expanse of snow. Even the towering maples that lined the sidewalk, usually resolute sentinels against the changing seasons, were bowed under the weight of the snowfall. Heavy with snow, their branches drooped like weary arms, obscuring any glimpse of the sidewalks beyond. The world outside was a monochromatic canvas, a stark contrast to the warm glow inside her cozy, festive den.

A strange sense of isolation gripped Sarah's heart and made her shiver. The blizzard hadn't just blanketed their yard; it had cut them off from the world, creating a temporary bubble of quiet solitude amidst the howling wind.

Pixie put her little paws on the low windowsill and scanned the landscape outside as if looking for something. Suddenly, one bark, and then another, and her tail began wagging furiously at the sight of a sudden burst of movement outside. A small group of children, bundled in layers of brightly colored snow gear, materialized through the swirling snow. Their laughter, muffled by the wind but bright and infectious, pierced the wintry silence. They raced down the street, their sleds leaving bright red slashes across the pristine white canvas. One little girl, bundled in a pink snowsuit that looked like a marshmallow come to life, struggled valiantly to drag a miniature snow shovel almost twice her size. The sight brought a smile to Sarah's lips. Even with the world seemingly shut down by the blizzard, these children found joy in the simplest things.

Sarah smiled and reached down to caress Pixie.

"You might have to go outside, Pixie," she warned with a grin, but instead of Pixie, she heard a groan from behind her. Cory, his sleep clearly disturbed, stumbled into the room, his hair tousled and his eyes half-closed.

"Ugh," he mumbled, shuffling towards the window for a peek. "Seriously, Mom? Did it have to snow this much?"

He cast a disgruntled glance at the scene outside.

"And, of course, we're the unlucky ones stuck without a snow blower." He slumped onto the couch beside Sarah, a look of resignation etched on his face.

Sarah chuckled, warmth spreading through her chest. Even in the face of potential danger and a massive snowstorm, her son's typical teenage grumbling managed to restore a touch of normalcy to their situation.

"We'll manage," she assured him, squeezing his shoulder gently. "Besides, think of the snowball fights we can have once this settles down."

A ghost of a smile played on Cory's lips. "Yeah, there's that," he conceded. "Don't think I'm going to let you win, though."

I believe I will take care of napping by the fire, Pixie decided and hopped back off the window frame again.

Sarah gently cuffed her son on the arm when a sudden flicker of light and several simultaneous electronic beeps interrupted their moment. The room lurched to life, banishing the shadows and replacing them with the warm glow of the overhead lamp. Sarah felt like the fist clenching her heart finally let go; the power was back. The long night of the blizzard was over, and nothing had happened to her little family.

∞

With a stretch and a yawn, Sarah set about making breakfast. The rhythmic sizzle of bacon in the pan mingled with the muffled sounds of scraping and shoveling coming from outside. Glancing out the window, she saw Matthew and Cory bundled up in winter gear, their combined efforts carving a path through the snowdrift that had practically buried their front door.

She desperately wanted to contact Lily, share the news about Travis Harrington, and see if she was alright after being trapped at the bookstore during the blizzard. Reaching for her phone, she dialed Lily's number for the fourth time in the last hour, a silent prayer forming on her lips.

The dial tone echoed in her ear, followed by a recording informing her that the call could not be completed. Disappointment fought with renewed worry as she shoved the phone back into her pocket.

"What's wrong," Emma asked, pouring some cocoa. "Still can't get Lily?"

"No," Sarah shook her head. "I just hope she's okay. Maybe the storm...or her phone and the bookstore just don't have any service. Could be..."

Emma came and offered the cocoa to her mother. "Or perhaps she turned it off to conserve the battery."

"Yup." Sarah took the cup and forced a smile.

And yet, a knot of worry tightened in her stomach once again. The lack of communication only amplified the unsettling feeling she couldn't quite shake.

She glanced back at Matthew and Cory, their laughter echoing faintly through the window as they playfully pelted each other with snowballs. A fierce determination hardened her resolve. She wouldn't let this uncertainty paralyze her. Moments of happiness, these were where she gathered her equilibrium.

A flurry of laughter and snowflakes erupted as the door creaked open again, admitting Matthew and Cory along with a gust of wintry air. Their faces were flushed and red, their hair dusted with snow, and their spirits high. The aroma of sizzling bacon and brewing coffee filled the air, a welcoming counterpoint to the chill they carried in.

"Looks like we made a decent dent in that snowdrift," Matthew declared, shrugging off his snow-laden coat. Cory mirrored him, a playful grin plastered across his face.

"Though, a snowblower would have been nice," he added with a hint of mock grumbling.

Sarah chuckled and let out a hard breath. Their lighthearted banter was a balm to her worried spirit. She dished up plates of steaming pancakes, golden brown and fluffy, the perfect antidote to the crisp morning air.

Just as Sarah was about to join them at the table, a sharp trill pierced the morning calm. The caller ID displayed an unfamiliar number, but the prefix—it was a local Rosewood Hollow number. Could it be Lily?

With trembling fingers, she answered the call.

"Hello?"

A crisp, professional voice crackled through the receiver.

"This is Detective Penny Harding from the Rosewood Hollow Police Department. Is this Sarah Anderson?"

Sarah's breath hitched. This sounded way too official. A tremor ran through her.

"Yes, it is, Penny," she stammered, her mind racing. What could the police possibly want with her?

"Everything all right out on Maple Street?" the detective asked, and Sarah exchanged a look with Matthew.

"Yes. It's nice of you to check, though I'm doubting this is a courtesy call."

Penny Harding did not answer immediately.

"Well... with the blizzard, we thought it would be best if we at least tried to do what we could to keep things on an even keel around here. And, finally, everything electronic here seems to be working just fine again."

"Isn't that something," Sarah choked out, trying her best to sound unconcerned and friendly, just as she was about to drop a bombshell on the woman. "Matter of fact, I was going to get in touch with you. Now is as good a time as ever to tell you this. The person who killed Luke Devin—"

"Let's not talk about Luke Devin and your friend Lily," Penny cut her off. "As if I didn't have enough to deal with with that storm, now I have a personal complaint against you."

"What?" Sarah pulled up a chair and took a cup of tea from Matthew. "No, I wanted to tell you all about Travis—"

"Travis Harrington and his harassment complaint against you, yes, of course, you did, Sarah. What on earth were you thinking? Harassing the man in his own restaurant, accusing him of god knows what, and threatening him with an animal, he said." Penny's voice hitched at the end of the sentence. She was obviously reading off a written statement. "I'm assuming that would be your dog there."

"Pixie, a five-pound Papillon," Sarah said, not bothering to hide the sarcasm. "I guess it would be. That man is guilty as the day is long. Listen…"

"No, you listen for a change, Sarah. Travis Harrington is a business owner here. Even though it's the about last thing I need this morning, I'm taking his harassment complaint seriously. Do you understand? I don't need any more trouble in this town. I have enough on my hands as it is. Now, please tell me you understand."

"No," Sarah said stubbornly. "I don't. There never was any harassment. Travis Harrington is not actually—"

A siren from somewhere in the police station interrupted their call, blaring into Sarah's ear until she held the phone five inches away from her face.

"Detective Harding? Penny? Travis is not who he—"

"Sarah, I have to go. We'll pick this up later, all right? Until then, just stay out of trouble—please. Take care of your family, and don't try to get involved in police work. That's the best thing you can do for yourself right now."

"No, but—"

No use. The line went dead, and Sarah let out a frustrated growl.

"She hung up on me," she complained, placing her phone down on the counter. "Just hung up on me. Can you believe this?"

"Police, they don't give a rat's…," Cory said around a mouthful of bacon. "Remember when they thought Katelyn had stolen that sapphire? Same thing. Nobody wanted to hear anything else."

He gave Matthew a quick sideways look and shook his head, digging back into the bacon.

"This is good. Thanks, Mom."

"You're welcome." Sarah poured coffee for herself and sat at the table without touching the food. "I have an actual solution to a current case right here in my hands. Who knew the hardest bit would be getting the information to them and into their thick heads?"

Sarah felt a dizzying wave of nausea wash over her.

"Harrington launched a complaint against me for harassment," she said, her voice shaking. "This is insane; I did not harass that man, nor did Pixie. I asked a question. About Lily and Luke and he got his defenses right up. Tell me if that screams guilty to you?"

"Look, harassment is a serious accusation," Matthew began, carefully putting down his fork. "I'm sure they won't leave it at just his statement. Once the situation with this blizzard is under control, I assume they will ask you to come down to the station and give your side of the story as well. We can clear everything up then."

He put his hand over hers, but the simple gesture did nothing to calm her nerves. Her stomach churned with a mixture of fear and indignation. Fear that Vincent Carlisle, a man she knew to be dangerous, had twisted the situation and made her appear to be a vindictive aggressor. Anger that the police would take his word over hers.

She slumped onto the chair and covered her face. Tears welled up in her eyes, blurring the image of Matthew and Cory looking at her with concern etched on their faces.

"Mom? What's wrong?" Emma asked hesitantly, her voice trembling with worry.

Sarah took a deep breath, trying to compose herself.

"I just wanted to see the man, look into his face while I asked about Luke. And with that, I've made everything so much worse. What if they believe his story and charge me?"

Cory's face scrunched up in a seriously pissed-off look. "Charge you? As in, give you a fine? For asking a question? You gotta be joking, right? Figures that witch Harding would take Mr. Moneybags' side." He made air quotes with his fingers on the last part and rolled his eyes hard.

Sarah recounted every bit of her short conversation with Penny Harding, the disbelief in her voice evident. As she spoke, a chilling realization dawned on them all. This wasn't just some random complaint—this was a calculated move by Vincent Carlisle. He was trying to silence her, to paint her as unstable, to discredit her accusations.

"He's trying to turn the tables on us," Matthew concluded, his voice grim. "He knows we're onto him, and this is his way of getting ahead of it."

Panic now clawed at Sarah. "But what's going to happen if the police actually believe him? What if they issue a restraining order or a fine, or whatever? It would get through to Michael, and he…" Her face turned another shade of white, imagining what the kid's dad would say once he found out. "And even if it doesn't, I won't be able to protect myself or you if Carlisle shows up here, ready to do who-knows-what!"

A tense silence descended on the usually bright, cheerful kitchen, interrupted only by the sounds of the snowplows outside. The pancakes on the table grew cold, the playful banter from earlier a distant memory.

Sensing Sarah's mounting distress, Pixie leaped onto her lap with a comforting whine. Burrowing her head against Sarah's trembling hand, the little dog offered the silent, strong support only she could.

We won't let that happen. Remember, you are strong, Sarah. Far stronger than anyone here.

Strong, Sarah thought and hugged her little dog a little tighter. If only she felt strong.

A faint shiver ran down her arm, a fleeting sensation of cool air that seemed to emanate from nowhere and disappeared as soon as she noticed it. For a fleeting moment, she wondered if it was Amelia, offering a ghostly touch of comfort amidst the spiraling panic.

You are stronger than anyone here.

Sarah took a deep breath, downed her coffee in one giant gulp, and straightened her back. She'd faced down a ghost and a thieving neighbor in this house. She'd nabbed a stolen sapphire from a gang of art thieves and returned it secretly to a highly guarded museum right under the guards' noses.

'Mom, you're so badass,' her own son's words.

"You are not getting me this easily," she said, and made a fist, and Pixie jumped to the floor again.

That's it – that's the spirit. Go, Sarah.

Fueled by a surge of defiance, Sarah stood and put her hands flat on the table. The fear wouldn't win. This wasn't about proving who harassed who; this was about protecting her family from a predator in disguise.

"Watch me," she declared, her voice stronger than she felt. "We're not going to let him bully us. I'm going down to the police station right now. I'll walk if I have to. They can't ignore me if I'm standing right there. And I will stay there until somebody listens."

Matthew, sensing her resolve, nodded in agreement.

"Then we're going with you," he said, his gaze unwavering. "They'll have a hard time ignoring a whole family showing up on their doorstep."

The cozy breakfast scene had morphed into a war council. The pancakes on the table sat forgotten, their golden-brown cheer starkly contrasting the grim determination etched on Sarah's face.

Cory and Emma looked at one another, first with surprise, then Cory started to grin.

"Yes," he said, offering his hand to his sister for a fist bump. "We're going with you. Try and stop us."

Sarah opened her mouth, then thought better of it. She shook her head with a broad smile. Under the table, Pixie ran from one to the other and put her paws on their knees, barking up a storm.

A wave of gratitude washed over Sarah. This wasn't just her fight anymore; it was a family effort. Together, they could face down this storm of lies and manipulation that Vincent Carlisle had unleashed.

"Okay then," Sarah finally announced, a newfound strength warming her voice. "Let's get ready. We have to figure out how to get to the police station, and we're not leaving there until they hear us out."

"I think the snowplow just did our road," Cory announced, checking the situation outside. "Matthew and I can get the driveway done in another half hour."

"I'll help," Emma said and reached for her coat, and in the inside of five minutes, all four of them were out there, tackling the driveway and the garage gate buried behind a massive snowdrift, with Pixie cheering them on from the inside.

∞

Sarah grabbed her coat, the familiar chill of the winter air starkly contrasting with the fire now burning in her heart.

As they piled into the car, a lone snowflake drifted down, landing on the windshield. It seemed even the winter sky held its breath, waiting to see how this storm, brewing inside their hearts, would play out within the sterile walls of the Rosewood Hollow Police Station.

Chapter Twenty-Seven

The car tires crunched over the freshly fallen snow as Sarah stared out the window, her mind a whirlwind of emotions. The landscape that had seemed so idyllic and festive just that morning now resembled an abstract painting: stark streaks of white and gray blurring together. The winter wonderland had taken on an ominous, foreboding chill that mirrored the icy dread knotting her stomach. With each passing mile closer to the station, her heart pounded harder, dreading what lay ahead. She shivered, hugging her arms tight.

Matthew, his jaw clenched tight, kept a firm grip on the steering wheel, his silence a testament to his simmering anger. Cory and Emma, usually bickering teenagers, sat in the back, uncharacteristically quiet, their faces etched with concern.

Sarah glanced at them in the rearview mirror, and her heart swelled with love and protectiveness.

As they pulled into the station parking lot, the knot of apprehension became a massive lump in her stomach. The imposing brick building radiated waves of unwelcoming energy. But Sarah held her head high. Today, she wouldn't be intimidated. Today, she would be heard.

As they rounded a corner, the familiar sight of the Rosewood Hollow Bookstore came into view. All the windows were lit brightly and decorated, a beacon of warmth amidst the swirling snow.

Sarah's heart lurched. Lily, bundled up in a long crimson coat that seemed to defy the bleak winter landscape, was valiantly battling a snowdrift that threatened to engulf the bookstore entrance. A tiny pink shovel, dwarfed by the task at hand, was her only weapon. Despite the obvious struggle, a wide smile lit up Lily's face when she spotted them. She waved enthusiastically, her bright green scarf a beacon against the backdrop of swirling snow.

Sarah barely registered the greeting. Their destination, the imposing brick building of the Rosewood Hollow Police Station, loomed ahead. As they neared, Sarah noticed Lily freeze, her smile faltering. Lily dropped the shovel and practically sprinted towards them, her coat billowing out behind her like a crimson sail.

Pulling into the station parking lot, Matthew slammed on the brakes just as Lily reached the car. The window rolled down, and Lily leaned in, her breath coming in ragged gasps.

"Sarah, what on earth are you doing here? Why are you even out in this mess?" she asked, her voice laced with concern. "Stay home, celebrate Christmas."

Relief washed over Sarah, a wave breaking the dam of worry that had been building within her.

"We figured out who killed Luke. It was Travis Harrington. But the police," she blurted out, stumbling over the words in her hurry to get it all out. "They think I'm harassing Travis Harrington! He wants to file a restraining order against me!"

Lily's eyes widened in shock. "What... wait. That's insane! Travis? But how? No... I...!" She trailed off, her gaze flickering to the police station behind them. "You have to tell me how you..."

A tense silence filled the car as Matthew put the car in park. Sarah and the kids exchanged worried glances. The weight of the situation settled on them once more, and the cozy breakfast scene was a distant memory replaced by this grim reality.

As they all piled out of the car, a sudden crackle of electricity ripped through the air. The old-fashioned neon sign that proclaimed Rosewood Hollow Police Station, in a faded blue glow, flickered erratically, buzzing once before going completely dark and coming back on again just as quickly.

Emma took her hand and squeezed tight.

"Amelia," she whispered, making a shiver run down Sarah's spine. She glanced at her daughter, who suddenly smiled broadly, a mischievous glint in her eyes.

"You really think so?"

Emma nodded and looked up at the sign, now listless, silent, and harmless once again.

"I know so."

Sarah squeezed her daughter's hand hard and hitched the purse carrier with Pixie in it another inch up her shoulder. Holding her head high, she marched towards the heavy oak doors of the police station, her family behind her.

The spark of defiance inside Sarah grew bit by bit into a massive blaze.

Sarah pushed the doors with a resolute shove. A blast of stale, frigid air momentarily stole their breath, carrying with it the faint scent of old paper, disinfectant, and something vaguely metallic. The warmth of their bundled clothing quickly gave way to the pervasive chill that seemed to cling to the very walls.

The bustling police station of Sarah's imagination was nowhere to be found. Here, time seemed to have slowed to a crawl. The linoleum floor, dulled to a pale gray over decades of footsteps, gleamed faintly in the dim light filtering through snow-covered windows. Snowflakes, carried in on their boots, melted on the floor with a soft sizzle, leaving tiny puddles that mirrored the general air of neglect.

An old-fashioned neon light fixture cast a sickly yellow glow over the sparsely furnished waiting area. Two mismatched chairs, their worn leather upholstery cracked and peeling, sat awkwardly facing a chipped wooden counter. A fly, seemingly oblivious to the harsh environment, buzzed lazily against the flypaper hanging from the low ceiling, its sticky surface a testament to countless other hapless insects.

The silence, broken only by the intermittent crackle of a police radio on the counter, was thick and oppressive. It spoke of a place where activity was a rare visitor, a stark contrast to the urgency pounding in Sarah's chest. A lone figure, a burly police officer with a salt-and-pepper beard dusted with snow, emerged from behind a swinging door marked Off Limits. His gaze swept over them, a flicker of surprise followed by a frown of annoyance.

"Didn't think anybody would come out in this mess," he rumbled, his voice gruff and weary. The air crackled with a tension even thicker than the dust motes dancing in the weak light. Sarah took a deep breath, the metallic tang of fear mingling with the stale air.

The burly officer, Sergeant Thompson, by the name tag on his chest, eyed Sarah and her companions with skepticism that mirrored the grimy walls of the station.

"Well then. What brings you all down here?" he asked, his voice gruff but not unkind.

Sarah cleared her throat, her voice surprisingly steady considering the hammering in her chest. "We're here to see Detective Penny Harding," she announced. "My name is Sarah Anderson, and I believe there's been a misunderstanding."

Sergeant Thompson's brow furrowed. "Detective Harding? You have an appointment?"

"Not exactly," Sarah admitted. "But it's very important. She called me about some... harassment charges, and I need to clear my name."

A flicker of recognition crossed Sergeant Thompson's face. He glanced at the file folder clutched in his hand, then back at Sarah. "Harassment against a Mr. Travis Harrington, is that right?"

Sarah felt a cold dread pool in her stomach. "Yes, but it's a lie! He's the one who's guilty."

"That may well be Ms. Anderson, but Detective Harding is a busy woman, especially today. There's accidents and emergencies all over the place. If this isn't a pressing matter, I suggest you—"

"It is a pressing matter!" Sarah snapped, her voice rising with desperation. She felt a sudden surge of energy flow down her arms and into her hands, bringing them together at chest level. If Sergeant Thompson had looked, he would have seen tiny blue sparks running between her fingers. "This man is dangerous," Sarah said firmly. "And I need Detective Harding to hear me out."

Before Sergeant Thompson could respond, a voice chimed in from behind Sarah.

"Is there a problem here, Dylan?" Lily, her face flushed from the cold, stepped forward. "We all need to speak to Detective Harding. It's a matter of public safety."

Sarah shot Lily a grateful glance. As a lifelong resident of Rosewood Hollow, Lily, no doubt, had probably known Sergeant Thompson since kindergarten or something.

Sergeant Thompson sighed, his voice heavy with weariness. He glanced at the small, cluttered office across the room, then back at the determined faces staring back at him.

"Alright, alright," he muttered, pinching the bridge of his nose. "But keep it brief. Detective Harding has a mountain of paperwork to get through, and it was just this morning we reopened the station after... Well, there were a few issues."

Relief washed over Sarah—briefly. As Sergeant Thompson led them toward the cramped office, she realized a new hurdle awaited them. "Wait," she interjected. We all need to be in there. This involves all of us."

Sergeant Thompson scoffed. "Look, lady, police matters are usually—"

"This isn't some ordinary police matter," Matthew cut in, his voice firm. "This man is a threat to our family, and we all have information that needs to be shared."

Emma, usually shy, stepped forward, her voice surprisingly strong. "He's dangerous. You have to listen to us."

Her hands, Sarah noticed, were also folded at chest level. Could the same thing be happening to her daughter?

Sergeant Thompson hesitated, the weight of their combined conviction hanging heavy in the air. He glanced at the determined faces staring back at him, then at the overflowing inbox on Detective Harding's desk. With a resigned sigh, he opened the door to the cramped office, ushering them all in with a muttered, "Just make it quick. Detective Harding won't be happy about this."

The cramped office that greeted them seemed to swallow the last remnants of warmth Sarah clung to. A flickering fluorescent light fixture cast an unflattering, greenish glow over the stacks of files that threatened to bury the lone figure hunched over a cluttered desk. Penny Harding, a woman whose sharp features seemed even more severe under the harsh light, looked up with a frown that could curdle milk.

"Sergeant Thompson," she began, her voice a clipped monotone, "I thought I specifically requested—"

Her words were cut short as her gaze landed on the unexpected entourage. Sarah, Matthew, Cory, Emma, and Lily stood huddled together, a silent force that seemed to fill the cramped space to capacity. A flicker of surprise, quickly masked by professional indifference, crossed Detective Harding's face.

"Ms. Anderson," she acknowledged coolly, "I see you've brought backup. However, this is a police matter—"

Just as Sarah drew a breath to detail the incriminating evidence they had gathered, a commotion erupted from the front office. A loud voice, laced with fury, pierced the tense silence of Detective Harding's cramped workspace. Before anyone could react, the door swung open with a bang, nearly slamming into Sergeant Thompson.

In the doorway stood Travis Harrington, a picture of outraged indignation. Snow clung to his hair and shoulders, melting in angry rivulets down his expensive-looking coat. His face, usually carefully sculpted with manufactured charm, was contorted with a mask of fury.

"Detective Harding!" Travis-Vincent bellowed, his voice booming through the small room. He stormed in, eyes wild, jabbing an accusing finger at Sarah. "This woman has been harassing me nonstop! She's stalked me, slandered me. She's single-handedly trying to destroy my restaurant and my livelihood!"

Sarah felt her pulse spike as his twisted lies unfolded, just as she'd predicted. Flipping the script, painting her as the unhinged aggressor. Her fists clenched, but before she could object, he plowed on in a frenzy.

"She's been spreading vicious lies about me!" Vincent's voice cracked with desperate rage. "Accusing me of crimes, and now she's shut my entire place down! Dead as a doornail. I demand you slap a restraining order on her immediately!"

A stunned silence fell over the room. Matthew's jaw ticked, hands balled up tight. Cory and Emma traded looks of disbelief, eyes wide. Worry etched across Lily's face as her hand found Sarah's shoulder in a supportive squeeze.

For a beat, Detective Harding seemed taken aback by the sheer force of Vincent's outburst. But she quickly recomposed herself, gaze flitting calculatingly between the irate man and Sarah's loyal friends.

"Mr. Harrington, please calm yourself. We were just discussing this matter with Ms. Anderson."

Sarah's anger blazed hot. "I didn't shut down anything! I've only been to your restaurant once!"

"Oh really? You're trying to tell me it wasn't you who sabotaged the entire electrical system?"

"Of course not. There's a storm..." Sarah began, only to have Vincent wiping away her protest.

"A storm that missed all of my neighbors? All it did was shut down my restaurant. Get real, Anderson. You tried to accuse me of some... crime, and when that didn't work, you sabotaged my restaurant."

He adjusted his coat and turned back to Penny Harding, radiating an air of smug confidence. "This woman needs to be held accountable for her slanderous actions."

"Electrical system, huh," Penny Harding said, coming out from behind her desk.

"Look, we've had the identical issue here at the station for the better part of a week now, and from one day to the next, it was gone." She raised her hands and lowered them again gently as if trying to tamp down the problem. "Let's not go accusing anyone when there's likely an innocent explanation."

Innocent. Sarah had enough. In one flash, she had enough of the detective's indifference, Vincent's lies, and the futility of standing there in this cramped office without accomplishing anything.

"Certainly," she said, folding her hands and gathering all of the energy she could feel coming to her. "Did you not have trouble with your furnace just a few weeks ago, Mr. Carlisle? And Luke Devin fixed it for you?"

Vincent froze and fixed Sarah with a look of sheer hatred. Penny Harding blinked, looked down at her paperwork, and back up at Sarah and Vincent.

"Oh yes, Mr. Vincent Carlisle," Sarah repeated. "Although I have to admit, Travis Harrington sounds a bit classier."

What happened next, neither one of them could have expected.

"Vincent Carlisle," Sergeant Thompson mused, scratching his beard for a minute. "Wasn't that some criminal who escaped from Atlanta correctional... Oh!"

Time seemed to slow in the quaint little office. The chatter of voices and mild disagreements faded into an uneasy quiet as Sarah witnessed a scene she'd only imagined in her more fanciful daydreams. She watched, bewildered, as Travis—or Vincent—became very visibly angry.

His usually pleasant features twisted into an unsettling scowl, and his eyes flashed with an intensity she'd never seen before. An angry huff escaped his lips—the sound startlingly out of place in their cozy surroundings. His mouth stretched into an unpleasant grimace that made Sarah take an instinctive step back.

A small gasp escaped Sarah's lips as Vincent's hand, with surprising swiftness, reached out and grasped her shoulder firmly. A jolt of surprise and discomfort shot through her as he spun her around, causing her to stumble slightly. Pixie's carry bag slipped from her shoulder, the little dog becoming entangled in the straps and half-open zipper as she wriggled to get free.

Chapter Twenty-Eight

Chaos erupted in the tiny room. Sergeant Thompson, lumbering towards Vincent with a shouted warning, was backhanded aside with shocking strength, crashing into the group by the door. Lily gasped. Matthew lunged forward, only to be restrained by Cory, and Emma's piercing scream sliced through the tense silence.

Everything seemed to move in slow motion, the cacophony of sounds warped and muffled. In that endless suspended moment, Sarah felt the scorching waves of Vincent's vicious anger rolling off him in stifling bursts. She desperately tried to summon that strange energy in her hands as before, but it eluded her.

Another vicious yank on her hair, and then she felt it—the razor-sharp edge of one of Vincent's prized chef's knives pressing into the tender flesh of her throat. A thin line of crimson welled up, trickling down to stain the white folds of her scarf.

"Let her go, Vincent." Detective Harding's voice was level but strained, her hands raised in a placating gesture. "Let Sarah go, and we'll talk calmly. Don't make this worse."

"Everyone leaves this station!" Vincent's roar bordered on unhinged. He jerked his head towards the door. "Everyone except her. If I can walk out of here unharmed, I'll release her outside of town."

"You know I can't allow that," Penny replied, her tone taking on an artificially soothing lilt Sarah had never heard from the gruff detective before. "Just let's talk this through rationally. Maybe it's all been a misunderstanding? Let Sarah go, and we can sort it out."

"Do not come any closer, or I swear I'll..." The knife dug deeper, parting Sarah's skin. She couldn't stifle the whimper that slipped out.

Matthew let out an inarticulate roar of fury, fighting against Sergeant Thompson's restraining hold as the larger man forcibly shepherded him, Lily, and the kids out into the main lobby at a nod from Harding. Their protests faded as the door swung shut, muffling Cory's string of curses.

Vincent yanked Sarah's head back further still, her vision graying out as dizziness washed over her. "Car keys," he snarled.

"In my pocket."

Fumbling with numb hands, Sarah managed to extract her keys from her pocket, bile burning her throat as his questing fingers ripped them out of her hand. If she stumbled, if she lost her footing even an inch with that lethal blade at her neck...

"Good." He gestured at the detective with the knife. "You, officer. Take a seat at your desk, hands flat on the table. You know what happens to her if you try to follow. If I even sense someone on my tail..."

Twisting with what little leeway she had, Sarah drove a desperate elbow towards Vincent's midsection. But he was too fast, his fist tightening in her hair as he violently wrenched her head back. Blinding pain lanced through her skull, her own blood flooding her mouth as her teeth savaged her tongue.

"Try that again, and it will be the last thing you do."

Sarah crumpled, stumbling in a haze of copper-tinged vertigo, the metallic tang of blood overwhelming her senses. Just a little longer. She had to hold on just a few more seconds…

Just one more second.

Pixie? Pixie, you're still here? Hide. He is…

Vincent's grip tightened on her upper arm, his fingers digging into her flesh like steel claws. A low growl rumbled in his throat, a sound less human than animal. It sent shivers down her spine, a primal fear urging her to fight back.

"This ends now, Sarah," Vincent snarled, his voice devoid of the charming facade he usually wore. "You'll regret ever crossing me. You ruined everything. I had a good thing going: a restaurant and customers. Everybody loved it until your meddling family had to come in and ruin everything. You'll pay for this. You will pay."

Desperation clawed at Sarah's insides. Detective Penny Harding, who had picked herself up from the floor, tried again to reason with the increasingly unhinged Vincent, her voice laced with a strained calm.

"Let her go, son. This isn't the answer."

Vincent scoffed, the harsh, humorless sound making Sarah's blood run cold.

"Stay out of this, Harding," he spat, his wild gaze never leaving Sarah. "This is between me and her. Run if you want. You can't help her."

Penny opened her mouth, undoubtedly to offer another placating reply. But before she could get a word out, the flickering fluorescent light fixture overhead sputtered and died with a final flicker, plunging the room into an impenetrable inky blackness.

Sarah's heart pounded in her ears, her gasps seeming to echo deafeningly in the smothering dark. She felt Vincent's iron grip on her hair slacken momentarily as he, too, was engulfed by the sudden absence of light. This was her chance.

Gritting her teeth against the throbbing ache in her skull, Sarah mustered every ounce of her waning strength. She wrenched her head forward, tearing free of Vincent's grasp, then whipped her arm up and back in a vicious arc. Her elbow connected with something soft. His stomach, she realized with a surge of grim satisfaction as he let out a pained grunt.

Not wasting a split second, Sarah spun and dropped into a clumsy crouch, sweeping her leg out in a wild kick at his feet, hoping to upend his balance. A loud crash and a string of curses told her she'd found her mark.

Sarah scrambled away, palms skating frantically across the rough industrial carpet, searching for any makeshift weapon, any hard surface to grab. Her fingers closed around something heavy and cylindrical—a metal desk leg, maybe? Clutching it in a white-knuckled grip, she hauled herself upright, straining her senses for any sound, any movement in the pitch-black void surrounding her, just as Vincent's hands fisted in her hair again, and he pulled her hard against his body once more.

Emma's scream, a strangled, high-pitched thing, echoed from outside the door, followed by the blessed thump of retreating footsteps.

Sarah's heart hammered a frantic rhythm against her ribs. Vincent's grip on her hair and arm tightened, his body a furnace pressed against hers. The darkness felt thick and oppressive, a living thing coiling around them. Her ragged breaths were the only sound that dared to break the suffocating silence.

Then, a wave of cold, unlike anything she'd ever experienced, slammed through the room. It was so sudden and intense that it stole the air from her lungs, forcing a gasp to escape her lips that materialized in a ghostly wisp. Simultaneously, an ethereal glow pulsed beside her, revealing Amelia's spectral form. The ever-present twinkle in her eyes had been replaced by a steely glint, a laser focus that sent shivers down Sarah's spine.

"Let her go, Vincent," Amelia's voice echoed in the room, a chilling counterpoint to the suffocating darkness. It wasn't just sound, but a tangible force that resonated with absolute authority.

As if on cue, time itself seemed to grind to a halt. Vincent, in mid-snarl, his hand still clamped tight on Sarah's arm, froze in a tableau of monstrous rage. His eyes, dilated with terror, bulged from their sockets. He tried to scream, but no sound emerged. His face, contorted in a grotesque mask, was a predator caught dead in its tracks.

The air crackled with a strange energy, a faint blue aura shimmering around Amelia's translucent form. Sarah, the only one unaffected by this temporal anomaly, stared at the scene before her in stunned disbelief.

Suddenly, a tiny ball of fur emerged from beneath Penny Harding's desk. It was Pixie, shaking violently, paws daintily picking at the air in what could only be described as disdain.

Let's get out of here, Sarah, Pixie rasped in her mind, the voice faint but resolute. *This won't last long.*

But Sarah couldn't move. Her gaze remained locked on Vincent, who vibrated with silent fury, ice crystals melting on his face from the sheer intensity of his rage.

Then, a guttural roar erupted from his chest, shattering the time lock. His hand, still fisted in Sarah's hair, yanked back with a sickening snap.

"Leaving so soon?" he snarled, his voice dripping with venom. His gaze flicked to Pixie, peeking from under the desk, but missed Amelia, who had condensed into a pulsing sphere of white light in the corner of the room.

A desperate plea, barely a whisper, reached Sarah's ears. "Pixie... Sarah. A hand, please."

Confused, Sarah blinked, then understanding dawned. She stretched out her free hand, aiming for the glowing orb. A bolt of white light erupted from her fingertips, seeking Amelia, connecting with the sphere's center and feeding its furious spin.

At the same time, Pixie mirrored Sarah's action. Her tiny paws formed a begging gesture, another beam of light shooting forth, joining the growing ball of energy. It spun ever faster, coalescing into a perfect triangle, a conduit for raw, crackling power.

The energy crackled and spat, the beam finally reaching Vincent. He let out a bloodcurdling scream, the knife clattering to the floor with a sickening thud. He crumpled to his knees, burying his head in his hands as if trying to shield himself from the blinding light.

Chapter Twenty-Nine

S arah felt the last of her energy drain, and dropped to her knees, still holding her hand out in the direction of the dark corner where Amelia had appeared.

She vaguely sensed Penny Harding jumping to her feet, kicking the knife away and into a corner, simultaneously opening her door, and yelling at the top of her voice for backup, backup.

Everything happened at once then.

Matthew, Lily, Cory, and Emma crowded in the door, wanting to get to her, only to be stopped by the resolute Penny Harding.

"Stay out there. Nobody is coming in here unless I say."

"But…"

"Lily, just shut up, please," Penny yelled uncharacteristically. "You're still officially a suspect, too. Sergeant?"

"Yes, Ma'am?"

"Get me a first aid kit for Sarah, then get this guy's fingerprints." She pointed at Carlisle, still sitting on the floor in the fetal position, repeating the word no over and over. "Get a kit on this guy. Let's check if his fingerprints match the escaped convict. And you..." She wheeled on Sarah, "Want to tell me what just happened?"

Sarah reached out and allowed Pixie to jump into her arms, rocking the little dog back and forth.

Keep it together. She didn't see anything.

Amelia?

I don't think so. She was frozen.

"I don't know, I was just focused on him," Sarah said, brushing her hair from her face. "The power... must have arced or something, maybe?"

"Arced?"

Penny reached out and helped Sarah to her feet.

"What the heck does that even mean."

"I don't know. Didn't you see anything?"

"No." Penny struck her desk. "Number one, I was in the dark just as much as you were, and number two, I was... frozen." The detective shuffled and rubbed her hands, remembering the feeling of the time freeze. "Like something was immobilizing me," she muttered. "Then a... light... and then... I just don't know."

"The triangle..." Sarah said, forcing as much fake surprise into her voice as she could muster just then. "What was that?"

"I just don't know," Penny said again.

Sarah looked down at her hands, where a tiny remnant of little blue flickers remained. Finally, she bent down to scoop up Pixie, hiding her hands in the long, fluffy fur.

Pixie gave her a little lick on the cheek and snuggled in.

Nice energy strike. You seem to have a thing about hitting things with full power.

Did I... do that? Sarah thought.

With a bit of help from Amelia.

"Where is Amelia?"

"Who," Detective Harding asked, and Sarah bit her lip, realizing she had spoken out loud.

"Emma, my daughter," she said, forcing a smile.

The overhead light flickered ominously, casting Penny's face in a dance of shadows for a second. Sarah watched, a knot of unease tightening in her gut. Detective Harding muttered under her breath, a snippet of a forgotten saying catching Sarah's ear, something about ghosts of Christmas past.

"I'd really like to join my family again," Sarah finally said, her voice barely a whisper in the tense silence.

Penny shook her head, a grimace creasing her features.

"In a minute, I'm sure Sergeant Thompson is looking after them," she mumbled, rubbing her hands together like someone trying to generate warmth against the chill that seemed to have settled in the room.

"First things first, your statement. Are you up for that right now, or do you want to see a medic first about that cut?"

"I'm good, nothing serious."

Sarah offered a shaky nod. Relief washed over her when Penny steered the conversation back to the case. She poured out her story, detailing her unwavering belief in Lily's innocence, the suspicious newspaper clippings in Luke's apartment, and the lingering scent of the exotic spice at the crime scene—a scent she'd later encountered in Travis' restaurant before she knew of his true identity as Vincent.

Keeping Pixie's pivotal role in cracking the case a secret, Sarah hedged her bets when it came to the spice. A white lie here and there was a forgivable sin in the pursuit of justice, especially during the most wonderful time of the year. And explaining to this detective how she could communicate with her papillon, that would take more time than either one of them had just then.

"The door to the bookstore was locked from the inside – that was the crucial detail," Sarah pressed, straightening her spine in an attempt to project certainty. "Both Matthew and I were certain about it. So, the killer must have used another exit. Matthew, bless his inquisitive mind and several old blueprints, discovered a hidden maintenance access behind the fireplace separating Lily's bookstore from the one next door. The one that's now empty."

A flicker of surprise crossed Penny's face.

"But how on earth would Travis..." she began, then stopped short. Her eyes widened as Sarah finished the thought with a triumphant smile.

"My son," Sarah declared with a hint of maternal pride, "is a research whiz. He unearthed a photo from a gala event held back when the shop next door was still an art gallery. Travis catered the event. The fireplace was roaring, and the food spread was laid out right next to it. A pretty good deduction that Vincent, posing as Travis, had lit that fire for ambiance and probably knew about the secret passage. At least that's what we thought."

Penny stared at her hands, her lips pressed into a thin, grim line. Finally, she let out a heavy sigh.

"I confess," she said, her voice heavy with regret. "I did let my initial gut feeling about Lily cloud my judgment. Wrapped up in the Christmas spirit, I wanted a tidy conclusion and failed to keep an open mind. A terrible lapse for someone in my position."

"You go out there and tell Lily about that, Detective," Sarah said gently. "But that's pretty much all I know about the terrible story."

Penny nodded and clicked off the little recorder on her desk. "Thank you. You'll be able to join your family in a minute. Are you sure you don't want a doctor to check on that cut?"

"It's just a scratch," Sarah touched the bandage at her throat, remembering how she'd used her hand once before when Pixie was hurt. She took a breath, sent a pulse of energy against her skin, and could feel the cut close and the skin even out over it.

A sudden, sharp rap on the door shattered the tense silence. Now looking a lot more ruffled and worried than he had earlier, Sergeant Thompson poked his head into the room.

"Detective Harding," he rumbled, his voice a low growl. "Just got the results back on those prints. Our not-so-charming guest is definitely Vincent Carlisle."

Sarah felt a surge of relief overwhelm her just then and closed her eyes with a deep sigh—finally, some concrete evidence. Penny, however, remained stoic, her jaw clenched tight. "Thank you, Dylan," she said curtly. Tell the officers to prep him for a formal interrogation, Sarah here." She nodded at Sarah and Pixie. "She can join her family when she's ready. Stay available, though, will you?"

She turned to Sarah, a mix of curiosity, disbelief, and plain old embarrassment playing over her face. "Your theories are all nice and tidy and intriguing, perhaps even well-researched, but you will excuse me if I want to check every last detail. Cross all my t's as it were."

Sarah pressed her lips together and nodded. "You will find that everything happened just the way I told you."

"You let that be my job." Penny Harding put a hand on Sarah's shoulder. "Which, if I may remind you of that, you should have done in the first place."

Sarah only nodded and scrambled to gather Pixie's carrier from where it lay, trampled on the floor, and her purse, flung into a corner.

She barely whispered a greeting and darted outside, where Matthew, Lily, Emma, and Cory stood waiting in the tiny anteroom of the police station.

Matthew was the first one to throw his arms around her and Pixie and squeeze her tight as if he never meant to let her go.

"I thought you were gone," he whispered in her ear. "When that man had a knife to your throat."

"Nothing happened," Sarah whispered back. "Nothing happened, I'm all right."

"But Vincent... the knife. How did he...?"

"Amelia showed up," Sarah whispered under her breath, and Matthew lowered his head.

"Did Detective Harding...?"

Sarah shook her head. "I don't think so."

She waved away the approaching paramedic and peeled off the bandage herself, disposing of it in a nearby trash can.

"See, I'm all good. Sergeant Thompson, is it okay if we all leave now? I'd really... I think I've enough of this place for the moment."

"Sure, go ahead."

The police sergeant and the medic stared at her wide-eyed for a moment. Sarah smiled and brought her hand to her throat, pulling up her scarf to hide the already-fading cut.

"Told you it was nothing, right?"

They almost ran out of the station the moment Sergeant Thompson nodded.

"Bookstore," Lily said and steered them across the road. "Cookies and Coffee—that is what we need right now."

Chapter Thirty

"I called a handyman service because the furnace at my restaurant was broken," Vincent said, fidgeting with the grainy black and white film. "They sent Luke Devin, and I knew the moment he walked in, he recognized my face."

"You knew him from Atlanta Correctional," Penny Caldwell asked, and Vincent nodded slowly.

"As a chef, I was assigned to kitchen duty, and he worked in the mechanic's shop, but our paths crossed now and then—in the yard and the gym. We weren't friendly, but I knew who he was."

Lily clenched her hands, staring at the TV screen in Sarah's den. It was probably against a dozen or more rules to let them watch the tape of Vince's interrogation, but Detective Caldwell was still pretty embarrassed about her lapse in judgment. She had made it happen.

Sarah reached over and put her hand on Lily's arm.

"You all right," she whispered, and Lily nodded.

"Then you broke out," Detective Caldwell asked, and Vincent nodded.

"I was assigned to an outside work detail and... just walked away."

"Devin didn't know?"

"Nobody knew," Vincent continued. "I just... walked away. I am a decent chef, so I worked my way north. Basically as a line cook for cash."

"The list of restaurants in Devin's apartment?"

Vincent nodded. "The bastard..."

"Mr. Carlisle."

"Luke Devin figured it out. I have no idea why he sat down and found most of the restaurants I worked at, but he did."

"He wanted to do right," Lily whispered, and Sarah squeezed her hand.

"When I got to Rosewood Hollow," Vincent continued. "I thought, here was a small town where I could stay and nobody would find me. I saw the old shut-down Indian restaurant and decided to create a new identity and reopen it. It worked, for a while."

"I have eaten at your restaurant," Penny said bitterly, as if the very fact offended her personally. "You are an extremely talented chef. If you were not a criminal..."

Vincent looked down at his hands and shrugged. "Five years," he said softly. "Five years and nothing happened. I thought I could keep going like that forever. Then Devin walked in."

"And you decided to kill him?"

"Not right away." Vincent Carlisle leaned back until the handcuffs clinked against the solid bar on the table that restrained them.

"No. He had to be a do-gooder. His own fault, really. He wanted to give me three days to settle my affairs and turn myself in—three days, or he would do it for me."

"That might have been a mistake, but it was still generous," Penny said, nodding for him to continue.

"I was trying to figure it out. When I went for a walk through town, I saw him going into the bookstore. Probably to fix something. He was always fixing things for people," Vincent shook his head and sneered. "I went in just to talk to him—just talk—but he wouldn't let up. Insisted I turn myself in. We fought; I had one of my knives on me because I'd had it sharpened, and it just happened."

"It just happened? You stabbed him?"

Vincent only nodded.

"I'm going to need you to say the words, Mr. Carlisle."

"I had the knife in my hand, and I just… stabbed him," he said almost softly. "I don't know what made me do it, desperation perhaps."

"But what happened with the fireplace," Lily asked and leaned forward, just as Penny asked the same question.

Vincent shrugged. "I was gonna leave, then a group of carolers came by."

"Carolers?"

"I guess so. They were right across the road. No way I could leave without everybody seeing me, so I went back into the office, looking for a back door."

"That one is alarmed," Lily whispered.

"The only door would have set off the fire alarm. I panicked until I remembered the fireplace… and that little passage into the other store."

"Which was empty," Detective Caldwell supplied.

"Yup. I locked the front door so you'd have a harder time figuring it out, went next door, climbed out a window in the back, and forced it closed again. And I thought nobody would ever know."

"They wouldn't have if it hadn't been for your spices."

Vincent cocked his head slightly, and though the camera didn't capture Penny's face, Sarah knew she was smiling.

"Grains of paradise, very specific. Someone smelled it at the crime scene."

"The spice merchant at the Christmas market." Vincent sighed and let his chin drop to his chest. "I usually order it online, but he had a fresh and beautiful supply I couldn't resist. It was in my pocket…"

∾

Sarah heard the front door open and quickly pressed the stop button on the remote. She had not wanted her kids to see the tape of Vincent's confession.

Cory and Emma burst in, a flurry of laughter and snowflakes clinging to their winter coats. Bags, clearly full of boxes wrapped in garish wrapping paper and outlandish bows, hung precariously from their arms.

"What are you all watching," Cory asked, and Sarah shook her head.

"Nothing important."

"Guess what?" Cory announced, a mischievous glint in his eyes. "It's snowing again!"

Matthew chuckled. "Looks like you and I have to do some shoveling again."

Cory groaned and dramatically covered his face with both hands.

Sarah, bundled in a cozy sweater and holding a steaming mug of hot chocolate, watched them with a heart brimming with love. The nightmare with Vincent felt like a distant memory, replaced by the comforting warmth of family and the promise of a peaceful Christmas.

"Alright, spill it," Sarah teased, gesturing toward the overflowing bags. "What have you two been up to?"

Emma, her cheeks flushed with excitement, peeked out from behind Cory's shoulder. "We may or may not have convinced Mrs. Claus to help us with some last-minute shopping," she confessed, a hint of a giggle in her voice.

Cory, unable to contain his amusement any longer, burst into laughter.

"Let's just say Santa might be delivering a few extra gifts this year," he added, winking conspiratorially at his mother.

The aroma of freshly baked cookies drifted in from the kitchen, courtesy of Lily.

Pixie trotted out of the kitchen, still licking the last cookie crumbs off her snout, a mischievous twinkle in her intelligent eyes.

Looks like our Christmas is shaping up quite nicely, wouldn't you say, she said to Sarah. *A little holiday magic, a sprinkle of justice, and a whole lot of family. Just the way it should be.*

Gazing at the twinkling Christmas lights and the faces of her loved ones, Sarah couldn't help but agree. This Christmas, despite its rocky start, held the promise of a new beginning.

By the fireplace, she could see just a hint of a magical sparkle, and she said a silent thank you to Amelia and Simon. She and the ghost had had a little talk just after she'd saved her at the police station.

"Most of it was you, Sarah," the ghost had said. "You still don't understand how much power you really have. Every now and then, you need a nudge to figure out how to use it."

Sarah automatically made a fist with her right hand, closing her left hand over it. One day, she would figure out where all of this power came from, why she had it, and how she could control it.

Lily came out of the kitchen, dusting her hands on her apron and giving Sarah a little nod.

"Cookies are ready," she announced. "If anyone—"

Cory and Emma were a mere blur, heading for the kitchen.

"Help yourself, why don't you." Lily laughed and let her eyes wander into the den, the Christmas tree, and the mountain of presents beneath it. "Thank you for letting me celebrate with you guys. So much better than being alone."

"Please, what are friends for? Merry Christmas." Sarah lifted her cocoa in a toast.

"There is just one thing you never told me."

"Which is?"

"What exactly happened at the station when the lights went out? Vincent Carlisle was on the floor quivering with fear when the lights came back."

Sarah smiled, remembering the triangle, and the crackling blue energy of her own fury.

"It's Christmas; can we please not talk about that," she said with a smile. "Sometimes we don't have to understand every single thing. It's... just magic."

Coming Soon

Thanks for reading! Please leave a review and watch for **Pixie's next adventure in** the next Magical Papillon Mystery.

For more fun and updates follow Pixie on TikTok, @papillon_pixie

Want early access to Pinch of Peril? Email me here to get on the list for release updates – **sabine-author@pm.me**. Or use the link below to sign up to get notifications of the release date Pixie's next adventure.

https://docs.google.com/forms/d/e/1FAIpQLSf6wLjWBuZqqJJg uR-_mtBVCHYE1UtbqxHE1uxpKWOPnlY8hA/

Scan to Sign Up

Also by Sabine

Cozy Mysteries: The Magical Papillon Mystery Series
Whispers in the Attic
The Mirror and the Matrix
A Pinch of Peril
The Rosewood Hollow Express: A special Christmas story featuring Pixie and the Andersons. Available in ebook and audible formats in December 2024.

∞

Financial Thrillers: The Cannabis Preacher Series
Sermon One
Sermon Two
Sermon Three
Sermon Four
Box Set
Joyce AI: She knows Everything About You!

∞

Romance Novels (Pen Name, Sabine Keevil):
SoundMaster Romance Series:
Guitars & Cadillacs
Foolish Pride

∞

Coming Soon
Ghost Mountain Gold (Financial Thrillers)
This Time (SoundMaster Romance)

Reviews for Other Books

Writing as Sabine Frisch:

<u>The Cannabis Preacher Series</u>

GoodReads Review: "The subject matter and title intrigued me having been around some of these sorts of dealings. From the beginning of this book had my attention; I picked it up to "just have a look" and suddenly found myself eight chapters into it. As the main characters were introduced, I started to feel that I had met all of these people before.Read on as Connor, the main protagonist, battles his demons up and down the shady side of Wall Street. There are just so many moving parts for any one control freak to manage. The greatest deal of all time starts to get out of control but every time he seems about to fall, he finds a way to land on his feet.We keep guessing:• Is he our hero or his own worst enemy?• Is this a runaway train or a slow-motion train wreck?• Will he end up in Financial Heaven, Regulatory Hell, or just a Fool's Paradise?Read to the end of this fun little tale and wait for the movie to come out."

Writing as Sabine Keevil

The SoundMaster Romance Series

<u>**Guitars & Cadillacs**</u> (Semi-finalist in the BookLife Fiction Prize Contest, 2023)

Editorial Reviews:

"Sabine Keevil has constructed the perfect fantasy romance in her novel Guitars & Cadillacs, the latest in the Soundmaster Romance Series... At the same time, she appeals to that part of us that longs to see the behind-the-scenes footage of celebrity lives."-Rachel Jagt, Rambles.net

"Ms. Keevil is a good storyteller, I'll say that right out. She has a good grasp of storyline, she's succinct and to the point, her characters are engaging, and she knows where she's taking them."-Laurie Joulie, Take-countryback.com

"Guitars & Cadillacs is the entertaining story of the fire and fury stirred up by the relationship between Reanne (Parker) and fictional country superstar Colton Wright...Offering surprise twists, intrigue and mystery...Keep turning the pages to see what happens next in the well-paced plot."- Pat Mandia, Country Weekly, the world's #1 Selling Country Music Magazine

<u>**Foolish Pride**</u>

Editorial Reviews:

"Keevil spins an engaging romantic tale and does a credible job of taking us backstage into the minds, lives and hearts of her characters."
-Pat Mandia, Country Weekly Magazine
"Canadian author Sabine Keevil (Guitars & Cadillacs) has done it again -- she revisits the world of SoundMaster with originality, humour and a large share of romantic spirit.

One of Keevil's strengths as a writer is her ability to create realistic characters, even in the midst of a story about the world of big money show business. She is unpretentious and honest and her characters are likeable from the beginning...Even in two nights, the characters became beloved -- a sure sign of a good story." -Rachel Jagt, Rambles - a cultural arts review magazine

Spotify Playlists

Enjoy the following Spotify playlists with music mentioned or inspired by my novels.

Guitars & Cadillacs:

https://open.spotify.com/playlist/71ymCTx5YJPzro WBg4gWHF?si=fcf531d7a84b46cc

Foolish Pride:

https://open.spotify.com/playlist/1lR5rhB840RyeecFLvb1pG

The Cannabis Preacher:

https://open.spotify.com/playlist/4P90ZeynKOI7gyGUcVF HJE?si=484f28ffa7fb4b2a

Magical Papillon Mysteries

https://open.spotify.com/playlist/46FQGJn3T7qnAnoau63 BxU?si=379b6a6be4874ef3